ANTOINE BELLO

The
Missing
Piece

Translated from the French by Helen Stevenson

A Harvest Original • Harcourt, Inc.

Orlando Austin New York San Diego Toronto London

Requests for permission to make copies of any part of the work
should be mailed to the following address: Permissions Department,
Harcourt, Inc., 6277 Sea Harbor Drive, Orlando, Florida 32887-6777.

www.HarcourtBooks.com

First published by Gallimard in 1998
First published in English by Serpent's Tail in 2002

This is a translation of *Éloge de la pièce manquante*.

Library of Congress Cataloging-in-Publication Data
available upon request.

ISBN 0-15-601337-1

Text set in Minion
Designed by Linda Lockowitz

Printed in the United States of America
First Harvest edition 2003

A C E G I K J H F D B

Contents

Contents • vii

The Enigma

Between March and September 1995 five murders were committed, casting a dark shadow over the professional U.S. speed puzzle circuit. In each case the modus operandi was the same: a massive dose of Pentothal was administered to the victim prior to the amputation of a limb—each time a different one. Attached to the body, the murderer left a fragment of a Polaroid photograph depicting the corresponding limb of a different man. Naturally enough, the police inferred that the limbs shown in the photographs were those of the assassin. This hypothesis, while not exactly furthering the inquiry, received vigorous backing from a large section of the population. Each time the murderer's photographs were made public, an impressive number of respectable citizens came forward, claiming to have recognized the left leg or right arm of a neighbor, or any other suspicious individual they happened to have seen hanging around their local Greyhound bus station.

In the course of their inquiries, the police were also drawn into the tight-knit world of the puzzle. Earlier, this community had undergone a number of important changes, as outlined below.

Although still in its infancy, the professional puzzle circuit had become increasingly popular with the public at large. According to a poll published in late 1994 in *Newsweek*, it had become America's favorite sporting discipline, on a par with baseball, and way ahead of basketball and football.

At the head office of the American Puzzle Federation, the body in charge of the circuit, it was always said that the idea for stopwatch competitions originated with multimillionaire Charles Wallerstein.

Wallerstein was the owner of the Ubiquis group, which he inherited from his father. Under his direction it grew into one of the most powerful and successful trusts in the United States. In 1990, Wallerstein, who had never made any secret of his interest in puzzles, took over control of the American Puzzle Federation, at that time little more than an empty shell, having existed for thirty years under the management of two sisters, the venerable Misses Inglethorpe. Six months later, the magnate announced his intention to organize puzzle tournaments, thus reviving an old American tradition his communications consultants traced right back to the 1960s. The first contest was held in Las Vegas on 16 September 1991. Several others followed, allowing the Federation to demonstrate the concept and test media reaction. When this proved favorable, Wallerstein himself launched a professional circuit, which united in battle some thirty players from seven different countries in its first season.

Although he had long been a puzzle collector, Wallerstein could hardly claim to be an expert. In a bid for further legitimacy, therefore, he signed up the services of several ex-members of the Puzzology Society.

The seriousness of this organization was beyond question. Established in 1935, the Society of Puzzle Lovers, renamed the Puzzology Society in 1968, existed purely and simply "to promote the ideals of the puzzle in all its forms," to quote the exact terms of its founder, Pete Carroll.

For more than thirty years, the Puzzology Society had brought delight to collectors in search of rare pieces and, on a simpler level, to amateur enthusiasts, who reported the joy they experienced on slotting into place the final piece of a particularly tricky Margaret Richardson.

In 1965 a small group of Harvard students steered the Society in a decisive new direction. Dazzled by the extraordinary possibilities opened up by the very idea of the puzzle, they decided to transform the association into a forum for the formulation and exchange of ideas, placing at the head of the agenda of their weekly meetings such abstruse subjects as "Light and shade in the work of John James Audubon" and "A critical examination of the Fissler Theorem of the nonfinite nature of the puzzle."

The adoption of this new, considerably more rigorous position attracted the attention of several academics, and, along with that, some of the more brilliant students at East Coast universities. In its heyday, the Society had more than two hundred active members and almost a thousand sympathizers. It published a quarterly, the *Puzzological Review,* copies of which it was proud to dispatch as far afield as Alma-Ata. Its finest hour came in 1969, when, in collaboration with the *New York Times,* it organized a competition around the theme "the most difficult puzzle in the world." Of the three hundred entries received, the one that found favor with the jury was a most singular work submitted by a Frenchman, Paul Rousselet. An honorable mention went to Thomas Carroll, son of Pete Carroll, who also happened to be the administrative secretary of the Society.

From that time onward, the Society entered a period of progressive decline, despite the strenuous efforts of Upton Sutter, a young academic who was elected president in 1977. The Society never entirely recovered from the departure of its key members, who moved away from the area once their studies were complete. Men like Dunlap and Earp, for instance, went off to live in the sticks as soon as they achieved their medical diplomas. The Bostonians began to tire of their endless debates, of which some of them, to tell the truth, had never been able to make much sense anyway. Only a few old faithfuls hung on, most of whom were distinguished not so much by their brilliance as by their taste for somewhat rarefied debate.

What shook the members from their torpor, in the end, was a crisis. In 1990, one of their number, Plunket by name, came up with the idea that went on to become the Gleaners Project. The thinking behind it was to provide an empirical response to a question that cropped up time and time again during the course of the Society's debates: Is there a universal equilibrium configuration for the puzzle?

To find out, Plunket proposed, in the first instance, an experiment to be carried out on a brick wall. Was it not possible that two laborers working on the same wall might achieve a stable equilibrium, in which any action undertaken by the one would immediately be negated by that of the other?

It was an ambitious project, and it received a budgetary allocation that might have been considered more than generous at a time when funds were comparatively short. The consensus that had been in place at the time of the project's commissioning completely fell apart in the face of Plunket's report, presented to the committee two months later. The method of procedure adopted in the experiment was manifestly flawed and, accordingly, any results had to be considered invalid. In the light of the facts, any analogy with the puzzle seemed at best dubious. Matters were not helped, furthermore, by the fact that the Gleaners Project considerably exceeded its allocated budget. In short, it was a fiasco, and it was not long before certain members began to demand that heads should roll. They pointed out, and not without some justification, that Gleaners represented a perfect illustration of what precisely had been wrong with the Society for a good number of years. They went further, and placed a question mark on the very role of the Society: the puzzle was in a state of widespread decline; what had the Society ever tried to do about it?

The Society, they argued, in its current form at least, was no longer in a position to respond effectively to the challenges of the contemporary world. In order to stamp out the revolt, Sutter had no choice but to call an election, which he won by a very narrow margin. His opponents resigned. They "refused to be accomplices to murder" and "declared their intention to join the ranks of those who, as early as 1990, had not been afraid to put themselves on the line in defense of the ideals of puzzling." Some weeks later, they were said to have joined the cause of multimillionaire Charles Wallerstein.

The success of the professional circuit vindicated the decision of the defectors. The early contests revived public interest in the jigsaw puzzle; very gradually, after twenty years of total stagnation, the rate of sales began to rise. A few of the old manufacturers, such as Jaymar Specialty and Saalfield Publishing, rose from the grave. Others were set up from scratch, Ubik Inc., for example, a hundred percent subsidiary of the Ubiquis group, who produced the puzzles used in competition for the commercial market.

The Americans were also introduced to Olof Niels, the Danish player who, after six tournament victories, was crowned champion in 1992. The speed puzzle had already been around in Europe for several years. Better trained and more used to competition pressure than their American colleagues, the representatives of the Old World ran rings around everyone in the first season. Wallerstein, realizing that European supremacy was likely to dampen the public's new-found enthusiasm for the sport, commissioned Cecil Earp to go and hunt down some national talent for him to pit against Olof the Viking (the nickname soon given him by *JP (Jigsaw Puzzle) Magazine*, on account of his imposing stature and shock of blond hair).

Later on, when Spillsbury became a superstar, Earp would often relate the improbable, not to say miraculous, circumstances in which he'd first come across this young man. Eighteen years of age, slightly retarded, Spillsbury had lived in a psychiatric asylum ever since his father had been thrown in prison for the murder of his wife. Earp looked on in astonishment as Spillsbury assembled the 520 pieces of "Keeper of the Flame" in eighteen minutes and thirty-four seconds. Using his left hand, he would pick up a piece at random, and place it in position on the table, apparently without a moment's reflection. The key to his prodigious skill lay with his phenomenal photographic memory, which meant he could identify the correct position for each piece at a glance.

During the 1993 season, Spillsbury won all fourteen contests. There was a fear the public might begin to complain of predictability. Not a bit of it. Millions of Americans took the gawky, half-orphaned youth to their hearts. He himself seemed to find nothing special about his particular gift.

The 1994 season was more of a challenge for Spillsbury. On several occasions he had to struggle to achieve his win. His first defeat came in the final of the Las Vegas Contest, the last of the season, against Olof Niels. The Dane's exertions throughout the season had finally paid off. On Niels's own admission, Spillsbury was still the best, but from now on he would have to put up a fight to keep his crown.

One month later, on 8 March 1995, to be exact, the corpse of the Dutch player Krijek, number six in the provisional rankings of the professional circuit, was discovered in a hotel bedroom in Baltimore. Krijek had succumbed to a massive injection of Pentothal. His left leg had been amputated and replaced with a fragment from a Polaroid photo.

Three weeks later the American architect Irwin Weissberg, who had just completed plans for a "Puzzle Center," suffered the same fate, identical in every detail save that in his case the right, instead of the left, leg was missing.

On May 15 Charles Wallerstein lost his loyal assistant, a young man in his early thirties named Blythe. Blythe's right hand had been cut off.

On 7 July, the Polaroid Killer, as the press quickly dubbed him, removed the right arm of the Russian, Kallisov, one of the rising stars of the circuit, according to Cecil Earp.

It should be pointed out that one week earlier, the members of the Puzzology Society had elected Thomas Carroll as their new president. During the course of an extraordinary general meeting, just as the members were all set to reelect the indefatigable Sutter for a fifth term, Carroll threw his own hat into the ring. He spoke for almost thirty-five minutes, outlining the history of the Society, from those heady evenings in the family home in Springfield, through to the appalling risks run by those who indulged in unwise speculation, without forgetting to mention the dubious Gleaners affair. More than ever before, he said, the ideal of puzzling needed defending. He pleaded for a return to grass roots, and proposed that the exchange market, which had been inactive for thirty years, be reinstated. Once it had recovered from the initial shock, the committee supported Carroll's candidature almost unanimously.

Olof Niels scarcely had time to dwell on this lesson in filial loyalty. On the morning of September 3 he was found by his girlfriend, sitting at a table on which was spread the thousand-piece "Survivors of the War in the Pacific." His posture seemed unusually sloppy. In front of him was a Polaroid of a left arm, the very same arm that was missing from his body.

It should be said in defense of the police and the FBI that the private detectives engaged at huge expense by Wallerstein did not succeed in throwing much light on the case. At best they drew a little more public attention to the circuit, and this in turn boosted the profits of their employer. That year the advertising revenue for the Las Vegas tournament exceeded even that of the Super Bowl, so much so that certain malicious gossips spread the word that Wallerstein could have masterminded the series of murders himself. More subtle commentators raised questions about the enigma of Spillsbury's disappearance. By unfortunate coincidence, the murderer seemed to choose his victims from among the young prodigy's most fearsome opponents.

In the interests of thoroughness, we should also mention the murder of the Frenchman, Paul Rousselet. After designing "the most difficult jigsaw in the world" in 1972, he was recruited by Wallerstein to create the unpublished jigsaws used in championship matches. He too got his dose of Pentothal, but was spared amputation and the accompanying Polaroid, which led some to suppose that the murderer had begun to run out of steam.

All this was several months ago.

This is the broad outline; obviously, the reality is a little more complex.

The Puzzle
(in forty-eight pieces)

Singles Competition:
The African Revival

Mind Games Magazine, July 1986

From our special correspondent in Stockholm:

"This is the victory not of a single individual, but of the entire African continent. Some people might look on it as revenge, but they'd be wrong: the puzzle is here to unite, not to divide us." The success of Cameroonian Georges Mombala, who yesterday was crowned world champion of the 500-piece men's singles competition, seriously—splendidly—confounds all those who were convinced they'd never see an African on the podium at international level. Let's just go back a little way.

The 1978 world championships in Lagos, the first ever to be held on African soil, ended on 8 August. In the final section, the 3,000-piece male singles, the title was won by Per Vansson. In his closing speech, Umberto Lampini, then President of the International Federation, declared: "The warm welcome extended to the foreign delegations, the public enthusiasm, the promising performances by the African players, are all key factors in assuring that the African people will be an increasingly significant force on the global puzzle circuit in years to come." Fine words, spoken to please the half dozen or so monarchs who had attended the Lagos competition, but scarcely disguising President Lampini's anger. Viewed as a whole, the championships were a complete disaster. The European delegations were billeted twenty miles from the venue. Half the competitors, including Vansson, got sick from the local food. The playing conditions were deplorable from start to finish and were not helped by the breakdown of the air conditioning on the very first day. The spectators had no idea of the rules, but noisily cheered on the African competitors. Some were laying bets during the game, in open contempt of competition rules. Most important, the Federation was staggered by the dismal standard of the African players. Not one of them achieved a ranking in the top fifty. As for the group competitions, they became an exercise in humiliation, with Togo and Algeria suffering disqualification for failure to complete their puzzle within the allotted time. Sedition began to stir in the bowels of the Federation. At the next meeting of the executive committee, the Canadian delegate demanded Lampini's head on a plate. Request granted. Manfred Dretter, the new President, privately admits that the experience in Lagos has taught the Federation a lesson. Over the next eight years, it adopted a policy of stamping out the unconventional elements in the African approach, an abuse of authority which this publication has consistently condemned.

All the more credit, therefore, to Georges Mombala, whose name, as recently as yesterday, was known only to specialists and those journalists who covered the recent African championships held in Bangui. Mombala, a French teacher from Yaoundé, and a member of the Cameroonian Federation since 1983, demonstrated throughout the week that intuitive sense which is the unmistakable hallmark of true talent. Halfway through the prequarterfinal, well down against the Mexican, Ramirez (we haven't heard the last of the Mexican delegation, who, had it not been for their failure to mark a victory, would surely have been among the medalists), he recovered his ground by fixing twenty-one pieces in only sixteen seconds. Again, in the quarterfinal, he gutted his opponent, the Frenchman, Cornillet, in the very first minute, by putting together a fifty-piece monochrome run, right under his nose—the most difficult part of the entire puzzle.

Mombala's game shows a refreshing spontaneity at a time when the widespread similarity of training methods threatens to detract from the interest in competition puzzling. What a difference between the two finals! On the one hand, an impeccable encounter between Strön and Renko, each using exactly the same selection process and memory technique. As a result, the method used by each player proceeds along identical lines, with the difference of only an occasional piece, here or there, between them. Monotonous perfection, zero theater, and a corresponding lack of enthusiasm, even occasional downright frustration, among the spectators. In the other match, the style could not have been more different. The game of both Mombala and Krijek is based entirely on enthusiasm and vivacity, and could be summed up in a single sentence: Neither man ever lets the puzzle grow cold. Each piece automatically leads to the next, and so on right through to the end. Mombala's games are like snakes, coiled up initially, on a single piece, suddenly unleashed, slithering madly across the table, before finally curling up once more, exhausted, inert, around the contour of the completed puzzle. His opponent was no slouch either. The contestant from Amsterdam, whose style places him clearly in the tradition of the great Dutch colorists, showed exceptional speed of execution. But even a Krijek, with his stunning track record at the bottom edge of the picture, and his victories against two successive world champions, could not stand up to Mombala's mad scamper. He was left with thirty-four pieces on the table at the end of one of the shortest semifinals in the history of the game.

It was expected that the final would be a pure formality for Mombala, as indeed it was, all over in twelve minutes flat, with never a moment's doubt as to the outcome. Those who see in Strön the successor to Per Vansson are doing the boy no favors. His rough edges and lack of self-confidence are still much in evidence, and as yet he has no major title to his name. The hapless Strön seemed paralyzed by the ease of Mombala's game, fumbling around in the easy passages, allowing his opponent simply to soar to victory. We should congratulate Mombala, too, on his modesty, on his choice of a consensual—one might almost say ecumenical—note in his speech of thanks, and on his unconcealed joy, which, in contrast with the formal nature of many medal ceremonies, was a pleasure to witness.

What lessons for the future can we draw from this victory? The first thing to be said is this: the Mombala phenomenon has brought a breath of fresh air to the singles competition, which, over recent years, had been in poor shape, suffering from the total lack of personality of its champions. Second: the African style, whose basic features we were already dimly aware of, has now become a reality. From now on, it is a force to be reckoned with. Boys like Kumba, N'Donge, Diallo, will follow in Mombala's footsteps. As yet they are still blundering and impetuous, but you can be sure that before long they will be channeling their creativity and astonishing us with their sheer audacity. Third—and this time, on a note of regret: the African continent, so rich in individual talent, does not yet have the teams it deserves. Once again the group contests revealed a lack of organization and cohesion among the African delegations. Although at the very height of his form, Mombala was unable to carry the Cameroonian team with him—indeed, the team seemed to be playing together for the first time. But Europeans and South Americans should not be drawing comfort from this: the day Africa does overcome its difficulties, it will be very hard to beat.

The Golden Age of the Puzzle:
A Retrospective

Walter Nukestead is Professor of American Civilization at the University of Salem, Oregon, where he specializes in the history of the puzzle. As the nationwide professional circuit of multimillionaire Charles Wallerstein gets underway, Nukestead tells Jessica Woodruff why he is counting on a new vogue for the puzzle, invented almost three hundred years ago.

NEW YORK TIMES: *Mr. Nukestead, how long have you been a member of the Puzzology Society?*

WN: I attended my first weekly meeting on 20 May 1963, thirty years ago next spring.

NYT: *Today you live in Oregon. Do you still attend the meetings?*

WN: Not every week, naturally. But I do make the trip once, maybe twice, a month, depending on the agenda.

NYT: *What drew you to the Society in the first place?*

WN: I was studying American Civilization at Springfield, trying to find a subject for my PhD. I was told about the Puzzology Society by a friend who was already a member. At that time the only puzzles I'd ever seen were the ones of Santa Claus my grandfather used to give me for Christmas. I found it hard to believe that serious-minded people could get together to talk about such a trivial subject, so I invited myself along to a meeting. The speaker on that occasion was a sociology professor from Harvard, one Gedeon Hochkiss, who predicted there would be a revival of interest in the puzzle in the not too distant future. I had a chat with him at the end of the conference and he persuaded me to write my thesis on the subject of the puzzle. Shortly after that I became a member of the Society.

NYT: *Why did Hochkiss believe there would be a revival of the puzzle?*

WN: He'd noticed that most board games go through cycles of enthusiasm followed by neglect. The average length of the cycle is thirty years, corresponding, roughly speaking, to a single generation. Naturally enough, a father who himself played dominoes as a child is likely to buy a set for his children, and they too, thirty years after that, will give one to their own children, and so on. In the case of the puzzle, it's particularly clear-cut. The first wave of popularity was in 1908–9. America had been importing puzzles from England for almost a hundred years, but up to that point they had been the exclusive preserve of the rich, who could afford hand-cut models.

The first decade of the 1900s saw the creation of the first puzzle lending libraries. For a modest subscription, people could borrow as many puzzles as they pleased. The middle classes embraced the new craze immediately, but within a few years had lost interest once again.

The craze in the thirties was by far the biggest ever. It came precisely at the time of the Great Depression and died out with the success of the New Deal. From one day to the next, hundreds of businesses began manufacturing puzzles, themselves competing with thousands of unemployed workers who had set up on their own, producing several puzzles a day. Mechanized production spectacularly reduced overheads. One manufacturer in Baltimore launched a series at ten cents a unit, which was a huge success. At the height of the puzzle's popularity, the Parker Brothers, Einson-Freeman and others like Milton Bradley sold up to ten million puzzles a week. That was when Pete Carroll founded the Puzzology Society.

NYT: *So, there had already been two puzzle crazes. Was that sufficient reason to predict a third?*

WN: Hochkiss had made a study of many other games. Over the years he had gathered data on dominoes, hopscotch, patience and so on. This enabled him to predict the success of the hula hoop, which may surprise those who believe the hula hoop to have been an invention of the 1950s. In point of fact, Hochkiss had previously made a study of a game already popular with the Pilgrim Fathers, which involved spinning a barrel hoop around the hips. The "barrel game," as the cowboys used to call it, had gone repeatedly in and out of fashion, until the First World War, when it disappeared completely from local town gatherings. In the early fifties, Hochkiss sensed the moment was ripe for a "barrel game" comeback. He outlined his arguments in an article in the periodical *American Studies*. Within a few months, millions of adolescents were wiggling their hips, all quite convinced that the hula hoop was a twentieth-century invention. Hochkiss was sure we would see the same thing happen with the puzzle.

NYT: *Was he right?*

WN: Yes, although the craze in the 1960s was less spectacular than that at the time of the Great Depression. Historians generally give the credit to Springbok Editions, a firm in New York. Sales figures for puzzles hadn't moved for about ten years. In 1963, Springbok created an initial stir by marketing circular puzzles (originally a British idea). A year later, they launched a series based on reproductions of famous paintings. It may seem surprising, but it was the first time a publisher had departed from the classic set pieces drawn, up till then, from American history and the baseball leagues. Fra Filippo Lippi's "Adoration of the Magi" was an immediate hit. It was followed by "Convergence," an abstract painting by Jackson Pollock, which Springbok claimed was the most difficult puzzle in the world, and which sold a hundred thousand copies in just a few weeks. The Allbright-Knox Gallery in Buffalo, where the painting hung, received thousands of visitors, who all came just to see the "dreadful Pollock" they had spent so many hours on.

Other firms jumped on the Springbok bandwagon. The fashion for puzzles lasted about five years, then the market dropped once more to its original level. The Society's list of permanent members, which peaked at one hundred and eighty in 1967, remained stable for two or three years, then started to decline again.

NYT: *Can we look forward to another surge of interest in the nineties?*

WN: It's already begun. The professional circuit created by Charles Wallerstein is about to enter its third season. Out of the circuit has grown the monthly *JP Magazine,* whose circulation is going up and up. Some of the television channels broadcast competitions at peak viewing hours and the sales figures for puzzles are set to rise again. Even so, I would make a distinction between this craze and the two preceding ones, in that this one has quite clearly been planned. Wallerstein doesn't just want a one-off success, he's looking to establish his circuit long-term. As a result you won't get the same level of enthusiasm we saw in 1965–9, and to an even greater extent, during the Great Depression.

NYT: *What's the position of the Puzzology Society with regard to the JP Tour?*

WN: Very reserved, let's just say. We are unanimous in our condemnation of the idea of the speed puzzle, which is simply designed to cultivate stars, and attract media attention. A number of our members, including the President, are even calling for the abolition of the circuit. We have been studying the puzzle, in all its intricate and theoretical glory, for sixty years. Suddenly, overnight, someone plucks some Scandinavian off his ice block and tells us he's the living incarnation of our discipline.

I understand the feelings of my colleagues, but at the same time I do hope Wallerstein's arrival on the scene, even if it does entail some rather dubious touting for popular support, may be beneficial for the science of puzzology. However, I should point out, that this has proved not to be the case.

NYT: *You were saying just now that the on/off cycles correspond generally to the generation cycle. Could there be any other factors?*

WN: Yes, of course. As early as 1965, Hochkiss showed how the economic climate, technological progress and social change impacted on the length of the cycles. I cannot recommend his *Histori-*

cal Materialism and Its Application to Board Games highly enough. It was written at the height of the Korean War, and got Hochkiss into some hot water with the CIA. He examines a number of well-known games and shows how their success or failure depends almost entirely on the economic conditions under which they were produced, marketed, etc. Thus, according to him, the vogue of 1901–9 can be attributed to the new lending libraries, which made puzzles available to all. In the case of the Depression, several factors came into play at once: the first automated printing machines cut manufacturing costs by ninety percent; businesses, always keen to find new means of advertising, produced thousands of puzzles bearing their own logos; millions of people who had been laid off found themselves with spare time on their hands, and discovered in puzzles an effective outlet for stress.

In a previous article, Hochkiss even put forward another, more profound, if debatable, explanation. In his view, one of the features of the Depression was an explosion of society, with the result that the average American lost all his bearings and experienced a sense of chaos hitherto unknown. The completion of a puzzle could give a sense of bringing order to chaos, restoring the world as it was meant to be, that is, as it was before the crash.

NYT: *What was Hochkiss's analysis of its popularity from 1965 to 1999?*

WN: He had no time to make one. He died two months after we met. However, I consider the question in my thesis. In my view, there were two main reasons for the extraordinary success of the Springbok puzzles. Their range of well-known paintings represented a complete departure from the aesthetic mediocrity of the usual subjects. Although after the war there was no shortage of creative talent or of researchers in the field, their work never reached the general public. Second, Springbok appealed to two classic American values, sportsmanship and a sense of challenge, by offering the public what were supposedly the most difficult puzzles in the world. Pollock's "Convergence," for example, offers the puzzlist no guidelines whatsoever. Along similar lines Springbok also issued a series of monochromes with evocative titles: "Little Red Riding Hood's Hood" (entirely red), "Three Bears in Close Up" (entirely brown), and "Snow White Without the Dwarves" (entirely white).

But the puzzle craze of the second half of the sixties didn't just stop with the Springbok titles. I think the success of the puzzle during that time was also a reaction against the increasing influence of television. Some people consider television to be emblematic of the counterculture. Personally, I wouldn't go that far. Nevertheless, the public appreciated the traditional and genuine character of the puzzle (many models were still made out of wood), a character that placed it in direct opposition to the hegemony of the signifier and the ephemeral world. I recall a member of the Society, now deceased, who drew up a map of the puzzle, based on the number of sets sold each year per capita. The greatest concentration was noticeably in the vicinity of university campuses, and in towns that were hotbeds of social unrest: Berkeley, Los Angeles, etc.

NYT: *Any reasons you can suggest for the current popularity of the puzzle?*

WN: Nothing comes out of nowhere. The current interest is quite simply another "application" of Hochkiss's historical materialist matrix. Wallerstein isn't exactly noted for his philanthropy. He went into this whole business for the simple reason that he reckoned it would make him money. He will now try to break the fatal cycle, according to which the puzzle should slump into obscurity for another twenty-five years. Powerful he may be, but I doubt even he can alter the course of history.

Murder at Point Bonita:
A Serial Killer at Work?

Richard Bronner, *San Francisco Examiner,* 11 March 1995

The identity of a murder victim found Tuesday evening at Point Bonita was revealed at a press conference held today at the HQ of the San Francisco Police Department. One of the victim's legs had been amputated. He was of Dutch origin and was identified as Rijk Krijek, a well-known figure on the professional puzzle circuit set up by multimillionaire Charles Wallerstein.

A passerby reported the presence of a suspicious vehicle in the parking lot at Point Bonita at around 2330 hours on March 9. The police reacted immediately and on arrival found a red Dodge Shadow parked on the grass, facing the ocean, with its headlights blazing. The man inside the car was dead. His left leg had been severed across the top of the thigh. He was wearing his seat belt. In his pocket the police found a fragment of a photo, showing a left leg.

On the day of his death, Krijek played against the Swede Uppal in the first round of the San Francisco competition. After an easy victory he went back to his hotel, the Hilton, at the junction of Taylor and Lombard. At exactly 1612 hours he received a telephone call from a public phone. The call lasted two minutes. The hotel receptionist saw Krijek come downstairs a few moments later. He left the hotel at the wheel of his rented car. It was the last time he was seen alive.

The autopsy showed that the cause of death was a massive injection of strychnine, administered shortly after the amputation, and not, as the forensic pathologist had stated, a hemorrhage. Traces of a Pentothal-based anesthetic were also found to be present. This product, more commonly known as "truth serum," is often used for its anesthetizing properties in the medical world.

Lieutenant Deroney, who is leading the investigation, agreed to go step by step through the murder scenario. The murderer called Krijek at his hotel and arranged a meeting with him. He anesthetized his victim, probably catching him off guard, then amputated the limb before finishing him off with the lethal injection. The absence of any trace of blood or sign of a struggle in the area immediately around Krijek's Dodge led the police to believe that the assassin had committed the act elsewhere, probably at his own home. Then, once darkness fell, he set out for Point Bonita and arranged the body in a macabre tableau. In support of this theory, Lieutenant Deroney, who is already known to the citizens of San Francisco for his contribution to the Havilland affair, observes that the absence of any stains on the seats of the Dodge proves that the body was put in the car only shortly before it was discovered.

The police are naturally concentrating their investigation on the mysterious caller. They were able to establish that he called from a public phone in a shopping mall not far from the hotel, but routine questioning carried out in the vicinity has as yet failed to reveal anything new.

Lieutenant Deroney explained that for the time being he was ruling out the possibility of a purely gratuitous crime. "The murder method proves the murderer knew Krijek, or was sufficiently familiar with him to get him to agree to a meeting. We therefore intend to concentrate on the victim's past, in collaboration with our European colleagues at Interpol."

Asked for his personal opinion on the case, Deroney admitted that certain aspects of the investigation seemed not to square with the theory that this was a purely private quarrel.

"Whoever he is, the murderer took unbelievable risks. Krijek could easily have informed a third person before going to keep his appointment. Also, in organizing his little setup at Point Bonita, at a time of day when many people are still out walking in the park, he exposed himself far more than he needed to."

Deroney contradicted a rumor connecting the Point Bonita murder to previous, similar, unsolved cases. "We are dealing here with a murderer whose method has no precedent. This particular combination of calculated risks and exhibitionism seems to point to a serial killer, and in the light of this, I would urge the citizens of San Francisco to exercise the utmost prudence at all times."

Enter the Competition for the World's Most Difficult Puzzle

Bram Thouless, *Puzzology Review,* July–August 1969

Gerald Honorton said it all the way through his campaign: "Vote for me to run the Puzzology Society and I'll set up an initiative that will hugely increase the popularity of the puzzle in our country." And, sure enough, no sooner was he elected—he took office on 21 June—than Honorton announced a competition for the "Most Difficult Puzzle in the World."

A debate as old as the puzzle itself

To be fair, the new president cannot take all the credit for this idea. The most difficult puzzle in the world is something of a shaggy dog for the Society, one of those subjects that crops up from time to time in debate and that no amount of discussion or theorizing ever seems quite to wear out. A long article in this journal in 1966 dwelt at some length on "Convergence," the reproduction of the painting by the same name by Jackson Pollock.[1] At its launch, Springbok Editions presented "Convergence" as "the most difficult puzzle in the world." Three years later, we asked whether the slogan was still valid, which in turn led us

---

1. *Puzzology Review,* No. 7, March–April 1966.

to consider two further, more general questions: What *was* the most difficult puzzle in the world in 1966, and what criteria should be used for judging the difficulty of a puzzle? Two apparently straightforward questions. Much ink, however, was spent in the discussion of both.

When canvassed by the *Review*'s editorial team, the Society's members were broadly agreed that the reputation of "Convergence" had now been pretty much usurped. Almost without exception, each respondent named at least one puzzle which he or she personally considered more difficult than "Convergence." The name that came up most frequently was that of the manufacturer Mrizek, no doubt on account of their method of cutting along color lines. DeLacy and Chatham were also mentioned, although they cannot actually be credited with any breakthrough in the field of manufacture.

But our fundamental point was this: How shall we judge the "difficulty" of a puzzle? One obvious answer comes immediately to mind: by the length of time it takes to solve it. However, a moment's reflection reveals the inadequacy, not to say sloppiness, of this response. To solve the fifty-eight-piece puzzle, "Funny Animal," by Mrizek, requires a minimum of around twenty minutes. Can we really therefore say that it is "easier" than "Feeding the Ducks" by the Parker Brothers, a 214-piecer, which even a child can complete in three-quarters of an hour? On that basis, the larger a puzzle, the more "difficult" it would be. And yet with his theorem (see boxed section), Fissler has shown that the very concept of the "largest" puzzle in the world is a meaningless one.

So where could we go from here? The traditionalists maintained that the "hardest" puzzle would be the result of bringing together a whole range of different elements which, for all that is familiar (noninterlocking pieces, cutting along color lines, false corners, etc.), remain as challenging as ever, particularly when employed simultaneously. The idealists, led by Jones and Vorech, objected to this view, politely dismissing it as "simplistic" and "outmoded."[2] In their view, solving the most difficult puzzle in the

---

2. In *Minutes of the Weekly Meeting of the Puzzology Society,* No. 1862, 16 June 1969.

world is not an immediate prospect: the creator God has scattered its pieces throughout the work of nature, and we have no idea even what the picture looks like.

Sponsorship by the *New York Times*: A Stroke of Luck for the Society

President Honorton's initiative offers the entire company of the puzzle faithful an opportunity to pick up the debate where they left off. In fact, the competition is open to everyone, including shareholders and manufacturers. The closing date for entries is 28 October 1969. The rules have deliberately been kept loose, allowing maximum freedom for bold and imaginative entries. No restrictions have been imposed on the format of the puzzle, its dimensions, shape or number of pieces, choice of subject or materials. Submission of the image itself is not obligatory. It has been decided not to impose any conditions on the actual nature of the puzzle, which may be traditional, contemporary, literary or any number of things. In any event, the jury alone will be entitled to judge whether or not, in each case, the work presented constitutes a puzzle.

It is certain that, without the collaboration of the *New York Times*, the organizers of this competition could not have allowed themselves such breadth or scope. Jessica Woodruff, Editor-in-Chief of the Arts section of the paper and a long-standing friend of the Society, secured the paper's commitment to the contest, and will be covering the awards ceremony, to be held on Saturday, 18 November in the Grand Auditorium of the Faculty of Human Sciences at Harvard.

A copy of the competition rules may be obtained by calling 707-3211 or by writing to the Society at 9 Rosamond Street, Boston, MA 20740.

May the best player win!

STANLEY FISSLER'S
BIG MISSED CHANCE!

Giuseppe Rinaldi, an Italian craftsman from Verona, took his place in the Guinness Book of Records last year, thanks to one of his original compositions, a puzzle of 36,000 pieces. But surely we should bear in mind the teaching of Fissler's theorem, which, stripped of its complex mathematical language, may be expressed as follows: the infinite nature of the maximum number of pieces in the biggest puzzle in the world renders any attempt to manufacture such a puzzle completely pointless.

Fissler, an astrophysicist at MIT, first addressed the question of the infinite puzzle in 1936. He proposed a circular puzzle, to which a new border is added each day. This new layer would remain the outer layer for only a single day, before it was superseded, at the outer edge, by a new series of pieces, the new border, and so on. It becomes apparent that the concept of the largest puzzle in the world has no meaning, since there always exists the possibility of increasing its diameter to create a new puzzle, which is bigger than the previous "biggest."

In the face of such virtuosity, the reader will no doubt be surprised to learn that Stanley Fissler was a mediocre scientist. This fact is all the more disappointing, given that his puzzle theory contains in embryo the basic principles of modern astrophysics. The circular puzzle represents the perpetually expanding universe, while the border to which a new layer is constantly being added brings into question the very notion of the "frontier" in a space without limits. Fissler died in 1961, without ever having picked up on this analogy, glaringly obvious though it is. Two of his colleagues later won a Nobel Prize for the same idea.

NINE WISE MEN FOR
ONE TITLE

The nine competition judges have been appointed from, in equal numbers, the Puzzology Society, the *New York Times*, and personalities from outside the field who have shown an interest in puzzles. The rules require them to meet on 29 October at nine o'clock to review the entries. After the initial selection of ten finalists, the overall winner will be chosen by majority vote. In the event of a tie, the vote of the chairman of the jury will count double.

President of the jury
Upton Sutter, 29, Junior Lecturer in Urbanism, Harvard University.

From the Puzzology Society
Frances Sheehan, 36, Professor of Ancient Greek, Harvard University.
Malcolm Crandon, 27, PhD student in quantum mechanics, MIT.

From the New York Times
Jessica Woodruff, 38, Editor-in-Chief of the Arts section.
Louisa Barker, 31, Editor of the "Mind Games" section.
Valentina Warcollier, 32, Editor of the "Visual Arts" section.

From the general public
Harry Mockenhaupt, 62, retired, collector.
Charles Wallerstein, 32, President of Wallerstein Inc.
Tracy Sargent, 46, Librarian, Harvard University.

Krijek–Herrera

Radio report by Leonard da Fonseca on WNDZ
Federation Tournament, 4 October 1992

"Welcome, ladies and gentlemen, to the very temple of the puzzle, the inner sanctum of the wooden piece, or, more precisely, the Sports Palace of the Mirage Hotel, Las Vegas. On the program for this afternoon, in that queen of all disciplines, the thousand pieces, four matches, which will bring together eight players from three different continents, all in all, the crème de la crème of the world's elite. In less than two minutes now, we will witness, in the presence of Charles Wallerstein himself, no less, the first quarterfinal: between the Dutchman Krijek, number one in group five, and the Colombian Herrera, number one in group four. And what a truly astonishing delegation, these Colombians, with three of them making it through to the last eight of the competition! Only this morning, their coach was saying that before long puzzlists would be overtaking coffee as Colombia's leading export! Those of you who are familiar with the circuit will already know Herrera of old; now you just need to learn the names of his compatriots: Parara and Neto. Only forty years on this earth between the two of them! At 1600 hours they'll be competing for a place in the semifinal. We saw the thrashing Parara gave Jean-François Cornillet in the quarterfinals, such a likable player, Cornillet. For the last few months, by the way, he's been training in the States. Chin up, Corny, to use his teammates' name for him! As for Fernando Neto, now there's a player who leaves nothing to chance. Yet up to a month ago, no one had even heard of this young Colombian peasant, a distant cousin of Herrera, so we're told, come now to try his luck in America, encouraged, no doubt, by his big cousin! Oh, I'm being told now they're not cousins; Neto is actually Herrera's brother-in-law. I must say, it's an easy mistake to make, muddling up these huge families, and, to be honest, cousins made sense to me, blood relations and all that. After all, these things run in the genes. Anyway, what we can safely say is that Neto comes from the right sort of background. His technical prowess quite literally blew our Scandinavian friends away! With odds of only thirteen to one from the bookmakers at the Mirage, he gave Eriksen not a whisker of a chance. Eriksen too, you will recall, came out on top in his group, group seven. I must say the Viking warriors certainly had a rough time of it in the first round: Sundström, Eriksen and Uppal had their noses rubbed in the dust by the virtual newcomers. In two years of competition, it's the first time we've seen anything of the kind! Jonas Lundqvist, their coach, was practically choking on his salmon!

Oh, now here come Krijek and Herrera, accompanied by the tournament officials. Krijek's wearing cream canvas trousers and a sea-green sweater, in impeccable taste. He looks relaxed, but totally concentrated, a strange mixture of inner composure and outward ease. Herrera, on the other hand, looks slightly tense. His fingers are constantly at his shirt collar, as though to check he still has room to breathe. The two players take their seats, side by side, as the title of the puzzle they have to solve appears on the giant screen. There it is! "Hauling Twenty Mules Out of Death Valley," a work from RCA Wrightington Editions, vintage 1967. Not, I humbly admit, a publisher I've ever heard of. As I speak, the lid of the box is still closed, but a priori, it's a subject that should very slightly favor Herrera, with his preference for figurative themes. In under a minute now, the umpire, Mr. Wallis, will unveil the pieces, arranged in staggered rows, or "quincunx," on a tray inset on the tabletop. Krijek is deep in thought: trying, no doubt, to picture that scene—twenty mules emerging from the desert, unless, of course, he's done the puzzle before, which I strongly doubt, since the Federation does pride itself on its competition puzzles being entirely unknown. Herrera crosses himself, yes, and his hand trembles slightly as he does so. But his fans need not fear: in ten seconds' time, the trembling will have vanished, as his hands take off in flight over the pieces.

They're off! The umpire has just set off the mechanism that simultaneously releases the pieces and flashes the image on the players' screens. What can I say? Let's see, first impression, reproduction of a fairly standard oil painting. A convoy of mules and carts is seen emerging from a long, rocky mountain pass, which opens out onto a vast salt desert. In the foreground, a few cacti and the obligatory coyote skull, picked clean by vultures. In terms of the actual subject, nothing here that should present a particular problem to players of the stature of Herrera and Krijek. This is definitely going to be a match all about color. The mountain range that forms the backdrop of the picture has been painted using the entire range of browns, yellows, ochers... the great Death Valley, pride of all America!

It looks like Krijek's made the fastest start. The clock says fifty pieces in one minute, nine seconds; that's six seconds in front of Herrera. Quite a lead! But it's early days yet; we'll be getting a clearer idea around the 200 mark. Just a word about the technique of each of these players. They both use what we call the morphological technique, or, to be absolutely precise, a variant of it, the concave morphological method. Those listeners who've been following our broadcasts since the beginning of the competition will be familiar by now with the initially rather bewildering terminology. For those of you joining us for the first time today, let me just tell you that, according to the morphological method, the player allows himself to be guided by the form, rather than by the color of the pieces. Don't even bother trying this at home! The morphological method requires an extraordinary degree of skill in the recognition of shape and outline. But to get back to the game, Krijek is still out in front, though by a slightly narrower margin now, if I'm not mistaken. Yes, I'm right, he's more than four seconds ahead, at the 150-piece mark! Herrera's looking good, I'd say, he's mastered his early match nerves, and is now slotting his pieces together with all the regularity of a metronome. He's got the entire front section of the caravan in position, and five or six mules, while Krijek, on the other hand, has taken the lead on the mountains. A fact that would seem to suggest that he still adheres, to some degree, to the colorist technique, the backbone, after all, of the glory days of the Dutch team. Indeed, up until last year, the sole guiding principle in puzzle assembly, for our Batavian friends, was color. Along with all the other competition players, except for Cornillet, a more recent convert, Krijek went over to the morphological method last year, but his game has visibly retained a few vestiges of his earlier colorism. As I speak, he's making rather heavy weather of the sky. He's just spent two seconds dithering over an apparently insignificant outline piece. Oh, now he's put it back again! He's actually trying to force a salt-lake piece into position. Whether it fits or not, it's a crude error, and one that may well cost him dearly. There they go, one after the other, he's lost five precious seconds, and Herrera is lapping them up! Now he's tackling the reddish mountain slope too, with rather more success than Krijek, by the look of things. Oh yes, look at the deftness of that stroke! Sublime! It's hard to tell exactly, but I *think* he's caught up with Krijek. Yes! It's up on the giant screen. Herrera's eleven pieces ahead of Krijek at the 350-piece mark. As the Dutchman dithers away up there in the sky and the clouds, the chronometer takes its pitiless toll. But it's not all over yet, we're only a third of the way through, and we've seen Krijek pull something out of the bag on more than one occasion in the past. Now he's picking up a rhythm again, he's looking more like what we expect from a player of his caliber. Sky-mountains-bush-mule-mule-salt-lake-mountain—that's a fine sequence; we may get an exciting finish after all. Yes, as I was saying a minute ago, Krijek simply never accepts he's beaten. In the same competition last year, he was up against Tackl in the quarterfinal, always a tricky customer, even if he has lost some of his sparkle of late. At the 600-piece mark, after a simply breathtaking early break, Tackl was ahead by a "mere" thirty-eight seconds! At this level of the game, that's a pretty unassailable lead. So what does Krijek do? He keeps his head down and simply plugs away at his game, totally ignoring the crowd's jeers. As well he might, for Tackl falls promptly into the classic trap of pushing his luck too far. Instead of easing off, as any puzzlist would in the face of an assured and easy victory, he begins to work at double speed, maybe with the idea of nudging up on Mombala's record! With the result that he gets totally screwed up in the final straight and mixes up two virtually identical pieces. By the time he realized what he'd done it was too late, Krijek had made up the distance and in fact had gone four pieces ahead. That's the kind of comeback kid the guy is! But I'd be surprised to see a guy like Herrera make a blunder as basic as that. You only have to look at the minute delicacy with which he's slotting that coyote skull together, even as I speak; the movement's measured and precise, one piece no sooner down on the table than the hand is racing off again. Pure poetry! A fifteen-second lead to Herrera at the 500-piece mark, no slackening of the pace for the Colombian. Krijek's going to have a job catching up now! These Colombians really do have a sense of rhythm we Anglo-Saxons lack. As indeed do the Brazilians! Happy children of the sun—first they invent the samba, then soccer, before long they'll be conquering the JP Tour! Oh yes! A colleague was telling me recently how he'd been at the Brazilian Championships, held in Recife last month. He came back raving, simply blown away by the game he'd seen there—instinctive, flamboyant, untainted by the sophisticated techniques and devices so common in the Northern Hemisphere. To hell with colorism and the morphological method! Let's get straight to what matters—speed, speed and more speed! What's more, down there, puzzling really is a genuinely popular sport: stadiums bursting at the seams, four hundred thousand registered players, all amateurs! The champion, Ghimalaes, is an electrician from Belém, to give you some idea. They've given him some Portuguese nickname that means streak of light, or lightning, or some such . . . incredible acceleration! This colleague of mine tried to get some idea of Ghimalaes's maximum speed. You may not believe this, but in Brazil, they don't even display the clock! All that counts is the beauty of the game. In the final he measured it at sixty-three pieces! Faster than Mombala, even if you can't strictly compare manual and electronic timekeeping. According to my colleague, the day the Brazilians decide to enter the JP Tour, they'll carry off every title there is. But I've got ahead of myself a bit: Krijek's making a strong comeback, he's only one second behind now, at the 750-piece mark, and, most important, the mountains are behind him! He's got a dozen mules, two carts and a few bushes to go, while Herrera, on the other hand, has been a good deal less systematic: he hasn't actually got any area of the picture sewn up properly yet, and he's scarcely dipped into his salt lake. He's realized things are getting out of hand now. He's sweating profusely, mumbling indistinctly, praying, I expect; the Colombians are devout by nature. I think it's unlikely his Hail-Marying will do him any good at this stage, Krijek's effortlessly getting his mules lined up there, the cart'll be with us in a moment. A new score goes up: he's seven seconds ahead now. I think that finally puts the lid on Herrera's chances. He really missed the boat at the 400-piece mark, when he kept on going back to the sky when he should have been making headway on the rocky path. Oh well, no doubt his brother-in-law will be there to offer comfort later on.

Mr. Wallis, the umpire from New Zealand, is about to raise the blue flag. He hasn't had much to do during this match, the players were deeply absorbed in play, and play was quite proper and correct. And indeed the best umpires are not necessarily those who use the whistle most; in fact, I might almost say the reverse is true. So, we're almost there. Krijek glances sideways at his opponent. Less than a hundred pieces to go, he knows that victory must now be his. And how proud they stand now, our convoy of mules. All too often we fail to give these small companies their due, when so often they are much more creative than the big ones! The JP Tour is to be warmly complimented for the way they've brought them to the fore. Oh my God! Herrera is suddenly leaping with an astonishing final fling into the salt lake, seeming almost to take pleasure in the subtly different shades of white that make it such a fiendish challenge. Teeth clenched, he slots home his pieces, automaton-like. But sadly he's too late, and he knows it. Still, what do you expect? That's the famous South American sense of honor for you! Now I'll be very interested to know what his speed over that last 100-piece stretch was, the computer will be giving us that very shortly.

That's it! Krijek punches the air. And the Dutchman might well feel pleased with himself, he's come from way behind. Now for the second time running, he goes forward to the semifinals of the Federation competition, where he will meet the winner of the Niels–Asherwood match. He wins by fourteen pieces; it's a clean, clear-cut victory. Herrera looks distraught, he's got his head in his hands. He'll look back on that mountain pass for some time to come; that's where he just somehow went limp, if you'll pardon the expression. His trainer, Pedro Alamondo, joins him on the stage, puts his arm around his shoulders, consoles him. So much emotion in that gesture ... But we must leave you now, for a few moments. We'll be back with you right after the break.

6

Letter from Harry Dunlap to Cecil Earp

Cambridge, 11 August 1969

Hello Old Thing,

When I picture you offering up that athletic body of yours to the rays of the Indiana sun, while I sit here poring over this damned anatomy book, I do rather wish I'd put in a bit more work during the year. The date of the resit has been set for 23 August, which means I've got just two more weeks left to catch up on nine months' work, which, to put it mildly, was sporadic at best. Old Tyrell's enjoying it anyway. I saw him yesterday in the library. He started sniggering when he saw I was getting out *his* psychology treatise. "I had imagined, judging by your relaxed attitude in my lectures, that you had long since digested the contents of that!" he lisped. The swine! I could happily give him a proper stuffing! After all, he'd be only marginally less ugly than that gorilla he had us dissect in such gruesome detail during the second term!

At least one good thing's come out of all this. If I hadn't screwed up my written papers in June, I wouldn't have had the pleasure of seeing Honorton launch his competition for the so-called "most difficult puzzle in the world." I'm enclosing Bram's article from the *Review*. Nothing particularly startling in it, if you ask me, apart from what he has to say on the subject of this man Fissler—as in Fissler's Theorem—but otherwise just some twelfth-rate astronomer. To be quite honest, I was convinced—as you were too, if I remember correctly—that Honorton would try it on somehow as soon as he was elected, but I must admit, I wasn't quite expecting this. He's taken everyone by surprise, including the members of the Committee. But no one has actually objected, which probably shows it's not such a bad idea. Akers thinks it's a bit of a prostitution, but you know what a snob he is. Once I even heard him complain that the cutting technique used in "Sir Grenfell on Board Strathcona" was "vulgarly populist," if you please!

The funny thing about all this is that, to start with, Honorton was going to exclude all members of the Society from the competition. I suppose, all things considered, it's fairly logical, particularly since we have three seats on the judging panel (what a weird idea to make Sutter the chairman of the judges! I don't even like to think about how he can have wangled that one). That really set the cat among the pigeons. Even so, the way they run down Milton Bradley sometimes, I'm surprised how eager some of our dear colleagues are to design their own puzzles. Pribam (yes, you did read that correctly, Pribam!) threatened to kick up a scandal if he was prevented from making his own practical contribution to the history of the puzzle (sic) on the sole grounds that he was one of the most eminent theoreticians in the field. He found a surprising ally in Carroll, who came out of his usual shell to applaud Honorton's initiative, at the same time urging him to reconsider his decision. Which, in the end, he duly did, though he solemnly requested that Sutter exercise complete and total impartiality. Knowing the man as you do, you will no doubt appreciate the full savor of this request!

So, it's been three weeks now since the competition was launched, and there's been talk of nothing else since. So many people turned up at the last Committee meeting, we had to leave the doors open. I strongly suspect certain Society members of rearranging their vacation dates. Up and down the faculty corridors they go, looking frightfully busy; in fact all their business amounts to is spying on their chums in the hope of rooting out THE idea, which will hopefully make up for their desperate lack of imagination. When I spoke to Carroll yesterday, he told me all the books had gone out of the library. Akers alone has got twelve! Carroll was having a laugh about that. He's got everything in his head. I asked him what he was cooking up; he wouldn't say, but I bet it will interesting.

In spite of all this secrecy stuff, I'm pretty sure our friends are desperately short of inspiration. Mark created a real stir with his study on habitual assembly techniques. According to his article, 83% of players (85% of women and 81% of men—interesting distinction) follow color patterns, before any consideration of either theme or form. They all immediately drew the conclusion that the most difficult puzzle would have to be cut out along color lines—which is, after all, hardly a revelation.

Apart from that, everyone's wondering about the possible theme. What we'll most likely see is an endless succession of "Skies," "Crowds," or "Poppy Fields." Norman is pinning great hopes on a photo taken by his brother-in-law in the north of Finland at two o'clock in the afternoon. He says he defies anyone to get the first two pieces in under an hour. We'll have to see.

There's definitely a lot of scope in the actual shape of the pieces. Do you remember that Zig Zag puzzle "Doghouse" that I did with Melinda, where each separate piece was a dog? It was incredibly difficult, and I wouldn't be surprised if that didn't prove to be the way to go. I'll talk to Bob about it, at least if I manage to get hold of him between now and the prize-giving. He tried to bum fifty dollars off me on Sunday. From what I could make out, he wants to sign up some guinea pigs to try his ideas out on. Fond as I am of Bob, you will understand when I say that I turned down his proposition.

On reflection, the success of the competition is not that surprising. After all, we've all got something to prove in this area. Honorton makes no secret whatsoever about what he's after. Sutter is lining up for the 1977 election. Guys like Akers and Pribam see it as an opportunity to make their names as *the* big puzzle thinkers of the latter part of the century. Carroll wants to do honor to his father's name; apparently the awards ceremony has been set for the anniversary of our friend Pete's death. As for me, if only I could chuck my studying...

And I haven't even touched on the financial aspect: I need only tell you there's a Wallerstein on the panel and you can guess there's a lot of money to be picked up. All the top makers, Parker Brothers, Milton Bradley, Springbok and the rest, have got their best designers on the case. Objective: to be able to put on the boxes "By the creator of the most difficult puzzle in the world," with all the millions of dollars that would bring in!

If there's one person who really ought to enter, it's you. Norman asked me yesterday what tack you were taking. He looked very surprised when I told him that to my knowledge you weren't planning anything at all. But he's right: you know so much about the history and the technique of the game, I'm sure you'd come up with something brilliant. Besides, you're pretty crafty, which is more than can be said for a good number of our friends in the field. Think of your future, old pal: an honorable mention wouldn't do you any harm. Anyway, I've said enough, suit yourself, it's not my place to tell you what to do.

Say hello to the cows for me, and come back soon: the level of conversation here is reaching an all-time low.

Harry

Extracts from the Minutes of the Board Meeting of the APF
(American Puzzle Federation)

Committee meeting, 7 February 1992

5. Decision regarding the future of Nicholas Spillsbury

WALLERSTEIN: You've all received a copy of the February status report? If I get what you're saying, Cecil, your young protégé could already wipe the floor with about three-quarters of the players on the Circuit. Is that right?

EARP: That's quite right. Only this morning I timed him at eleven minutes twenty seconds for "Dating Susie," which is equivalent to an absolute speed of seventy-seven.

DOBBS: And I guess a relative speed of thirty, thirty-two?

EARP: Thirty-three, to be exact. It's quite simple: only Niels scores higher than that, over the season so far.

BLYTHE: And how much room is there for further improvement, in your opinion?

EARP: Considerable room, I'd say. In only a week I've seen his RS go up by pieces.

DOBBS: It doesn't make sense. No training gives results like that, that quickly.

EARP: In theory, you're right, Diana, but you have to understand what's special about the Spillsbury case. There's practically no limit to the number of pieces this boy can locate at any one time. With a single glance, he can tell you the position of any given piece, and where it belongs in the puzzle. All he has to do after that is fit it into place—and that's where Nicholas lacks dexterity. It's a pity—he loses, in assembling the puzzle, virtually all the advantage he gained with his extraordinary visual skills.

BLYTHE: What do you suggest?

EARP: We just need to develop his skill. He's making such rapid progress, it suggests that it's simply a question of practice.

DOBBS: Why don't we just throw him in the deep end? He can do his training on the job.

EARP: Personally, I think we'd achieve more by putting off his first public appearance for a while. If he progresses as fast as I expect, no one will be able to touch him.

BLYTHE: And then we'll have the emblematic figure we've been looking for. And better still, he's American. . . .

WALLERSTEIN: Nice work, Cecil. He's right, Diana. We'll let Niels, Krijek and the others fight it out for the title in the first year. It'll be all the more spectacular to have a young unknown turning up on the scene at the start of the second season.

Editorial by
Katherine Houtkooper

JP Magazine, No. 1, September 1991

Last Thursday evening, an hour after putting this, our first issue, to bed, the *JP Magazine* team celebrated the event with a glass of champagne. It was an emotional occasion for us all. At last, after all these years, the great puzzle magazine we'd been waiting for. Of course, many of us have been collaborating on fanzines since the early seventies, often working the entire evening to produce a simple sheet that would give you the secondhand price listings for the week. But the puzzle deserved something better than mere college magazines.

Appearing as it does today under the aegis of the American Puzzle Federation and its President, Charles Wallerstein, *JP Magazine* comes to you with all the guarantees of quality and professionalism that will without doubt make it the journal of reference for amateur puzzlists throughout the country. A magazine that will put emotion before analysis, published under the double banner of sport and pleasure, and that, we sincerely hope, will appeal equally to children and parents, yes, and grandparents too, as they unite together around the family table.

As you may already know, on 17 September, the Federation will be launching the JP Tour, a professional circuit whose members will be competing in the speed stakes, to solve puzzles both known and unknown. The speed puzzle is an extremely popular discipline in

Europe, Africa and South America, but is virtually unknown in the United States, where it is still a minority pursuit. Here at *JP Magazine* we are convinced that a sport that produces both dramatic spectator entertainment and outstanding individual performances cannot remain unknown for long.

We will therefore be keeping you informed of developments on the JP Tour, which will be moving on after Las Vegas, first to Minneapolis, and then to Philadelphia and Baton Rouge, Louisiana. But we will be doing more than just covering the Tour. We will be constantly filling you in on the legend of the puzzle and its pioneers, from the tragic Englishman John Spilsbury, whose untimely death in 1769 deprived him of all knowledge or enjoyment of the success of his early puzzles, right through to today's pioneers, with their work on tiered puzzles and the musical puzzle. Moreover, it is impossible to talk of the puzzle without mentioning the subjects it portrays. To that extent, any interest in puzzles will of necessity plunge you into the world of American history, back through the years to the time of ocean liners and the first cars, via the great sporting events of the century.

In addition to all this we'll be bringing you more practical information, in particular a monthly price index, scrupulously compiled by our teams on the basis of information from more than fifty outlets in the United States. At long last you will be able to see just how much that Carroll Towne your grandmother left you is worth and whether the neighbor who wants to swap his first edition of "Convergence" for two of your Marjorie Bouvés is offering you a good deal.

Finally, page 155 of this magazine has been left blank. It's not a mistake. This page is yours. We want *you* to write to us, tell us what you think, what you love and what you hate, share your likes and dislikes, tell us what sets your heart pounding, what gets your stomach churning. The publication of this first issue is a victory of sorts. We will consider that victory complete the day we can say that you, the readers, have taken over *JP Magazine* to the point where you, and not we, are its true editors. Long live the puzzle! Long live *JP Magazine!*

Contents

Interview with
Charles Wallerstein

JP Magazine, No. 1, September 1991

Several months ago, Charles Wallerstein, the well-known multimillionaire, took over the presidency of the American Puzzle Federation, surprising those who thought his only pastime was reading the
financial pages. He quickly set about making changes: within two
weeks, from Las Vegas, he launched the JP Tour, a professional Speed
Puzzle Circuit.

JP MAGAZINE: *Charles Wallerstein, where exactly does your love of the
puzzle come from?*

CW: From the very core of my being. My dad was crazy about
transatlantic liners. Every year, for my birthday, he'd give me a
puzzle of a boat. At the age of six, I was given *"Pilgrim of Fall River"*
by the McLoughlin Brothers. At eleven I got my first European im-
port, *"Queen Elizabeth,"* by G. J. Hayter and Co. My mom and I
spent the entire afternoon on it; I stared so hard at the box lid, I
nearly made myself ill. In 1965 I set up the Wallerstein Foundation
in memory of my father. I went out and bought every single boat
puzzle, big or small, I could lay my hands on. One day a supplier
who was a bit smarter than the rest pointed out that other subjects
did actually exist: trains...planes...Mickey Mouses...If you'd
heard him reeling off that list, you'd have said he thought I was a

total cretin! At first I thought he was pulling my leg, but then he got out his own stuff and I had to admit he had a point. I ended up buying a case of his very finest.

JPM: *Who are your favorite makers?*

CW: I don't have favorites. I love everything good and I'm no snob. I can show you Davy Crocketts with a darn sight more character than some old Marjorie Bouvé that has all the collectors down on their knees. I don't look at how much something costs, and I never part with anything I've bought. Besides, there's no fortune to be made in puzzles.

JPM: *You've always been known as a collector. But the step from collector to president of the U.S. Federation...*

CW: Well, someone had to get serious! For several years now, the world of puzzles has been in decline. For some time, it had been just about kept going by an organization in Boston, the Puzzology Society. But that had become virtually defunct, and the few members it still had left spent entire meetings making critical surveys of geometric presentations of Topper's[3] coat. Not my kind of thing at all. The two Inglethorpe sisters did actually have a whole load of plans, but they were strapped for cash. So they called Zorro the magician to the rescue, and here's what we've come up with.

JPM: *So what exactly is on your agenda?*

CW: Our agenda can be summed up in seven words: get people back in love with puzzles. I'm not going to give you a great speech about it, but can you think of many games that teach patience, method and history all at once, as well as taking you on a trip down memory lane? Personally, I know of only one, and it upsets me to see it dying out. Did you know that sales of new editions have been decreasing steadily for almost twenty years? That small manufacturers are folding, one after the other? That collectors put only a few puzzles a year onto the secondhand market? According to the experts, there are three or four ways we can turn that trend around. Quite frankly, we're going to use them all.

---

3. Hopalong Cassidy's horse (editor's note).

First of all, your magazine, which should be an absolute godsend to all those folk who love the old "wooden piece." They love puzzles, we're going to give them what they want: match reports on every round of the Tour, advice on their collections, tales of the greats, it'll all be there, including, in every issue, a secondhand listing, carefully compiled on the Argus model.

Deuzio, we'll be going out into the field, organizing a monthly forum, with lots of advance notice in the local press; it'll be completely free—yes, that is what I said, completely free, and open to everyone. Our valued readers will be able to put their questions to our specialists, compare their own treasures with the next guy's, and even trade puzzles on a kind of makeshift exchange. For the first meeting (Philadelphia, 13–14 October), we're looking to attract a minimum of ten thousand people!

Last—and by no means least in this nation that gets its kicks from greenbacks—the Federation will be encouraging independent puzzlemakers by awarding, every December, a hundred grand to the "most creative" U.S. manufacturer of the year. So, all you budding designers—pencils out!

JPM: *That's certainly some agenda! But now let's talk a little bit about your most spectacular innovation, the JP Tour. Where did you get the idea for that?*

CW: The wrinklies among you will perhaps remember that I was on the panel of judges in 1969 for the competition to find the most difficult puzzle in the world. I'd heard people talking at the time about a Harvard student who could do the trickiest puzzles at incredible speed. Obviously, I asked to see him. Well, it wasn't just talk. In just ten minutes this funny little chap, Jack Marietta, completed the 328-piece "Music Hath Charms"—one of those old-fashioned puzzles with weird-shaped pieces and a color range going subtly from light chestnut to dark brown. Hell on earth! At any rate, the kind of exercise that takes any normal person hours on end. Well, this Marietta, not only did he not even look as though he was particularly concentrating, but he even continued chatting to us while his great big paws dabbled around frantically among the pieces. Apparently, he discovered he could do it as a child. He used to challenge his brother to matches. What a hobby! And their sister held the stopwatch!

So, that's the formula for the Circuit: thirty-two players from all over the world, in a knockout contest held over one week, and first prize to whoever's got the most points at the end of the season.

JPM: *Where will you find the Circuit members? By placing ads?*

CW: Got it in one! Guys like Marietta are probably bursting to put their hobby to good use, to make some serious cash. If they're reading this now, they should get in touch with Diana Dobbs and Cecil Earp at the Federation. We'll set them tests, and the best of them will be included at the start of the first season, on 1 January.

But it's not just a local affair. It seems the speed puzzle is incredibly popular in Europe (particularly in Scandinavia), Africa and some countries in South America. In Denmark, inter-club matches attract thousands of fans every Sunday. These guys have developed all sorts of ultra-sophisticated techniques for picking up and memorizing. We'll be inviting the best of them to take part in the Circuit, starting with the Las Vegas tournament.

JPM: *Isn't there a risk they'll way outclass the Americans, if they've got more competition experience?*

CW: Quite probably. Well, our vanity will certainly take a knock! Especially since the Tour's only really going to get off the ground if there are Americans in the key positions. With that in mind, I've asked my friend Earp to take up his pilgrim's staff and trawl his way through the country in search of tomorrow's talent. It's his job to organize trials and local selections, put up ads in the few puzzle lending libraries that have survived the sixties, and all the rest of it. If, with all that, our boys haven't caught up with the best of the foreigners within a year or two, there's no hope left for the Yankee race!

JPM: *The Las Vegas Tournament will be broadcast on the Ubiquis channels. What sort of audience are you hoping for?*

CW: That's a state secret. No. Joking apart, I have no particular target in mind. We'll give the Circuit time to get established, become part of the viewers' lives. I'm not worried. There's plenty of room, alongside baseball, football and basketball, for a fourth professional circuit. Besides, believe me, once you've seen your first match, you'll no longer doubt: the JP Tour is the future of sport on television!

JPM: *And with all that, are you going to have time to look after all your business interests?*

CW: Oh, it's just one extra activity. I don't keep count any more. But you may have noticed, at the request of my board of directors, the Las Vegas final's been scheduled for a Sunday!

10

Letter of Application from Rupert Clockwise to Diana Dobbs

Des Moines, 7 October 1991

Dear Madam,

Having read recently in the papers that the American Puzzle Federation is currently embarking on the recruitment of several staff members, I am honored to submit my application for the post of official timekeeper for the professional speed puzzle circuit (JP Tour).

I am confident that my curriculum vitae will convince you that I possess all the necessary skills for the position. What it cannot hope to convey, however, is the genuine passion I have felt ever since I was a small child, for all things connected with timekeeping.

It began, most definitely, with my father, a humble watchmaker in St. Paul, who introduced me at a tender age to the subtle secrets of European, and particularly Swiss, mechanisms. "My boy," he used to say to me, as he took apart the watches left with him for repair by the genteel folk of St. Paul, "we have invented the telegraph, liberated Europe, and put the first man on the moon, but when it comes to tickers, we are total numbskulls." And he was right. To this day, even if the American watchmaking industry can be said to have made significant progress (it would be wrong not to acknowledge the work of people like Dunbar, or Lloyd), it has to be said that no Yankee mechanism will ever approach anything like Swiss precision.

At the age of eighteen I decided to turn down my father's offer of partnership, and to embrace the equally noble but less widely recognized profession of chronometer. Dad was perhaps a little vexed by my decision; my mother, on the other hand, was not surprised. "I always knew it," she told me, "even when you were a baby you had a clock ticking away in your tummy."

I have no need to tell you, madam, how thankless and yet demanding is the task of the chronometer. Our job involves a degree of control that alienates the sympathy of a certain section of the population. Certain sloppy members of our profession, its undeniable black sheep, have succeeded in tarnishing our image in the eyes of the general public. Let me tell you, Madam, that occasionally, in sports arenas, children have been known to pelt us with stones....

Finding myself without any obvious support in an extremely closed world, I was obliged to establish my own legitimacy. Excellence is not something that falls out of the sky. What talents I may possess (my lateralization skills are generally acknowledged to be impeccable) have never, in my own eyes, exempted me from the need to apply myself. Put your work back on the loom twenty times over... (Boileau, *L'Art Poétique*)... My entire work history to date should be considered in the light of this adage.

I began, quite naturally, with boxing, a sport in which the chronometer plays a limited, but essential, role. For three years (1976–1978, cf. CV), I officiated at the Boxing Club of St. Paul, where my role consisted entirely of ringing the bell at the end of each round (each round lasting, as is widely known, three minutes, except in the case of open-hand boxing, a variant of English boxing, very popular in southern Missouri, where the rounds last two minutes and twenty seconds). It was rather too rudimentary an occupation for my parents' taste and on several occasions they urged me to accept one of the attractive propositions I received from various athletic clubs. Although I am not insensible to the somewhat limited character of timekeeping in the sport of boxing, I would nevertheless strongly recommend it to any young people desirous of following in my footsteps, and would point above all to its unquestionable structural and pedagogic qualities. Toward the end of my time at the Boxing Club, I was able to call the end of a round with only the merest verifying glance at my chronometer (I resisted that particular form of vanity which might have urged me to rely on the human factor alone). It is an accomplishment on which I congratulate myself every morning as I boil my eggs.

In 1979 I finally decided I had learned everything I could in my current position. Several possibilities now lay open to me. My colleagues all looked to the forthcoming Olympic Games, in Lake Placid. My own feeling was that I was still too young to officiate at such an important event. "There will be other Olympic games," I thought (and as it turned out I was right); "for the time being, just think about adding strings to your bow." And so it was that I came to accept a position as a cycle chronometer in Europe.

Cycle chronometry differs from boxing chronometry in several respects. Firstly, you are measuring a sporting performance, whereas in boxing you are simply indicating the expiry of a period of time established in advance. Next, with the exception of against-the-clock races, about which I shall have a special word to say, one takes only one reading per day, at the finishing line of the race or stage of the race. One therefore works in pairs, in close association with the starter chronometer (I forgot to mention that I worked as an end chronometer, my American experience being sufficient to exempt me from the initial two-year traineeship during which junior chronometers are confined to indicating the start of the race). What I acquired, above all, during my five seasons in Europe, was a sense of exactness and a professionalism which, as I realized on my return, are still not to be found in American competitions. Fifteen years later, I still count the against-the-clock stages of the Tour de France among my most treasured memories. Thanks to them, I mastered the particularly complex technique of intermediate timings. Thus in 1982 I managed 402 timings on a single stage, that of Mont Ventoux (132 competitors, and two intermediate timings).

The day came when I felt I had nothing more to learn, and so I left the field of cycling. Time for a crack at the king of sports. This came about on 2 September 1983, when I signed a three-year contract with the legendary Santa Monica Track Club, stable to so many champions. Of all sports, track-and-field is undoubtedly the most varied and interesting. From the hundred meters through to the marathon, it requires the chronometer to employ the entire range of his many and varied skills. One of its principal disciplines is the relay race, an eminently precise discipline, over the chronometrage of which the greatest specialists are still in some disagreement (see my own modest contribution, *Relays and Team Races: Timing Movement*). It requires instant by instant attention (how often I have seen the Greeks raise their arms at the final tape, when in fact they are one, sometimes even two revolutions behind the Kenyans).

Some may remember from their time at the Santa Monica Track Club the moment when they shook Carl Lewis's hand, or wedged the starting blocks of Mike Marsh. I prefer to let my track record speak for itself: seven world records,[4] three Olympic records, eleven United States records and twenty-six best world performances. Of course, you will say that these achievements are not mine alone. Let me just ask you one simple question, which I myself shall refrain from replying to: What would Carl Lewis amount to without his timekeeper?

Since 1986, I have been working as a freelancer in over thirty different sports: track-and-field, swimming, tennis (on the end changes), football, basketball, hurdles, ice hockey and field hockey, Indy car racing, sack racing, downhill skiing, drag racing, chess, blueberry pie contests, and so on. I have now reached the stage where I wish to settle down, and offer my skills in the service of a single discipline, one sufficiently diverse and intense to allow scope for the deployment of my entire range of skills. In this respect, the creation of the professional speed puzzle circuit seems to constitute a unique opportunity, and I would be happy to work with you in defining the role I might play within it.

---

4. To which should be added one other, not accredited for fallacious reasons I prefer not to rehearse, set by Lewis in the two hundred meters in Stockholm, 1984.

As you will have gathered, I am completely mobile. I should expect to earn in the region of $45,000 per annum, plus fringe benefits.

I look forward to meeting you shortly.

Yours sincerely,
Rupert Clockwise

Extracts from the Minutes
of the Puzzology Society

Committee meeting, 4 December 1990

President Sutter opened the meeting at 1800 hours precisely.

1. Presentation of the Gleaners Project

MELINDA PLUNKET: I would like to share with you an idea that occurred to me this morning as I was on my way to work at the university, in the company of an old friend. You will perhaps have noticed the building site on the corner of Hancock and Derney. For several weeks now, there have been notices up announcing the start of building, but I have yet to see the slightest sign of any activity. This morning, since we had a little time on our hands, my friend and I took a walk around the outer fencing, purely out of curiosity.

The building work has not begun yet. There are no markings to indicate the eventual position of the foundations, and I saw no building materials on the site. The area was completely deserted, save for two men, both working on the same job, a section of freestanding wall about sixty-five feet long and around six feet high, right in the middle of the site. We must have stood there for about a quarter of an hour, just watching them. The first, armed with a mallet and chisel, was removing cinder-blocks, one by one. At the other end of the wall, the second workman was diligently adding new blocks, which he took from the back of a truck parked nearby.

At first, we couldn't figure out what was particularly unusual about two bricklayers working on an empty site, but suddenly a phrase came into my mind that made me see what it was about the scene that was strange. The phrase was: zero sum. One of the workmen was constructing, the other deconstructing. You will no doubt point out that they probably had good reason for proceeding in this way. No doubt the second worker needed to dismantle the wall in order to reconstruct it differently. That doesn't alter my argument. Even if the two men were not working on the same actual stones, one of them was undoing the other's work, each man destroying the other one's efforts.

Having said that, the one did not completely cancel out the other. First because the deconstructor was working slightly more quickly than his colleague. Second—and most significant—because the appearance of the wall changed as they worked, even if the number of component blocks remained more or less stable. During the time I watched, the left-hand side became longer by about a yard, while the right-hand side lost a layer in height.

We then asked ourselves what might happen if the two workmen continued indefinitely, one building, the other dismantling. Assuming they worked at the same speed, neither man would gain an advantage over the other. The number of blocks would remain constant, but the form of the wall itself would be perpetually evolving.

Let me now come to the idea I have in mind. Is it not conceivable that after days, months, years have gone by, the wall would inevitably tend toward a particular configuration and then become stabilized? That an equilibrium point would be reached, after which every new block laid by the bricklayer would immediately be pulled free by the dismantler and any block removed by the dismantler would immediately be replaced by the bricklayer? Naturally, I have no preconceived ideas regarding the actual nature of this configuration, but my hunch is that it would eventually emerge. But maybe I haven't made myself quite clear....

TOM DE LAZIO: On the contrary, you have made yourself perfectly clear, but what I don't understand is the point you are trying to make. This configuration you speak of—would it have some particular property?

MELINDA PLUNKET: It would constitute in some sense the "truth" of the wall. It's an idea derived directly from physics. Every oscillatory system possesses its determining frequency, regardless of circumstances. Standing looking at this very ordinary wall, it occurred to me that it possessed its own particular configuration, to which it would invariably be brought back by the conflicting efforts of the two workmen.

TOM DE LAZIO: As you have said, the real frequency of a structure is independent of circumstances. Could this be equally said of the wall? Are you quite sure that it would always reassume the same configuration, whatever the conditions of the experiment?

MELINDA PLUNKET: This is exactly the point I'm making. I would like to put this hypothesis to the test in one of our workshops. The idea would be to employ two men and give one of them a trowel and the other a chisel. We would then set them in front of a half-built brick wall for several days, during which time we would be able to judge whether an equilibrium configuration was being achieved.

NICHOLAS PASQUALE: One of them would be bound to work more quickly than the other....

MELINDA PLUNKET: It depends on the experimental procedure. By modifying its conditions, it would be possible to arrange for the two men to work at exactly the same speed. Besides, we could simply specify the number of blocks they were each allowed to handle.

DOYLE EVART: What's the connection with the puzzle?

MELINDA PLUNKET: Think back to the 1972 seminar in Lunenberg. We spent a whole afternoon discussing whether the essence of the puzzle lay in its completed or dismantled state. McRae drew an analogy with the tightrope walker, who is only really a tightrope walker when he is actually up on the high wire, between one platform and another. The true puzzle is one which is in progress, a point expressed by McRae when he said: "The starting and finishing points are in themselves of no significance; all that matter are the tiny separate oscillations that connect the two."

DOYLE EVART: But McRae was unable to define exactly what he meant by "in progress." He felt instinctively that the interlocking of two pieces was insufficient for a puzzle to be considered "underway," as with the tightrope walker's first step on the rope.

TOM DE LAZIO: McRae had no scientific training—he always tripped up on figures....

MELINDA PLUNKET: That's a separate issue. I believe that, if McRae had pursued his investigations, he would naturally have come to consider the question of the perfect form of the puzzle. In fact, he mentions it in his notes. I have found the exact reference. "Tidied away in its box, the puzzle is not yet [a puzzle]. Once completed, it ceases to be one. Between these two states, between box and the framed image on the wall, there exists a moment when the puzzle expresses its function to the full, at which point the fascination it exerts is at its height, and has not yet started to decline."

McRae himself did not give a name to it, but I call this moment "the truth of the puzzle," in the sense in which I spoke just now of the "truth" of the wall. If the wall experiment proves conclusive, we will be able to adapt it to the case of the puzzle.

DOYLE EVART: Why don't we start straight off with the puzzle?

MELINDA PLUNKET: Because in all probability, the experimental procedure with the wall will be a lot easier to set up than one for a puzzle. The bricklayers will be subject to physical constraints, whereas there is no limit to the number of pieces any individual can put together or take apart. I also think it will be easier to choose an appropriate subject for the puzzle experiment once we have seen the results with the wall.

PRESIDENT SUTTER: In your opinion, the true condition of the wall is independent of the initial conditions of the experiment. How do you take account of the number of blocks?

MELINDA PLUNKET: I haven't made myself clear. As I see it, there exists one "truth" for all walls of a hundred blocks, one "truth" for all walls of two hundred blocks, and so on. When I talk about initial conditions, what I mean is the arrangement of the blocks before the start of the experiment.

PRESIDENT SUTTER: How many blocks do you want for this experiment?

MELINDA PLUNKET: Four hundred would seem a suitable number. That would make a wall about sixty-five feet long and six feet two high.

PRESIDENT SUTTER: Have you worked out a budget?

MELINDA PLUNKET: No, not in any detail. But if we calculate for two workmen at $6 an hour, over two months, and add to that the cost of the blocks, cement and other materials, that should come to around $6,000.

PRESIDENT SUTTER: If no one has any objection, I propose that we accept Melinda's project according to Category B1, and assign it a budget of $6,000, which will come out of the research budget. John, any comments?

TREASURER: On the basis of our current commitments, the "research" fund will be overspent this year by $7,500. However, the income on receipts for the use of the "Approved by the Puzzology Society" label is far in advance of initial projections. I therefore have no objection to Miss Plunket's project.

PRESIDENT SUTTER: Doyle, you have expressed some interest in Miss Plunket's project. Would you care to be involved with it?

DOYLE EVART: I should be delighted.

PRESIDENT SUTTER: Miss Plunket, your project is accepted under Category B1, and will be referred to as the "Gleaners Project," in honor of Margaret Richardson's "Perplexity Puzzle." You will work together with Doyle Evart. We would be grateful for a weekly report through to the completion of the experiment.

Off the Cuff—Rae Koonis

JP Magazine, No. 26, October 1993

I like young Spillsbury. To be honest with you, I've liked him right from the start, ever since his very first campaign, in Orlando, when he gave a roasting to the last representative of the French school of elegance, blew away a raw herring-chomper, and sent a lumberjack from Jutland back to his chippings, just like that, one after the other. A really pleasant young man, no airs and graces, nothing swanky about him. Admittedly, he makes rather heavy weather of his acceptance speeches in presentations, and he's not the man to look to for a breakthrough in the study of fractal theory. But each man has his job to do, I hear you say, and Spillsbury's job is doing puzzles.

Except I have to tell you, there's a problem here, and I am indebted to my lovely wife for pointing it out. The other evening, I was sitting with a can of Coke in my hand, watching our home-grown Mozart quietly pulverizing the German, Trackl, otherwise known as Ice Cube, on account of his famous ice-blue eyes, which, rumor has it, cannot be met without blinking (my brother-in-law, who knows him well, swears he wears contacts. I refuse to believe it—another myth crumbles). Anyway, there I was, watching those great big paws of Spils's (suits him, don't you think, the nickname—sounds like a brand of beer) groping around on the board, and saying to myself, boy, you have to admit it, we do live in amazing times.

Just at that moment, my wife turns up, plonks herself in front of the TV, and casually lets drop this remark, which has been bothering me ever since: "There's a touch of the Frederick Winslow Taylor about the boy." I shall allow my wife's titanic erudition to speak for itself: do you know many grown women capable of coming out with the name of the god of automation just like that? Even so, her remark gave me pause for thought. I began to break down Spils's style (that's what they call alliteration, I believe) into simple gestures: pick up piece (two-tenths of a second), look at piece (one-tenth), identify piece (usually one-tenth, rising to three or four on a dull day), work out position (one-tenth), place piece (three-tenths). Total: roughly speaking, one second. You must admit that, worked out like this, there's not much room for improvement. Only a machine could go quicker, and even then, imagine, if you will, the amount of programming you would need (hey, boss, the robot's trying to stick the sun down at the bottom of the sea!).

All right, I'm not a nostalgic man, but you must admit that the puzzle as performed by Spils looks like a puzzle, and feels like a puzzle but, somehow, isn't really a puzzle as we know it. Serious accusation...Mozart could play the whole range of instruments, whereas I suspect Spillsbury has never even weighed a piece in his hand, never run his fingers over it in search of its essential mystery. I wouldn't be surprised if he didn't know the difference between a wooden and a cardboard puzzle. A sorry state of affairs for a man of his age, you must agree.

Thus ran my reverie, when suddenly Spils raised his fist in the air to salute his victory. Thirty-seven pieces ahead of the counter: you've got to hand it to him, fine play, fine play indeed. Then, during the slight delay while the producer fumbled to get the credits up, he began dismantling the puzzle, piece by piece, mechanically, in a manner that was almost a perfect negative image of his performance. Take my word for it, if you will, the dismantling was scarcely quicker than the assembly. In view of which I invite you, in your wisdom, to consider this question: How long before we get the first dismantling contests?

World Tour of the Puzzle

JP Magazine, No. 1, September 1991

As Charles Wallerstein reminds us in our interview with him on page 17, the speed puzzle is already a discipline in its own right in Europe, South America and parts of Africa. Time for a quick whizz around the puzzle world, before we meet the champions in the flesh in Las Vegas on 17 September.

Origins of the puzzle

It will be helpful to recall that the puzzle started out life in Europe, in the mid-eighteenth century. The man usually credited with its invention is a young English cartographer, John Spilsbury, who cut up his very first model, a map of Europe, for the purpose of giving a geography lesson (see our special feature, "From Map to Puzzle: The John Spilsbury Saga," p. 71). This explains why the first-ever puzzle manufacturers were based in London. At the beginning of the nineteenth century, the puzzle ceased to be simply a pedagogic tool, and other, less serious, subjects were adopted. At the same time, it began to find its way abroad, to the rest of Europe, notably to Germany, the Netherlands and France. Our own ancestors had to make do with imported British models until 1849, when Samuel McCleary and John Pierce set up the first workshop on American soil, in New

York. From that point on, homegrown production went from strength to strength, with three notable peak periods: 1908 to 1909, during the Depression, and at the end of the nineteen-sixties.

Surprisingly enough, the puzzle developed along different lines on different continents. In the United States and Canada it was a popular activity—every single person has probably done a puzzle at least once in his life. There have been many different derivatives—publicity puzzles, puzzle-based books for children, even chocolate puzzles at Christmastime. To the best of our knowledge, there has never before been any kind of speed puzzle competition.

The puzzle in Europe

In Europe the puzzle fared differently according to region. In England and Germany it developed along lines fairly similar to the U.S. Independent workshops vanished, one after the other, and print runs were rarely less than several thousand models at a time. The English have a Federation, a small association of volunteers based in Birmingham. The Germans, on the other hand, have no representative body. Hans Trackl, their top player, trains at a club in Luxembourg.

The tradition of speed puzzle solving is in fact much more entrenched in the Benelux countries (Belgium, the Netherlands, Luxembourg). Every weekend, several hundred players join in interclub matches. Virtually everyone uses the colorist method, that is, they follow the color patterns of the subject when assembling a puzzle. The finest exponents of this school are Krijek, Van Emp, Diedrich, Michiels; the first two will be competing in Las Vegas at the end of this month.

France is home to the last generation of true puzzle makers. In the Marais quarter of Paris can be found the workshops of several artisan puzzlemakers. Feuilland, the most famous of them all, charges up to a hundred dollars a piece! These extraordinarily high prices are justified by the exquisite refinement of the work, in terms of both design and the quality of the wood and oils used. In sporting terms, however, the French players are, on the whole, fairly weak;

untimely injury often seems to put an end to their ambitions at the international level.

Italy, on the other hand, and, to a lesser extent, Spain, produce players of impressive, if inconsistent, stature. For them the speed puzzle is a highly respected discipline, and it attracts betting on a scale that almost rivals horse racing. And finally, a note on transalpine production—far too much of it, and at best of no great interest.

The Scandinavian subcontinent

Scandinavia (a group of countries comprising Sweden, Denmark, Norway, Finland and Iceland), although technically a part of Europe, deserves consideration in its own right. Public enthusiasm for the puzzle has reached heights unknown elsewhere in the world, with the exception, perhaps, of Brazil. The annual meeting held between the universities of Uppsala and Malmö attracts several tens of thousands of spectators, and invites comparison with the unholy battles between the rowers of Oxford and Cambridge.

Sweden has four thousand registered players, Denmark twenty-five thousand, Norway eighteen thousand, with Finland and Iceland both somewhat marginal in this respect. Each of the three main countries naturally seeks to impose supremacy over the other two, the puzzle being one more outlet for a sense of competition that finds expression in numerous other political, economic and sporting contexts. Tension peaks at the SAS Open, the final of which is traditionally held on board a supersonic jet, which flies over each of the three countries in turn.

Impartial observers[5] are inclined to acknowledge a slight edge to the Danish game, which has no doubt facilitated Olof Niels's ascent to the highest echelons.

---

5. Such observers are rare. The publication, in December each year, of the *League Table of Scandinavian Puzzlists* (pub. Stockholm, Andersson & Andersson) nearly provokes an annual diplomatic incident.

For more than ten years now, Scandinavia has pretty well dominated the international scene. It should come as no surprise, therefore, to discover they have the largest contingent of players in Las Vegas. Niels, Eriksen and Jörring will be representing the Danish flag, Nyquist, Uppal and Mansson the Swedish one, while Trombdø, Skaal and Modt will be lining up for Norway.

The African wizards

Enough of Europe. Let's now turn to the African continent. The puzzle reached its shores only at the dawn of the century, introduced by the powerful colonizing forces of France and Britain. Local production is virtually nonexistent, and can be seen only in the traditional models of certain primitive tribes. Despite this relative paucity, some truly fine talents have emerged. In 1988, in Rome, the Cameroonian, Georges Mombala, became the first African player to clinch a world title (the 500-piece singles). His star may have dimmed a little since those days, but the French teacher from Yaoundé continues to be a serious contender. We expect him to take advantage of the school holidays in December to make an appearance on the JP Tour. The Africans have earned their reputation as "wizards" on account of their spontaneous, unpredictable, even, on occasion, fun-loving approach to the game. Dismissive of the sophisticated technique employed by their European colleagues, they tend to trust to instinct, and in some cases, the voices of their ancestors. Indeed, Diallo, the young hope of Senegal, is a holy man by profession, while N'Donge, from Zaire, regularly enters a trance in mid-match.[6] So what: if they have earned their places at the Las Vegas table in ten days' time, it's entirely due to their class as players.

---

6. N'Donge missed out, through this practice, on a place in the Africa Cup Final in 1989. He argued for a replay on the grounds that his tongue had turned blue. Accustomed to the shaman's eccentricities, the judges remained implacable.

South America

Our world tour ends in South America, where the puzzle has been practiced since the end of the last century. However, until now only three nations have succeeded in rising to international level: Brazil, Colombia and Peru. Not much to be said on the subject of the last two, save that they will be sending three representatives to Las Vegas (Herrera and Parara for Colombia, Los Bustos for Peru). The unknown element in this vast continent has to be Brazil. The most extraordinary rumors have been circulating concerning the standard of the Brazilian players, who are capable, according to some accounts, of achieving up to seventy or eighty pieces a minute. It has to be said, the puzzle is an international sport down there, almost as popular as soccer. Millions of kids train in the *favelas* in the hope one day of emulating their idol, João Brás Procopio e Barros, also known as Ghimalaes. However—and herein lies the main particularity of the Brazilian puzzle scene—all their champions are amateurs. For reasons which, at best, remain inexplicable, and despite the large amount of funding for certain competitions, the public would oppose the idea of any player living off his art alone. Although Ghimalaes wins several million cruzeiros per annum in prize money, he still works as a plumber in Belém. It is said that certain families will bleed themselves dry for months on end simply to be able to afford running water and have it installed by the maestro himself.

As we go to press, there is some doubt concerning whether Ghimalaes and his heir apparent will agree to take part in the JP Tour. They are currently in dispute with the Brazilian Federation. Let us hope for a positive outcome. It would be a real shame if cultural differences were allowed to come between the American public and some of the finest puzzlists on the planet.

The Most Difficult Puzzle
in the World—Results

New York Times, 20th November 1969

As reported in these pages,[7] a rather bizarre competition was recently launched to find the most difficult puzzle in the world. The *New York Times*, which for some years now has been a partner of the Puzzology Society, had agreed to sponsor the competition. Jessica Woodruff, editor-in-chief of the Arts section and a member of the panel of judges, reports on the winners. They were announced Saturday evening in the grand auditorium of the Faculty of Human Sciences at Harvard.

NYT: *Are there any broad conclusions we can draw from the competition, or is it still too early?*

JW: It'll be for history to separate the wheat from the chaff and judge as to the quality of our prize list. But one thing is for sure: the success of this first contest has exceeded our expectations. The panel of judges looked at nearly four hundred works, from forty-three different states and eleven different countries. And, significantly, a large number of those came from within the puzzle world itself. More than half the members of the Puzzology Society submitted an entry; and closer to home, on our own newspaper staff, three journalists got involved and actually entered the contest.

---

7. Edition of 3 August 1969.

NYT: *Does the quality of the prizewinning puzzles reflect the general level of the entries?*

JW: Oh, without a doubt. Originally we had intended to award only one prize, but the panel's discussions were so passionate, we decided to pick four runners-up as well.

NYT: *Indeed. Tell me a little about the winning puzzle, "Pantone 138."*

JW: Well, it's a work that is both extraordinarily simple and profoundly original, by a Frenchman, Paul Rousselet. It consists of a wooden tray, about twenty by twenty inches, on which the puzzle is to be assembled, and a thousand pieces, each of them strictly identical, half an inch square, colored bright blue, Pantone shade 138.

NYT: *That doesn't sound all that difficult....*

JW: That's what some of us said at first. But Rousselet didn't just hit on it by chance. There had to be more to it than that. Malcolm Crandon, one of the judges, pointed out that if the most difficult puzzles are the ones that give the puzzlist the fewest clues, then the Frenchman, who had succeeded in giving none at all, in terms of either color or shape, could indeed be said to have invented the most difficult puzzle in the world. We all felt that Malcolm had put his finger on something essential here, but that we needed to go further still. It was Valentina—our "Visual Arts" correspondent—who remarked that, by a sort of paradox, the most difficult puzzle in the world was at the same time the *easiest*. In fact, since any arrangement of the pieces which fitted into the tray could be said to be a solution, less than a quarter of an hour was required to solve the most difficult puzzle in the world.

NYT: *Forgive me for insisting, but that still doesn't make "Pantone 138" the most difficult puzzle in the world!*

JW: Oh, but it does! It was Charles Wallerstein, the well-known multimillionaire, who came up with the answer. What he said, essentially, was this: "I do not believe Paul Rousselet's intentions can be summarized simply in terms of specious considerations regarding the measure of 'difficulty' of difficult puzzles. There are several billions, or indeed, tens of hundreds of billions of ways of assembling

'Pantone 138.' But only one of them is correct. I am prepared to wager that Rousselet will take the secret of which one that is with him to his grave."

NYT: *Fiendish! And do we know what Rousselet does for a living, to come up with an idea like that?*

JW: He's the senior cutter with Feuilland, a Parisian producer of made-to-measure puzzles. He's master of old techniques that have fallen out of fashion, such as the juxtaposition of different woods. He is also responsible for the invention of a number of new methods; the multilayered puzzle, for example, a technique that is sadly neglected today, but that was all the rage in Europe in the fifties.

NYT: *In one sense, Rousselet was making a play on words. When you launched the idea of a competition based on "the most difficult puzzle in the world," I imagine you hadn't expected that?*

JW: Yes and no. We deliberately chose as broad a title for the competition as we could. If you go back and look at the conditions we set out, you'll see we were anxious not to rule out any genre, or any format a priori. Having said that, most of the entries were designed along "classic" lines.

NYT: *Such as Thomas Carroll's "Tulip Field," the first runner-up?*

JW: Exactly. Thomas Carroll was deeply moved, last Saturday evening, on accepting his prize. He dedicated it to the memory of his father, Pete Carroll, who founded the Puzzology Society thirty-five years ago. We decided to award a prize to Thomas because his "Tulip Field" represents a sort of synthesis of all known methods. The subject, to start with: a detail from the crowd gathered beneath the balcony of the Holy Father on Easter Sunday. This obviously has no connection whatsoever with the title of the puzzle, which was chosen simply to mislead the puzzlist. Then the shape of the pieces, which he cut individually around the contour of each member of the crowd. It's a technique as old as the puzzle itself, popularized by Mrizek, a well-known maker, and referred to as "color line cutting." Because each piece features a different person, and only one person, the solver has nothing to go on, and is wholly dependent on the shape of the pieces. But there's more. Carroll unearthed a trick that goes back to 1908: false corners. As you know, everyone begins a puzzle by looking for the four corners and the edge. So the idea is to plant in the puzzle a number of square-shaped pieces, just to trip up the nonexperts. The judges counted no fewer than fifty-four corner pieces in "Tulip Field"!

NYT: *Why did you decide to give a prize to a work like "In the Footsteps of Buddha"? Perhaps you could first just describe it for us, very briefly.*

JW: "In the Footsteps of Buddha" isn't a puzzle, in the usual sense of the term. It consists of a collection of two hundred and fifty "objects," all connected with the spread of Buddhism in Asia. So you find photographs, taped extracts of ritual chants, strips of map drawn by Marco Polo, prayer wheels, two traditional costumes, a treatise on the evolution of Chinese ideograms, and so on, all jumbled together. In a brief accompanying text, the author, Yoshiro Hakematsu, explains how he seeks to "convey to the judges the extraordinary complexity of what historians perceive as the enigma of the spread of Buddhism in the East." As you know, Buddhism originated in Northern India in the fourth century B.C., with the preachings of Buddha, the Enlightened One. It then spread throughout the rest of Asia along routes and by means that remain something of a mystery to us, split into two branches, the Great and the Small Paths, incorporated Zen philosophy, thereby gaining a foothold in Japan in the twelfth century, and so on. Hakematsu's great achievement was to depict this process of intellectual growth, while at the same time highlighting certain major currents that represent the fundamental precepts of Buddha's teaching.

NYT: *Are there many examples of this type of work around?*

JW: Not that many, no. In fact, they all belong to what's known as the school of the ideal puzzle, that's ideal in the philosophical sense of the word, existing only as an idea. It's difficult to sum up the idealists' approach in a few simple words. Broadly speaking, their view is that the puzzle as a physical object is now obsolete. They train themselves to assemble puzzles in their heads, dispensing with the actual material object, which for them represents a constraint. By developing this skill, the idealists believe they will learn to discern patterns and relationships not yet perceived. They are convinced that Nature itself is composed of pieces that have been flung down on the table, as it were, by the creator, and that their task is to reestablish the natural order of things simply by the power of thought. Idealists also conceive of life itself as a puzzle. In their view, the life story of every individual can be written in terms of the overlapping and fitting together of a whole host of everyday occurrences.

NYT: *As an outsider, it's hard to believe that a simple game like the puzzle can give rise to such complex theories....*

JW: And I haven't even touched on the dozens of schools of thought caught up in the puzzle debate! Take the transversalists, for example. They go along with the idealists in rejecting the physical object that is the puzzle, but their interest lies altogether elsewhere. They aim to create a new type of puzzle, they call it the transversal, which takes its pieces from transversal disciplines, or even from different periods in history. They aspire to a puzzle comprising pieces taken from the cinema, music, painting, newsreels...

NYT: *Fascinating. So how can our readers learn more about the puzzle?*

JW: By joining the Puzzology Society, the association that organized this competition and that does an admirable job of promoting the puzzle, both here in the States and abroad. Their monthly meeting is for members only, but the Monday-evening workshops are open to the public, on payment of a modest participation fee. I would like to invite all our puzzle-loving readers to come along, even if it's just for one evening. For some years now, the Society has been working to create a new discipline, and we are now on the verge of a major breakthrough. I'm quite sure I speak for our President, Gerald Honorton, in saying that all genuine supporters will be extremely welcome.

Puzzology Society
9 Rosamond Street
Boston, MA 20740
Tel. 707-3211

Prize winners

1st PRIZE
"Pantone 138," by Paul Rousselet, France

1st RUNNER-UP
"Tulip Field," by Thomas Carroll, United States

2nd RUNNER-UP
"In the Footsteps of Buddha," by Yoshiro Hakematsu, Japan

3rd RUNNER-UP
"Karigasmemi, Finland, Two in the Afternoon," by Norman Halcock, United States

4th RUNNER-UP
"Cones and Trapeziums," by Springbok Editions, United States

Extracts from the Minutes of the Puzzology Society

Committee Meeting, 28 November 1969

The meeting was opened by President Honorton at 1800 hours precisely.

1. Assessment of the competition for the most difficult puzzle in the world

PRESIDENT HONORTON: I should like first and foremost to congratulate you all on your cooperation over the last few weeks. A special mention goes to Thomas Carroll, our loyal secretary, who so magnificently defended the colors of the Society by carrying off the First Runner-Up prize, thoroughly deserved.

I consider this competition a great victory and, if I may be so bold, a turning point for our Society. It has been the occasion for us both to reinforce our status as the ultimate point of reference, and to gain valuable publicity. Our partnership with the *New York Times* ran remarkably smoothly. No doubt you are all aware of the article on the awards ceremony by Jessica Woodruff. If the *New York Times* has even half as many readers as Jessica would like us to believe, we should be seeing a considerable new wave of subscriptions over the next few months.

We can also take considerable satisfaction from the list of prizewinners. I must say I take great personal pleasure from the routing—the word is no exaggeration—suffered by the manufacturers. We were told to expect a cleanup—what we've seen is a clearout. Milton Bradley, Parker Brothers, Selchow & Righters, whose bragging filled the pages of our newspapers only a month ago, have bitten the dust. Only Springbok managed to save the honor of the profession with their Fourth Runner-Up title—generous, to say the least. What other conclusion can we draw from all this but that, from now on, the future of the puzzle lies in the hands of the researchers, not the sellers? The future of the puzzle lies with those who love her, irrespective of culture, race or religion—which brings me to my second cause for satisfaction, the three nationalities dominating the roll call of winners: France, the U.S. and Japan. First of all, France, spearhead of Old Europe, where our discipline has its roots, country of Dumarais, Léonceaud, Jacquemard, country of contradictions, the first ever slayer of privilege, where puzzles sell for five hundred francs each! Next, Japan, home of the samurai, so infused with the values of Confucius that the "puzzle collectivity" is esteemed more highly than the individual pieces that go to make it up. And, finally, our own country, once again showing its winning mettle the minute a place in *The Guinness Book of World Records* is at stake! The puzzle seems more cosmopolitan than ever before, the supreme language, a kind of miraculous Esperanto in a world beset with noncommunication.

Last of all, I should like to express my gratitude to the judges, who, in their infinite wisdom, have awarded prizes to works drawn from each of the great branches of our discipline. Carroll and Halcock bear the standard of the classic puzzle. Rousselet has undoubtedly opened up a new path, that of the concept puzzle. And Hakematsu, who has produced the great, universal work which the world of the ideal puzzle so greatly needed. As for Springbok, well, the word "geometric" is the only one that comes to mind to describe their "Cones and Trapeziums."

In short, you might call this president happy, were it not for one shadow that falls across the picture, and a long shadow at that, I'm afraid to say. According to Friday's edition of the *New York Times,* Paul Rousselet has sold world rights to "Pantone 138" to Jig & Toy, one of the numerous companies owned by Mr. Charles Wallerstein. Upton, can you confirm this information?

UPTON SUTTER: I'm sorry to say, President, I can indeed. The contract was signed on the evening of the awards ceremony, in Mr. Wallerstein's hotel room.

PRESIDENT HONORTON: But I had explicitly stated that the Puzzology Society should be responsible for the commercial exploitation of the prizewinning work, through its publications section. I asked at this very meeting for this stipulation to be printed in the conditions of the competition.

UPTON SUTTER: And so it is, but not in its entirety. Article 34 stipulates that "the award-winning work will be manufactured for the American commercial market within a period not exceeding six months." We forgot to make clear who would be in charge of this process.

PRESIDENT HONORTON: *You* forgot, Upton. And as President of the Judging Panel, it was your job to draw up the rules. Do we know how many copies of "Pantone 138" Wallerstein hopes to sell?

OLIVER AKERS: They're talking about a first print run of 50,000 copies.

PRESIDENT HONORTON: Which represents, at the lowest estimate, a deficit of $200,000 for our society. As you know, we were counting on that money for financing our future programs.

UPTON SUTTER: I really am sorry....

PRESIDENT HONORTON: And so you should be.

UPTON SUTTER: Maybe we could go after Rousselet, ask him to change his mind. After all, he could always say Wallerstein had hoodwinked him.

PRESIDENT HONORTON: Oh, that's a splendid idea, Upton! And why not just declare outright war on Wallerstein while you're up to it? Don't forget it was we who went out of our way to invite him to sit on the panel. In any case, your rules are so badly drawn up, we'd have no chance in a court of law. And, once again, Wallerstein would have the last laugh. No, there's nothing at all we can do.

UPTON SUTTER: I really am so sorry....

PRESIDENT HONORTON: Not so sorry you're offering to resign, I notice....

UPTON SUTTER: Please accept my resignation.

PRESIDENT HONORTON: Don't be ridiculous, Upton.

16

Homage to a Great Architect

From the *Saint Louis Express,* 5 April 1995

The funeral of Irwin Weissberg, who was murdered last week in Edmunson, was held yesterday morning in a private ceremony at the Baptist church in Hazlewood. A dozen close family friends came to offer condolences to Barbara Weissberg and her daughter Josephine, including multimillionaire Charles Wallerstein, for whom the deceased had built the Transatlantic Museum in San Diego in 1985 and just completed the plans for a "Puzzle Center."

The Reverend Willcox paid tribute to Irwin Weissberg as "a thoroughly upright man, who had placed his talent at the service of men and of science." The famous architect Percy Strauss, who gave the funeral address for his friend and colleague, also spoke in praise of an artist "whose airy yet complex edifices are all nostalgic paeans to the idea of escape, of a journey." After the ceremony, the Mayor of Edmunson announced plans for a retrospective of the work of the former architect. Weissberg won the respect of his colleagues in the profession with the renovation of the auditorium in Dallas, his defining work was the terminal at Galveston port (see article "Irwin Weissberg, Architect for Take off" in these pages, 30 October).

Two FBI agents arrived in Edmunson last Thursday. Irwin Weissberg would appear to be the second victim of a serial killer who has already earned himself the nickname "Polaroid Killer." Weissberg's body, discovered 30 March in a quarry not far from Edmunson, had had its right leg amputated. In its place, the killer had put a Polaroid shot depicting—a right leg.

The police refuse to comment on the progress of their inquiries.

Serial Killers and
Dismemberment

Louise Coldren, *New York Times,* 14 June 1995

Louise Coldren, psychiatrist and expert criminologist, has written
numerous books on serial killers. In her most recent work, *Serial
Killers and Dismemberment,* she considers the idea of deconstruction, which she likens to another fundamental characteristic among
serial killers: exhibitionism. Coldren applies her theory to the recent
case of the Polaroid Killer.

Seventy-seven percent of crimes committed by serial killers[8] involve
mutilation or dismemberment. Nat Sheridan, the "Minneapolis
Filleter," used to kill prostitutes, break their bones, and then chop
them into pieces. Conrad Bercovitch, "the milkman from Mobile,"
would deposit the limbs of his victims outside his ex-girlfriends'
homes. Even when the killer stops short of dismemberment he will
usually set about the victim's body, inflicting on it a variety of gross

---

8. According to FBI terminology, a serial killer is "an individual guilty of at least three
murders committed according to a similar modus operandi." Nevertheless, an increasing
number of criminologists, in particular those trained in psychiatric pathology, are
adamant that the serial killer always considers the sequence of his actions to be open-
ended. It might therefore be possible to characterize a serial killer as someone who will
continue to murder until he is caught. This is a point we will return to in the course of
this article.

abuses[9]: gouging out the eyes, cutting off fingers or ears, removing bits of genitals, and so on.

How can we account for this particularity? It was previously thought that the serial killer was a psychologically vulnerable character type, prone to unpredictable and irrepressible surges of violence. In such moments, it was thought, the murderer would lose all self-control and indulge in acts of the utmost monstrosity. In fact, this explanation is far too simplistic to have any substance: the majority of assassins are now known to be calm, intelligent people, perfectly conscious of their actions. Above all, this theory fails to take into account another very basic question: Why, if he had lost all reason, would a serial killer proceed specifically to dismemberment, rather than some other, equally revolting practice?

Dismemberment, negation of the natural process

This was the approach adopted by a number of New York psychiatrists in their ground-breaking work on the phenomenon of serial killers. The serial killer expresses himself through killing. In most cases he will be someone who is naturally quite shy, someone who, through the act of murder, manages to unleash desires and frustrations for which normal individuals find an outlet through the imagination, social contact, and, in some cases, artistic activity. If we accept this supposition, it becomes necessary to regard the circumstances of the murder as a coded message, coded by the murderer, that is, in his own particular language, and intended for the watching world. What, in such circumstances, might be the meaning of the act of dismemberment?

In our opinion, dismemberment constitutes the negation of the natural process itself. The serial killer is pitting himself against the

---

9. The weapons most frequently employed by serial killers are knives and axes, far in excess of firearms, which nevertheless feature in over three-quarters of murders committed in the United States.

great architect in the sky, the creator of mankind, whose work he is in some sense seeking to undo. For him, the act of destruction, or, rather, of deconstruction, becomes a creative act. This hypothesis is borne out by the remarks of the perpetrators themselves. In reply to a question from the judge as to why he removed his victims' bones, Nat Sheridan replied: "Your Honor, these women had fallen into sin, they would never have been admitted into the Kingdom of Heaven. No doubt you are familiar with the expression dust to dust. I ground down those women's skeletons, reduced them to dust, that's what I did, Your Honor. I committed them once more to the earth, and, even as we speak, they are seated at the right hand of God the Father."[10] Similarly, Matthew Russell, who cut off the legs of seven homosexuals in the Phoenix region in 1986 declared: "They [the victims] did not deserve to walk the surface of the earth." The serial killer undoes the world, partly because he is dissatisfied with the way it is, partly out of spite, to spit in the eye of God, the oppressor.[11] In all cases it seems more appropriate to talk of a *deconstructive* rather than of a *destructive* impulse.

This tendency is quite clearly in evidence in the case of the Polaroid Killer. The fact that each time he removes a different limb from his victim should be interpreted as an attempt to assert his power: the Polaroid Killer is showing that he can pull off *any limb he wants to.* He is not at the mercy of his impulses; he is in total control of them. The autopsies, moreover, have shown that amputation always takes place prior to the act of murder. The murderer clearly wants his victim to experience the absence of his limb, albeit just for a few minutes, and under the effect of anesthetic, to savor the full impact of his act.

---

10. Taken from the account by L. T. Bullow in *The Sheridan Affair.*
11. The criminologist John N. Powell interviewed the families of twenty-six serial killers convicted in the State of Texas between 1974 and 1982. In so doing, he revealed the determining influence of religious education in the psychological development of serial killers. Fifteen out of the twenty-six subjects had continued to attend Sunday school beyond adolescence.

Desire for posterity

If there is one pathological aspect that all serial killers have in common, over and above technique or motive, it is exhibitionism. The serial killer may commit murder in the dark, but what he desires most is the glare of publicity. The large majority are happy to confess their crimes, and avow their motives; without exception, they save the newspaper clippings that refer to their exploits. Harry T. Gozen, more commonly known as the "Butcher of Davenport," would film the death throes of the young girls he skinned alive. When the police came to arrest him at his home, he readily handed over the videos to the investigators.

This desire for posterity explains why the serial killer always gets caught in the end. After several months, he grows tired of being known only by a nickname; the media ascribe to him a crude psychology, inaccurate motives. There comes a moment when he longs to break out of the stifling anonymity that surrounds him, to give a public account of himself. He takes fewer precautions, less care in selecting his victims, or returns to the scene of a former crime: unconsciously, he wants to be arrested. Contrary to popular belief, it is never the police who break the serial chain, but the killer himself. He plans his own arrest in advance, as others might arrange a press conference.[12]

Once behind bars, he will behave like a veritable celebrity, willingly agree to interviews, write his memoirs, give straight answers to the prosecuting attorney. He will rarely repent of his actions, and will almost never make an appeal. When the verdict that would send him to the electric chair was read out, Robin Smith, "the Dakota Chainsaw Killer," asked what he would be required to wear for the execution.

The Polaroid Killer shows all the signs of hyperdeveloped exhibitionism. He does not commit murders: he stages murders. In San

---

12. Sometimes he will do both at once. The most famous example of this is the case of Rudolph Markham, the "Lumberjack from Saskatchewan," who confessed to fourteen murders, live on local radio.

Francisco he placed the body of the puzzlist, a former racing driver, behind the wheel of a car parked facing out over the Pacific. In Edmunson he set up his victim—now minus his right leg—in the position of a soccer player about to kick a ball. In Detroit he removes the right hand of Charles Wallerstein's assistant, before throwing him into a ditch and arranging him to look like a rock climber. By staging these macabre set-ups, the killer obviously hopes to achieve two things: to attract the attention of the media, who love this kind of show, and to distinguish himself from other serial killers, whom he is symbolically castigating for their lack of imagination.

But the most obvious sign of the Polaroid Killer's exhibitionist impulse, torn as he is between a desire for impunity and a desire for recognition, lies with the photographs he leaves in his victims' pockets. With each new victim, he yearns to see his own picture printed in the newspaper. He is realizing every serial killer's dream: his photo's on the evening news, and he's still out there, uncaught.

It is certainly too soon yet for us to identify the assassin: two legs and a hand are insufficient basis for an electronic identification, but with each murder the noose tightens around the Polaroid Killer. What better illustration could there be of the condition of the serial killer, proud to be sticking two fingers up at the police and at the same time longing to get caught?

Is there any chance the Polaroid Killer will be caught? If he sticks to his plan, he has only a few photos left to distribute before he gets to the face, at which point he will of course be arrested at once. One question, though, still remains unanswered. Will he stage his own arrest, as he has staged all his previous exploits?

Bjerringbro Mourns Its Champion

From our special envoy in Bjerringbro,
Skive Herald, 10 September 1995

A sad, sad day, yesterday, for Scandinavian puzzling, which buried its finest player, our fellow countryman, Olof Niels, brutally murdered last week in Tampa, Florida.

Niels was born and raised in the small village of Bjerringbro (1,400 inhabitants), twice won the SAS Trophy, and began to compete on the American professional circuit in 1991. He was head and shoulders above the rest in the 1992 season, and was the first overall title winner of the Tour, with a total of nine wins in fifteen tournaments.

Niels was a champion on a grand scale, but always remained a simple man. Each year he came back home to Denmark, to spend six weeks among his own people. Here he would purge himself of all the incredible pressures of the circuit by entertaining his friends, for the most part young local women, on his parents' farm. "An angel": the words of his mother, Katrina, as she sits slumped in despair in her own kitchen, her eyes red from crying. His father, Lars Niels, puts it more simply: "He was a great guy," he says, drawing heavily on his pipe. The rough-hewn peasant farmer insists we come with him to the barn, where we find piles of wood, neatly stacked. "Who'll cut my wood for me now that he's gone?" he asks, his eyes searching hopelessly for an answer, as though we might supply him with one.

It was hard to move in Bjerringbro yesterday afternoon without running into a friend or a neighbor of Niels who wanted to tell us what a "great fellow Olof was." We can well believe it, especially having seen the snapshot now displayed over the fireplace in the village tavern, which shows a strapping great figure of a man standing with a dead roe deer. "He seized life with both hands," commented the mayor, Skus Valfeld, who dandled him on his knee twenty-five years back. Words echoed by his colleague on the Danish team. "A real goer," said Eriksen. "Invincible," added the man who trained most closely with him, Poul Trombdø.

After the funeral, the national team players installed themselves in the tavern in Bjerringbro, where they drank beer late into the night. "Because that's what Olof would have wanted," Trombdø insisted, in a state of high emotion.

Olof Niels the Jutland Lumberjack

Jessica Woodruff, *New York Times*, 23 December 1992

When asked "What would you say you get out of the professional puzzle circuit?" Olof Niels doesn't mince his words: "A load of cash and some firm young flesh." The Jutland Lumberjack, as his opponents call him, always comes straight to the point; he says what he means, and he means what he says, with that curious mixture of candor and clumsiness that makes him the darling of his sponsors.

In fact the huge success of the JP Tour, launched last year by multimillionaire Charles Wallerstein, is due in large part to the personality of its most distinguished representative, the Dane Olof Niels. It's certainly an amazing story: the huge blond colossus, great talker, incorrigible womanizer, arrived in the States only a year ago to try his luck on the circuit, having carried off all the prizes in his native Scandinavia. In Bjerringbro, the small town where he was born twenty-seven years ago, anyone will tell you about the Mountain, just one of a string of nicknames he acquired at the age of thirteen, by which time he already stood six feet tall in his stocking feet, and weighed a hefty 176 pounds. Built like a sailboard, Niels knew of only two outlets for his incredible energy: the first was trees, which he felled with a great deal of puffing and heaving, and the second was the young girls of Bjerringbro, whom he'd no sooner pick up than he'd let drop again. Early on it became apparent that the local scene was too small for this wild lion of a man, and he began to venture farther afield, in search of new prey, both vertical and horizontal. From Randers to Silkeborg, from Skive to Arhus, the peasants soon learned to put fences around their land, while their wives locked up their daughters.

At seventeen, Olof abandoned his studies. Understandably, Mr. Niels did not dare question his son's decision—Olof was now a hefty six feet six inches and 242 pounds. "Broad Neptune Shoulders," a maritime nickname awarded after he swam the four miles across the Strait of Sletterhage, immediately found employment using his forest-felling skills. The landowners of the large estates in Jutland were delighted: Olof could do the work of four ordinary workmen. Accordingly, they were happy to overlook his unusual eating habits (the occasional live chicken) and his insistence on tumbling in the hay with farm girls every hour of the day and night.

This outdoor way of life might well have continued indefinitely if Christina, one of his conquests, had not had the brilliant idea of giving great big Olof a puzzle for his birthday. For one so adept at the destruction of Mother Nature, he puts it together with surprising, even impressive efficiency. His great big mitts bear down on the pieces, select, assess, and slot them into place at a hectic rate. Christina senses a miracle; the next day, just before she gets her marching orders, she manages to sign him up for a puzzle club in Lundsun, a suburb of Copenhagen. Oh blessed Christina, who did reveal unto the Jutland Lumberjack his true and only destiny!

The speed puzzle is an extremely popular sport in Scandinavia. Every year the SAS Open, sponsored by an anonymous airline with the same initials, brings together the top players from Sweden, Denmark, Norway and Finland. Denmark alone has twenty-five thousand registered players, out of a population of under five million. Needless to say, the talents of Blue-tooth Knut (so-called for the state of his dentition) were soon recognized. Led by Niels, Lundsun made its way through to the 1987 interclub final for the first time ever. Niels himself won the SAS Trophy in 1988 and 1989, after some truly Homeric encounters, the highlights of which the passengers of the airline company can still read about in the pages of their free in-flight magazine.

It is fashionable in some quarters to criticize Niels's style. Although it would be going too far to suggest, as some have, that he simply has none, it has to be said that his style is not distinguished by its purity. Niels is no colorist. But neither is he an adherent of the shape-based method. The fact that his fingers hang like sausages off his hands means he will never win on sheer dexterity. Lastly, it should be said that Niels is incapable of solving a puzzle unless he has the box lid there in front of him. In fact, if the Dane has one overriding characteristic, it's pragmatism. He makes the best of what he has, exploiting every possible method for its most obvious, immediate benefit. Whatever his weaknesses, his incredible energy puts them in the shade. The man has such a huge desire to win, the elements themselves, you feel, could not resist him. And who would, who *could* resist six feet seven inches and 284 pounds, a weight he carefully maintains by consuming nearly a gallon of beer a day?

In 1990, aged twenty-five, Olof Niels won the 1,000-piece at the world championships in Rome, wiping the floor, in the final, with the titleholder, Cameroonian Georges Mombala. Always a hit with young female fans, he encourages them to come and lend support in his dressing room before—and after—the match. Come summer, he withdraws to Bjerringbro, where he chops twenty-seven cubic feet of wood for his mother, and kills young deer with a single blow to the jaw. In short, our lumberjack was beginning to get bored.

The letter from the Federation arrived while Olof was somewhat out of it, resting in a convent after clearing the entire forest of the isle of Endelave with his bare hands. Charles Wallerstein invited him to take part in the first round of the tournament in Las Vegas. All his expenses would be paid and he would earn a minimum of $15,000, even if he went out in the first round. Olof, confident he could easily wipe out anyone they threw at him, agreed at once and took the next SAS flight out, accompanied by a bevy of young beauties, whom he introduced to the welcoming official at the other end as his qualified masseuses.

As one might have expected, Niels made a clean sweep of the contest. In the final he trounced the rough-edged Texan Brad Callaway, leaving him trailing by sixty-five pieces at the end of the game.

When a TV journalist from Ubiquis asked him what he thought of his opponent, Niels cracked a sincere smile and said: "I've met dairy cows whose eyes sparkled more than his." A statement like this coming from anyone else, particularly applied to an American player, would have caused an outcry and got him in hot water with the organizers. But Olof the Viking has a real gift for getting public sympathy, and he was immediately forgiven for his outspokenness.

Within the space of a few months, Juggernaut, as his male fans quickly dubbed him (his female fans favor more colorful nicknames, of a flavor that would seem to confirm popular rumor concerning the proportions of a certain part of Niels's anatomy), became the Golden Boy of the Tour, picking up along the way the first championship title, which was based on only the first half-season's play.

The 1992 season was rather trickier, even if the Jutland Lumberjack was widely expected to pick up a second title and certainly continued to sail through every round. In his frequent press interviews he tends to speak slightingly of his rivals, whether it's Rijk Krijek ("the Van Gogh of cardboard"—an allusion to the Dutchman's color technique), or the Frenchman Cornillet ("a has-been who's taken too many knocks to be dangerous"), or even of his young, and very promising countryman, Eriksen ("D'you think he's even shaken hands with a girl yet?").

He has not much to say for Wallerstein either, even though he is the only patron on the circuit: "You know where the man's coming from—he's not into giving handouts. For every dollar I manage to scramble together, he's probably earned himself ten." In fact, Charles Wallerstein must be pretty happy with his investment. While we continue to look for an American capable of winning the Tournament, Niels is for the time being an ideal figurehead for the sport of speed puzzling. At worst, a few superior killjoys will get hot under the collar at having to play the pimp with a supply of fresh young girls: during the actual tournaments, Niels settles into a rhythm of one girl before every match, and another two after, rising to three in the case of a defeat.

But who will rid us of the Jutland Lumberjack?

Extracts from the Minutes of the Puzzology Society

Committee meeting, 9 April 1984

President Sutter opened the meeting at 1800 hours precisely.

1. Decision to grant the use of the label "Approved by the Puzzology Society"

PAUL FAIRCHILD: On the eighteenth of March we received a letter from Mrs. Harriet Fairchild, who lives in Darget, Missouri. Mrs. Fairchild has a small puzzle collection that she proposes to exhibit at the Darget Fair on the tenth of June next. She requests permission to use the label "Approved by the Puzzology Society."

PRESIDENT: Do we know anything about this fair?

PAUL FAIRCHILD: It's known mostly for its blueberry-pie competition. They also hold an auction for the town orphanage. Mrs. Fairchild informs us that she will be donating the proceeds of the exhibition to a variety of local causes.

TREASURER: How much is she charging for entry?

PAUL FAIRCHILD: Two fifty.

TREASURER: Will we be receiving a portion of the receipts?

PAUL FAIRCHILD: On what grounds?

TREASURER: Technical support, expert advice on exhibits, our support of the association...Mrs. Fairchild should be spoiled for choice. Does she mention a forthcoming donation to the Society? Would she be prepared to pay the expenses if a Society member were to attend?

PAUL FAIRCHILD: She doesn't mention that in her letter. But maybe we could put it to her.

PRESIDENT: Don't go to any trouble. I know exactly the type of person we're dealing with here. Mrs. Fairchild does absolutely nothing to support our society. On the other hand, she's clear on what we can do for her. Please, let's not encourage this kind of thing.

BRAD MALONE: Mrs. Fairchild's name doesn't appear in any of the catalogs. Does she say anything about what's actually *in* her collection?

PAUL FAIRCHILD: I asked her that—she's sent a list of what she calls her "finest pieces." I brought it along to show you.

Mr. Fairchild hands out the list.

BRAD MALONE: Has anyone heard of this before? A collection based on puzzles by Whitman Publishing and Co.?

LIBBY CULLINS: Isn't Whitman that offshoot of Mattel that bought up the rights to *Sesame Street?*

BRAD MALONE: And to Walt Disney, not to mention the Wild West heroes. I've got a marvelous 1955 thirty-piece Davy Crockett of theirs.

TREASURER: She won't get fifteen dollars for it.

LIBBY CULLINS: She'd probably rather swap it for a dog-eared "Cookie Monster."

PRESIDENT: Mrs. Fairchild's request is hereby rejected. Paul—this woman wouldn't be any relation of yours, would she?

PAUL FAIRCHILD: Good Lord, certainly not!

2. Financial report for the first term

TREASURER: I'm pleased to say there has been a decrease in expenditure for this term, although of course it is partly due to the breakdown of the photocopier. On the other hand, I am concerned by the stagnation in income. It doesn't look too good. Since the acceptance of Ursula's piece on the twentieth anniversary of Springbok Editions for the *New York Times*, the main national dailies have rejected all articles by members of the Society. The label "Approved by the Puzzology Society" now only brings in between $2,000 and $3,000 a year. Donations are increasingly rare: only one check for $5,000 since the beginning of the year.

TOM LAZIO: Who was the generous benefactor?

TREASURER: Mrs. Creenshaw, as ever.

PRESIDENT: Any news on the state of her health?

TREASURER: Yes. All good, I'm afraid.

PRESIDENT: No prospect of a legacy, then?

TREASURER: I'm afraid not, no.... For the time being I'm going to have to ask each member to put up $1,000 to cover the running costs of the second term.

PRESIDENT: Anyone object to the treasurer's suggestion? No? Suggestion unanimously carried. Sol, collect the checks at the end of the meeting. Of course I should remind you that these sums are advances, and will be repaid as soon as our association's financial position reverts to one befitting its eminence.

Extracts from the Minutes
of the Puzzology Society

Committee meeting, 10 February 1992

4. Regarding the resignation of Walt Hewitt and Karen Fishbeck

PRESIDENT: Walter, do you know anything about Hewitt's and Fishbeck's resignations?

WALTER NUKESTEAD: Not a great deal, no. Karen called me last Tuesday to tell me she meant to resign. She said Walter Hewitt probably would as well.

PRESIDENT: Did she give you any reason?

WALTER NUKESTEAD: No, not exactly. She simply said she had been contacted by the American Federation and thought she could be more useful down there than here.

PRESIDENT: Riffraff! Now I understand what Hewitt was up to last November when he was pushing for an alliance with the Federation "in the interests of puzzling and its enthusiasts." And with hindsight it is quite clear to me what Mr. Wallerstein understands by the "interests of puzzling." I am at a complete loss for words to describe my repugnance for these speed contests he and his Federation are organizing throughout the country. Have you seen the kind of thugs they have competing? They're like fairground animals, incapable of stringing three words together on, say, "Some interesting aspects of the circular puzzle."

Of course, I've heard people remarking on the growing audience for puzzling. I'm delighted to hear it! First, there's been hardly any impact on sales, a rise of scarcely two or three percent. Second, and most important, what is the point of getting people interested in puzzling simply by appealing to their basest instincts? Our Society has been working for almost sixty years to further the cause of puzzling. We have always taken the long view. I myself, as president of the fortunes of this association for almost fifteen years now, set far more store by long and patient toil than by this kind of setup, with its obscene sensationalism.

Let me be quite clear about this: intelligence has no place in the strategy of the Federation. Wallerstein only thinks about one thing: profit, by any and every possible means, the more dubious the better. I invite any of you who have not yet got around to reading Charles Wallerstein's biography to do so. The kindest thing one can say is that the spiritual dimension has not exactly impinged heavily on his life.... When I think that some people simply see the revival of the Federation as the caprice of a harmless magnate! Gentlemen of the press, open your eyes! Wallerstein, as always, is following his life's guiding star: money, money and more money! And—don't forget—he stands first in line to profit from the new surge in popularity for the puzzle. We all know he bought up some of the small manufacturers for tiny sums, and immediately steered their catalogs toward a more lucrative type of production.

My friends, please, I beg of you, be on your guard before Mr. Wallerstein and his clique. You should expect to be approached. Wallerstein is not stupid. He knows where to come to find the really competent people in this country. It is obvious that the name of a single member of our assembly would suffice to lift the prestige of his federation off the zero mark, where it currently resides. He is prepared to pay huge sums to acquire the credibility he so sadly lacks, and he's not going to get it from any of those cretinous speed freaks. I can't say I am entirely surprised that someone like Hewitt had his head turned by the money. His creations were always distinguished by their crass materialism. Besides, I might as well tell you now, I always had the feeling Hewitt was the weak link in the chain.

The fact that Wallerstein struck there first just shows you how low-down and calculating the man is. Well, good riddance, Hewitt and Fishbeck. As long as he doesn't try to meddle with the elite...

NUKESTEAD: Well, exactly, we wanted to warn you about that. Wallerstein is contacting us one by one.

PRESIDENT: In person?

TREASURER: No, he always sends his assistant, a man by the name of Blythe.

PRESIDENT: The dirty rat! Well, Mr. Wallerstein, you will clearly stop at nothing! But money can't buy everything. You can't wipe out years of good and loyal service, just like that. The Puzzology Society is an order: you enter it as you would enter a religion; in the knowledge that self-sacrifice in favor of the collectivity allows you to participate in a movement that is greater than the sum of the individuals involved. Come, then, Mr. Wallerstein, and strut, like a peacock, under our window. You will soon realize what you are facing, for we are a solid block. Neither your dollars, nor your promises shall put us asunder. Once you realize the vanity of your cause, perhaps you will come crawling, as a penitent, for a truce.

TREASURER: So what should we do?

PRESIDENT: Well, we'll decide, when the moment comes, on the best way to refuse the armistice, but in the meantime we can always play around with a few ideas. First hypothesis...

Summing Up
by Charles Wallerstein

Annual convention of the Wallerstein group,
San Diego, 20 February 1991

Friends,

This convention is drawing to a close. If the bill the director of the Hyatt got me to sign just now is anything to go by, you didn't stint yourselves with your minibars, and good for you. If you could, however, just clear your heads for a few seconds, I would like to make an important announcement, which will give you something to talk about with your partners when you get back home tonight.

As of today, our group will no longer be known as Wallerstein. Its name from now on will be Ubiquis. A little reminder for those of you who skipped Latin class at school: *ubique* means everywhere. The term "ubiquity" refers to an ability to be present in several places at once. It can be applied, in the broad sense, to the whole spectrum of the Group's activities: air transport, international couriers, telephone, television and press.

When my father, Wayne, fitted out his first merchant vessel in 1920, he could have had no idea that the majority of his turnover would come from activities that at the time didn't even exist. But, without wanting to sing his praises, you must admit the man was a visionary: over the next forty years, he was always the first to pick up on the massive changes taking place in the transport and communication industries. Today, an activity like high-speed transport may seem commonplace to you; dozens of companies all over the world are in competition with Wal Express. And yet in 1956, when WW struck a deal with the powerful Teamsters union, and claimed he could distribute express mail quicker and cheaper than the Postal Service, no one took him seriously.

Last month I consulted an agency and asked them to devise us a new logo. As usually happens, the head of the firm asked me to describe the essence of the Group, i.e., to do his job for him. Still, I did go back and take a long look at the history of the Group, and discovered that it was basically consistent with the history of technology. It is the daily record of those men and women who glimpsed tomorrow's world before their time. Another thing stood out when I looked at our past—there are only two universal values, time and space. So I put that to the agency, and they came back a week later with these five words: "Here, everywhere, now, and forever."

Well, that's worth what it's worth (an awful lot, judging by the agency's bill). Personally, I think the phrase is pretty classy, and I may even consider having it put up over the entrance to our headquarters. As I said earlier, the change of name takes effect from today onward. Your printers are going to be busy. Have a good trip back, and see you next year!

Letter from Thomas Carroll to Upton Sutter

Boston, 2 December 1969

Dear Upton,

It may surprise you to hear from me in writing, when we see each other every Monday, but there are certain things that are better set down on paper.

First of all, forgive me for not having done so earlier, but I would like to thank you for organizing this wonderful competition. It was originally Gerald's idea, but it would probably never have got off the ground without you. Or without Pete, who watched us from up on high, and who, I am quite sure, supported you all the way. I was talking to Mom again about it yesterday, showing her the illuminated scroll you handed me on 18 November. These were her words, which will no doubt go straight to your heart: "How your father would have loved to have taken part."

Did you know that Pete himself organized a tournament, on a more modest scale, of course, but with the same idea? One Monday evening, about halfway through 1937, he asked all the association members—there were more than fifty of them at the time—to bring along the most difficult puzzle they had at home to the next meeting. It was a huge success! Everyone turned up with a box tucked under their arm, and the men spent the night doing a Jaymar Specialty brought along by Jones, as in the Jones bowling clubs. It was a fairly typical prewar Jaymar: 2,500 pieces, a huge steamer coming into harbor, about three-quarters of the image given over to the hull. Oh, they knew how to make them in those days! Believe me, we haven't come up with much new since then.... Anyway, my point is, Pete would have appreciated your efforts.

I should say, while we're on the subject, that I thought the way Gerald treated you last week was completely unfair. As if you were in any way to blame for the editorial error! What he omitted to say was that as president of the Society, he was the one who gave his imprimatur. And anyway, who would have thought a member of the jury would dare take advantage of a slight weakness in the rules? You can never completely protect yourself against untrustworthiness, that's another thing Pete taught me. "If someone is really determined to do wrong, there's nothing you can do to stop him," that's what he always said. I suspect Wallerstein had been working on this idea for quite some time. When Gerald invited him to sit on the panel of judges (after all, it was his idea in the first place, let's not forget that), he must have sensed the possibility of a deal and been rubbing his hands with glee. But Gerald is far too proud to admit that. He'd rather pass the buck to you, even when everybody knows you had no real control over the competition.

Which brings me to the main point of my letter. I find it very odd that you and the rest of the jury chose to give the first prize to a work like "Pantone 138." Let me remind you of the purpose of our Society, as defined by Pete almost forty years ago: "To promote the ideals of puzzling, in all its forms, to encourage a sense of enjoyment and fun and to use the puzzle to build bridges between men." Let me ask you: What enjoyment is there to be had from "Pantone 138"? Who could possibly get fun out of putting together a thousand identical pieces to make a monochrome square? As for building bridges, I would be very grateful if you could show me Rousselet's contribution to world brotherhood and the edification of nations.

You know where I stand: I've got nothing against those interminable discussions about hypotheses regarding the validity of

Fissler's Theorem, or the representation of authority in the puzzles of Margaret Richardson. I don't share your preoccupations, but I respect them; after all, Pete himself, in his day, always gave his say to Hansel the butcher, with his theories on puzzles in relief. But a competition is a serious matter, and of the five prizewinning puzzles, only two—possibly three, if you count the Springbok puzzle—are really puzzles as such. Hakematsu's box belongs in a folk museum or the Institute for Buddhist Studies in Lhasa, but surely not on the list of prizewinners in a puzzle competition. As for giving first prize to Rousselet, forgive me for saying so, but you've got to be kidding. I can't even begin to think what Pete would have said about "Pantone 138." Maybe he would have had a good laugh, or maybe a good cry, I don't know which. What are you trying to achieve by giving prizes to people like Rousselet? To put ordinary folk off puzzling, by making them think it's an intellectual discipline reserved for the elite? Tell me I'm wrong, Upton, my wise friend, you who have always shown such respect for Pete's legacy. I prefer to think the rest of the panel of judges cornered you. It was a wretched panel, all Gerald's choice. Half of them hadn't done a puzzle in their lives.

In short, I am asking you to disqualify "Pantone" and revise the list of winners accordingly. Don't be misled by what looks like unanimity. Quite a few of the Society members, as well as some ordinary puzzlists, have already asked me to do something about this scandal—and yes, scandal was the word they used, Upton; I think you should know that. Act quickly, before it's too late, to save the reputation of the Society.

Your devoted
Thomas Carroll

My Father, Pete Carroll

Extract from *Luminaries of the Puzzle World* by Thomas Carroll

My mother has often told me how, one day in March 1932, my father hung a sign over the front door of his surveyor's practice, on which was written the word CLOSED. At the height of the Depression, the real estate market came to a complete standstill. Land stopped changing hands and, from one day to the next, surveying joined the long list of obsolete professions. Some surveyors went on running around in fields and forests, planting their little wooden marker pegs, just to keep their hand in, and years later my father would unearth them for me, all swollen from rain.

He had been raised in Springfield, and had gone back to live there eight years earlier, after he'd finished his training as a surveyor. He had met up again with my mother, who was yet to become his wife. They married and had two daughters in quick succession, Clara and Laetitia, who were six and three respectively when my father shut down his practice, and so were a little young still to appreciate President Hoover's deadpan humor when he announced that recovery was just around the corner and invited all Americans to reach out and grasp it.

The whole irony of the story is that my father met his saving angel in Springfield, on the corner of Broad and Jefferson. Alden L. Fretts had worn out the seat of his pants with my father at Westfield Senior High. He was a promising lad who had gone on to become a student, then a designer, then unemployed, then a businessman. He had set up a little business manufacturing puzzles, which was known as far afield as Boston. He designed his own collection, the Yankee Cut-Ups, but he didn't know much about sales. He hired my father as a salesman and my mother as a "solver," a noble but vanished profession. At the same time, in fact, Gladys, Fretts's wife, opened a puzzle lending library. For a period of just over a year, Mom did each and every puzzle they produced, to check that all the pieces were there!

Once he'd honed his spiel by practicing on the neighbors, my father went out to look for customers, ringing every doorbell in the country, as far as Northampton. "Do you have a minute, Mrs. Jones? Pete Carroll, Alden Fretts Corporation. I would not presume to trouble you did I not have something of the greatest importance to tell you. Believe it or not, I'm here to talk to you about puzzles. Do you do puzzles yourself? Of course you do! What a question! Who doesn't, at the moment? But I have the feeling you take a greater interest than our average citizen. Oh yes, there are puzzlists and then there are puzzlists. Look at the stuff arriving from New York, for example, often with pieces missing or with pieces all identical, cut by machine. And as for historical accuracy, forget it! Have you seen the latest from Jaymar Specialty? A watercolor by Anna Dryhurst. In the blurb they have the nerve to describe her as a New Yorker! Anna Dryhurst! A local girl, raised in Ludlow, married in Chicopee! It's going a bit far, that is. But these people in New York, they've no respect. For them, everyone north of the Bronx is a hick, if you'll pardon me, Mrs. Jones. But I'm not here to give Jaymar's puzzles a bad name; their designers do that for them. I think you mentioned you go for quality? Ah, quality, that's what it's all about. One question, Mrs. Jones: How do you gauge the quality of a puzzle? You hear all sorts of nonsense on that subject—scientific tests, clever calculations, and all sorts of other highfalutin claptrap. And the answer is plain and simple. Just one phrase: a quality puzzle is one that never dates. If a puzzle is beautiful, you want to be able to hold on to it for twenty years. When Alden Fretts makes a new design, that's the only thing he cares about. His puzzles are always at least one-third outline pieces, which, as you know, are the most hard-wearing. Think back, Mrs. Jones: when was the last time you found an outline piece in an Einson-Freeman puzzle? Well, I won't wait for an answer to that.... But design is only the beginning. Alden Fretts personally supervises the way his puzzles are cut. And since the existing printers—who incidentally supplied all his competitors—seemed too slapdash for him; he devised a system that increased the accuracy of the machines tenfold. These probably seem like rather technical details to you, mere talk; let's move on to more serious things.... Take a look at this model. It's called "John Paul Jones Bids Farewell to His Boat." Notice, by the way, what I was saying about the outline pieces: here, look at this bell, this star, and here, look, a shepherd, an elegant lady with her parasol... Well, we haven't got time to look at them all; there are over two hundred pieces. But the reason I got out this model to show you is to illustrate what I was saying about quality. I was saying how Alden Fretts's puzzles are designed to survive the test of time. If you don't mind, I'll ask you to prove the point for me, Mrs. Jones, by just taking hold of the corner of this puzzle. If what I was telling you is true, the pieces should fit together so neatly that not one of them falls out. No, it doesn't matter where you hold it, maybe take it by the corner, any one will do. There. You see? Isn't that wonderful? You certainly look amazed, Mrs. Jones. I know you're just dying to go find a Milton Bradley and put it to the same test. But please, spare me the agony, wait till I've gone! Oh, and while we're on the same subject, allow me to show you another surefire way to recognize a Fretts. After all, imagine if you lifted up a puzzle one of your friends had done by the corner and the whole thing fell apart! She's going to be angry enough without your telling her she's been conned into the bargain. No, what I'm talking about is something much simpler. All Alden Fretts's puzzles have a signature, an outline piece with a little dog on it, called Pal. You'll usually find him in the bottom right-hand corner. Look, there's one in this model, here. Take a good look. Now, thanks to him, you'll be able to protect yourself from impostors. Remember: a puzzle without a Pal isn't a Fretts...."

And so on and so forth. In those days people had the time to talk to sales reps. My father was usually to be found with his puzzles spread out on the kitchen table and a glass of lemonade in front of him. Because, once Mrs. Jones had got the message that Fretts's puzzles were truly unique, she would buy a dozen of them straight off. Pal had found himself yet another home....

The bright star of puzzling waned in the final months of 1933, when it became clear that America was coming out of the Depression. Fretts's models fared only marginally better than the others. The recession had been like a sort of long, slightly crazy interlude, during which people had gone in for the strangest sorts of professions. In January 1934, that interlude came to a close, and everyone went back to what he had been doing before the recession. Fretts found work once more as a designer, and my father reopened his surveyor's practice. Twelve months went by, twelve months of grinding boredom, according to my mother. For two years my father had lived for puzzles and nothing else. Not content with selling them during the day, he spent his nights doing them, or designing new ones. It wasn't a question of whether he would maintain his commitment to puzzles. What drove him to despair was the thought that his neighbors no longer shared his passion, and that if he opened his mouth to talk to them about Pal, he'd be greeted with an ironic smile.

On 13 January 1935, he founded the Society of Friends of the Puzzle. Today, fifty years on, the purpose of the Society is still a subject of endless debate. People come and pore over the statutes with the precision of a textual critic, claiming to have forgotten that my father drew them up one evening on his kitchen table while listening to baseball on the radio. The first item reads: "The Society is committed to the promotion of the ideal of puzzling in all its forms." Certain commentators will naturally make much of my father's ecumenical approach. My own feeling has always been that he wasn't quite sure himself what he was getting at and that "the ideal of puzzling in all its forms" was a useful phrase that took account of any direction it might take in years to come.

Alden and Gladys Fretts were the first people to put up their token dollar to become lifelong members of the association. They were joined by about thirty other inhabitants of Springfield, a number of whom had been my father's former clients. I recently came across a blue leather notebook recording the minutes of the inaugural meeting. Here I read that "Meetings would be held about once a week, preferably on Fridays so that children could come along with their parents," that "Katharine Carroll would look after the cakes but that the members were kindly asked to take turns bringing drinks." And that "The agenda would be drawn up after the meeting, to take account of what had been said." These few lines, written in my mother's large, looping hand, are the only written records of the first fifteen years of the Puzzology Society. Fretts volunteered to keep the minutes, but he seems to have forgotten to do so seven times in a row, and no one thought to remind him.

I would have attended these meetings myself had it not been for the fact that I was born five years after the Society was set up. I spent a few years slumbering with the other babes in arms, but when I turned three, my father decided I was old enough to join in with the grown-ups and do my first "Santa Claus," a McGloughlin, with eighteen pieces, which kept me busy four Fridays in a row. Later, once I'd shown myself competent on locomotive engines and scenes from American history, I was admitted to the collective puzzle table. We started every meeting by doing a puzzle that one of our members had found particularly tricky, interesting, or simply enjoyable. We all huddled around the big table in the dining room, and would talk about what we were looking for, help each other out, and triumphantly shout out each piece as we found it. Then my mother served the cakes, an operation that inevitably got us split up into groups. While the women gathered around a cup of tea, the men lit up cigarettes and chatted. About puzzles they'd loved, or those they'd never managed to finish. About the different shades of Topper's coat—Topper being Hopalong Cassidy's horse. About the exhilarating atmosphere of Springfield, which had spawned two makers (Milton Bradley and Fretts) and now the Society of Puzzology. Sometimes the conversation would take a more serious turn. Everyone jumped on his particular hobby horse. My father would speak up for the noninterlocking designs by Margaret Richardson. Our neighbor, Kestelman, fulminated against the dismal quality of the Madmar Quality Co., which was no longer what it used to be. Fretts broke our hearts by announcing he would shortly be discontinuing hand-cut puzzles.

How many were we? Recently, I tried to jot down the names of all those who were of our number. I had no problem coming up with the names of fifteen or so families. I had more of a problem with the dozen or so women who used to join us on evenings when their husbands had gone off to the game. I've forgotten the name of the old grandpa who came along with his little grandson, Jeremy, and would spend the evening telling him how he'd won the geography prize by using the Silent Teacher puzzle-maps. Jeremy must be sixty now. And yet it still seems like only yesterday....

25

Letter from Thomas Carroll to Cecil Earp

Boston, 9 May 1991

Dear Cecil,

What a surprise to hear from you after so many years! If I'm not mistaken, it must be at least fifteen years since you left Boston. Dunlap has kept me informed of the main moves in your brilliant career. To be honest, your success is hardly a surprise. Your contributions in seminars were always the most limpid and erudite. On the other hand, I had no idea you were still interested in puzzles. Dunlap told me you always renewed your annual subscription to *Puzzle Journal,* a fine example of loyalty, one that certain of our old friends, who stuffed their puzzles away in a drawer the minute they quit studying, would do well to follow.

I would also like to thank you for your suggestion, although I am unable to accept. Things have been rather painful of late, as you can imagine. It is always sad to watch an association that has so many fond memories tear itself apart. And yet I would be the first to accept that the situation couldn't continue as it was. Diana, Hooper, and the others are right: the Society talks too much and does too little. I voted for them, and after the second round I really thought we had a chance of throwing Sutter over. But what can you do; now he's elected, I'm bound to help him in any way I can, out of respect for Pete's memory and the legacy he's left us.

And yet I would have been pleased to be involved in this new project with you. I don't know Wallerstein, apart from what you read in the papers, of course. Do you remember he was on the panel of judges for the "most difficult puzzle competition"? I've also heard he's got a fantastic collection of old puzzles; if he ever puts on a private exhibition, do let me know. His idea for a federation is very tempting, at least on paper. At any rate, it forces Sutter to react and to take up some of the proposals on Dobbs's list. Speaking of which, I heard that Wallerstein sent his assistant, someone called "Blythe" to talk to each of the "dissidents," one by one. What's he offering them? A place in the organigram of the Federation? Upton will be furious if he hears of it.

So sorry to let you down. My place is here, whatever happens. But that doesn't mean I don't wish you well. Long live the Federation!

Sincerely,
Thomas Carroll

P.S. Enclosed is a copy of my book, *Luminaries of the Puzzle World,* which came out in 1982. Please forgive me for not having sent it to you at the time.

Gleaners Project Report

26 March 1991

NOTE: In this document we assume that the genesis and purpose of the Gleaners Project are known to all. In the interest of readability, a more thorough treatment of certain subjects has been included in the appendices at the back.

1. Experimental protocol

This study was conducted between December 11, 1990 and March 19, 1991 on a building site at 406 Haverhill Street and involved Elmer Humphrey, 49, and Richie Wyatt, 36, both employed by the Bireley building company.

It was decided on the opening day that Wyatt should be the "constructor" and Humphrey the "deconstructor," roles the two men kept for the duration of the contract. They were not told the purpose of the experiment. Hours of work were from eight to twelve and from one to five, Monday through Saturday.

The first week was spent working out rules that would ensure that Wyatt and Humphrey would work at precisely the same speed. Thus we tested a number of combinations with particular reference to the following parameters: size and weight of the cinder-blocks, distance between the pile of cinder-blocks and the wall, capacity of the cement mixer, ratio of the cement, length and shape of the chisel, leverage and weight of the mallet, length and frequency of the rest periods. On the fifth day, we attained satisfactory results (a difference of one block per day in favor of Humphrey).

It should be noted that these specifications were defined with reference to the workmen, Wyatt and Humphrey, and to them alone. Anyone wishing to repeat the experiment with different workmen will not have the benefit of this procedure, which was set up very precisely with reference to the characteristics of the workmen concerned.

The complete experimental procedure appears as Appendix 1.

2. Initial configuration and equilibrium configuration

The initial configuration was randomly generated by computer. This comprised 238 blocks and took account of the rules agreed for construction (no two adjacent spaces in the first nine rows) and the required dimensions (a maximum of forty blocks long and ten high). Complete, the wall would thus comprise four hundred blocks. Throughout this report, their positions are designated by a code comprised of a letter from A to J and a figure from one to forty (A corresponding to the bottom row and one to the column farthest to the left). Thus the position at the intersection of the fourth row from the ground and the twenty-sixth column from the left is shown by the code D26.

The number of blocks moved in any one day varied. During module one, this reached an average of 36.4 blocks for Wyatt and

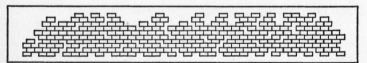

Initial configuration: 18 December 1990

35.2 for Humphrey, which means that the daily rate of wall renewal lies between zero and nine percent, depending or whether or not the work of the two men overlapped. The difference between the number of blocks added or removed in any one day at no point exceeded four (plus or minus).

These fluctuations were noted (see Appendix 2). With hindsight, three phases may be identified:

• Global phase (December 18–21)
Wyatt and Humphrey worked in a systematic fashion. The objectives they set themselves were overambitious. Wyatt began on the left-hand side of the wall and tried to complete each column up to a height of ten blocks. Humphrey began by dismantling the farthest column on the right. Then he changed strategy, and began working from right to left, but removing only two or three blocks per column.

• Local phase (December 21–January 3)
The global phase ended at exactly 1045 hours on December 21, when Humphrey decided to leave the right-hand side of the wall and come and work on Wyatt's territory. He knocked out some of the blocks Wyatt had laid over the previous three days. After an hour, Wyatt reacted, reconstructing, during the course of that afternoon, the right-hand column that Humphrey had knocked down on the first day. On December 23 and 24, Humphrey deliberately destroyed three days of Wyatt's work, while Wyatt responded in kind. By the evening of December 26, it can more or less be said that the wall had reverted almost exactly to its condition on the very first day.

On December 27, Wyatt went back to the left-hand side of the wall, and set about filling in a hole which Humphrey was currently creating. Not to be outdone, Humphrey began methodically knocking out each new block that Wyatt had laid. Thus began a war of attrition, which lasted seven days. The conflict had become a localized one. The two men stuck to each other like glue and their struggle began to focus on parts of the wall that took on a new symbolic significance: column thirty-eight, which was knocked out and rebuilt three times, the gap at EG–17/20, and the series of steps at EJ–1/5.

• Equilibrium (January 4–9)
On the afternoon of January 4, Humphrey finally won the battle of the steps. The wall now consisted of 266 blocks. It no longer resembled the configuration of the original wall in any way. From January 7 onward, Humphrey simply proceeded by removing each block that Wyatt had laid. On the morning of the ninth, the two men laid down their tools and shook hands.

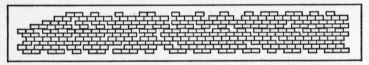

Equilibrium configuration: January 9, 1991

3. Notes on the equilibrium configuration

The design arrived at by Wyatt and Humphrey does not seem to obey any internal system of logic. The number of blocks finally settles at 268, thirty blocks more than the initial configuration. The vertical distribution is fairly regular (139 blocks in the five lower rows, 129 in the five upper rows) as well as a distinct imbalance in favor of the right-hand side of the structure (143 blocks in the right-hand half of the wall, seventy-five of those in the very farthest quarter).

The step sequence at EJ–1/5 is unquestionably the most striking feature of the structure. Also worthy of note are the two gaps at AC–11/13 and AC–27/29, which seem to mirror each other symmetrically, at an imaginary axis. The degree of dissimilarity (equal to the ratio of the number of blocks that changed position to the number of stones left from the original wall) is 17.48 percent.

A more detailed analysis of the equilibrium configuration appears in Appendix 3.

4. Permanence of the equilibrium configuration

This first experiment demonstrated the existence of an equilibrium configuration in a wall surface consisting of four hundred blocks, subjected to contradictory forces. The second stage of our experiment was to ask whether the equilibrium configuration was dependent on the initial configuration.

The results are extremely thought-provoking. The experiment, repeated four times over, never again produced the exact configuration of 9 January. Nevertheless, the degree of fluctuation observed over the course of the first five attempts never exceeded two percent (five blocks).

• Second experiment (10 January–1 February)
The configuration generated by the computer includes 156 blocks and shows 24.66 percent degree of difference when compared to the initial configuration. There is a deep gap between columns thirty-four to thirty-seven, running as far down as row F.

Wyatt and Humphrey abandoned any semblance of method. They indulged in light skirmishes for almost a week, before engaging in more serious, albeit still localized confrontation. The final configuration emerged over a period of sixteen days, assumed its form on 30 January and solidified definitively on 1 February. It included 265 blocks and differed from the configuration of 9 January by only five blocks. The step sequence at EJ–1/5 remained intact, as did the gaps at AC–11/13 and AC–27/29.

• Third experiment (2–8 February)
The new configuration contains 252 blocks and shows an 11.35 percent degree of difference when compared with the initial configuration.

There are no obvious moments of significance in this third repetition. Abrupt, nervous gestures lead to lightning strikes of extreme violence. The outcome of these major battles is decided on the third day. Note how on the morning of 8 February, Wyatt and Humphrey arrived once more at the equilibrium configuration of 9 January.

They then deviated from this by a difference of two blocks, before declaring themselves finished at 1128 hours.

• Fourth experiment (9–28 February)
The new configuration contains 183 blocks and shows a 34.92 percent degree of difference when compared with the initial configuration.

This repetition of the experiment can be described in terms of a single battle, fought for a period of thirteen days, over column thirty-eight. In the week of 18 February alone, this column was entirely dismantled seventeen times. On 23 February at one in the afternoon, Humphrey surrendered. In less than half an hour, the column was complete once more. The subsequent stages were a mere formality. On 2 March, Wyatt and Humphrey laid down their tools, leaving a wall which corresponded almost entirely to the initial configuration, with only one block's difference, at J38.

• Fifth experiment (1–19 March)
Unlike all the preceding configurations, this one was not generated by computer. We chose it because it was as different as it was possible to be from the configuration arrived at the end of module 1, while still containing the same number of blocks. When compared with this configuration, therefore, it shows a maximum possible degree of difference, that is, 49.25 percent.

Wyatt and Humphrey are visibly disorientated. They hesitate for several minutes before undertaking the slightest movement. This period of doubt lasts almost five days.

What finally gets the two men back on course is the step sequence at EJ–1/5. On 7 March, toward the end of the afternoon, Humphrey knocks out two blocks, at J5 and I4, which provokes an immediate reaction from Wyatt. The two men suddenly remember what it was they had forgotten. Wyatt's trowel finds its way back to column 38, while Humphrey's mallet returns to his symmetrical gaps. Bit by bit, the wall begins to resemble the reference configuration. Humphrey calls a halt to the work at 1100 hours on 19 March, at a point at which the wall shows a degree of difference of only 0.7 percent (two blocks).

Each movement of Experiments two to five is detailed in Appendix 4. Statistical analyses comparing each of the initial configurations with the equilibrium configuration are given in Appendix 5.

5. Conclusions regarding the equilibrium configuration

The five experiments described above incontestably demonstrate the existence of an equilibrium configuration, applicable to a wall of four hundred blocks subject to contradictory forces such as those described in the experimental protocol. The discrepancies observed in the five experiments are of little significance and are probably the result of external factors that are difficult to control (climatic conditions, diet of the two workmen, mood swings, periods of tiredness, etc.). The discrepancies were related to nondescript stones (always blocks within the body of the wall, never on the edges or in proximity to the principal motifs).

The number of blocks in the equilibrium configuration (which we have chosen to define as an average of the five configurations achieved) is 267, that is, the nearest whole number to 266.67, one-third of 400. The similarity achieved should not be considered purely coincidental. But apart from this fact, the equilibrium configuration remains impenetrable. It confounds those who expected to see the emergence of simple geometric patterns: the step sequence EJ–1/5 and the two symmetrical gaps at AC–11/13 and AC–27/9 are the only really clear patterns which can be made out at first glance. The configuration is strikingly provisional in appearance; no one column or row is complete; no one column or row is entirely empty either.

The pattern of the configuration is currently being subjected to more in-depth analysis, the results of which will be given at a future meeting.

6. Comments on the protocol

On the whole, the protocol drawn up between 11 and 15 January worked quite satisfactorily. One detail, however, does compromise the relevance of the experiment: from 9 January onward, Wyatt and Humphrey were aware of the equilibrium configuration and were therefore able consciously to strive toward it. Although the abilities of the two men should not be underestimated (their sound common sense struck us on repeated occasions), it seems unlikely that either of them managed to memorize the pattern of the wall down to the smallest detail. On the other hand, it would be unrealistic to imagine that Humphrey or Wyatt could have forgotten such obvious features of the pattern as the symmetrical gaps, and, above all, the step sequence at EJ–1/5. Several times we had the feeling that the two men, in particular Humphrey, were actively trying to recall the configuration of 9 January in order to reproduce it. This is a danger that could in future be avoided by one of two methods: either by serving the two men at regular intervals with a product that erases the memory of the preceding weeks; or by changing the protagonists each time the experiment is repeated (which would, however, require a complete redefinition of the protocol). Financial constraints and the limited scope of the task we had undertaken ruled out either of these solutions, which would necessarily have to be considered if the Gleaners Project were to be expanded in any way.

7. Comments regarding a possible expansion
   of the Gleaners Project

The Gleaners Project could conceivably be expanded to investigate whether the equilibrium configuration was directly dependent on the two subjects. By forbidding all communication between Wyatt and Humphrey, we hoped to eliminate one factor that might have distorted the experiment. Despite this, the results obtained do not rule out the possibility that two different workmen would not have arrived at a different configuration, or even that they would have arrived at any sort of equilibrium at all.

It might also be interesting to calculate the correlation between the rate of difference between the initial configurations and those arrived at, and the length of time required to reach equilibrium. The five pairs of results obtained, even if they do not constitute a statistically valid sample, would seem to suggest that a particular relationship exists between the two variables.

8. Comments regarding a possible transfer of the protocol to the case of the puzzle

In view of the way the Gleaners Project evolved, we are concerned that the utmost prudence should be exercised as regards the possible transferral of the experimental procedure, or protocol, to the case of the puzzle, as had originally been envisaged. In our view, there are a considerable number of obstacles that might compromise the success of such a transfer. First, it is impossible for two people to work on the same puzzle without getting in one another's way. It would therefore be necessary to make changes to the protocol so as to allow the two subjects to take turns.

This brings us to a second objection: whereas it was possible to slow down the two Gleaners workmen by modifying the physical constraints (weight of the blocks, consistency of the cement, and so on), there is no way of restraining puzzlists in their frenzy to complete, or, indeed, dismantle, a puzzle, except by imposing an arbitrary limit on the number of pieces they are allowed to act upon. Even then, such an expedient might well encourage the players to develop all sorts of perverse strategies, as found most frequently in the game of Go.

The third restriction, and undoubtedly the most important, is connected with the extreme variety that exists among puzzles, whether in terms of their dimensions, subject or type. The Gleaners experiment was carried out on a wall of four hundred blocks, but could equally well be repeated tomorrow on a different edifice, with only a few very slight modifications to the protocol. This is by no means the case for the puzzle. To start with, it would certainly take many months to arrive at the "truth" of a model such as "Pantone 138." But, most important, what conclusions could one possibly hope to reach in the case of a model such as "Watch out, Gramp!" or "Shattered Hopes"? Each new attempt would require a fundamental revision of the protocol, and could only hope to achieve results that were at best hypothetical and no doubt of an extremely partial nature.

For all these reasons, we believe the Gleaners experiment should not be extended to the puzzle. On the other hand, we have undoubtedly much to learn from the study of cinder-block walls.

9. Comments on the Gleaners budget

The committee voted to assign $6,000 to the Gleaners Project. We regret to have to inform the association that this sum has been considerably exceeded. There are several reasons for this.

It had been envisaged that the salary of the two workmen would account for the greater part of the expenses. In our calculations we allowed for an hourly rate of $6. Now, the professional guidelines followed by Bireley Inc. set the minimum hourly wage at $8.45, a figure that rises to $11 to account for various obligatory deductions. The agreement also stipulates that hours worked on Saturdays should be paid at a rate of an extra 25 percent, a fact we were unaware of at the time the protocol was drawn up. In total, the cost of labor should come out around $13,300.

To this sum should be added the cost of raw materials, again more expensive than had been envisaged. It turned out that the cement we had chosen on account of its exceptional kinetic quality was the most expensive of all those used by Bireley Inc.

Finally, a number of incidents entailed unforeseen expenses. In each case, we made a point of settling the matter in the best interests of the Society.

We estimate the total budget for the project at around $18,500. We would ask our colleagues to excuse this overspending, which was due to circumstances entirely beyond our control.

Melinda Plunket   Doyle Evart

Citizen Wallerstein's Dirty Tricks

Val Nuss, *The Impertinent*, 2 February 1992

No doubt about it, Charles Wallerstein seems to be modeling himself on Citizen Kane to the point of caricature. His taste for ostentation has been common knowledge since the publication by *The Impertinent* of exclusive pictures of Ubiquis, his palace built in stucco and pink marble. Like his illustrious role model, he is known to be expert in the art of manipulating public opinion, a process made considerably easier by his ownership of a national network of eleven cable TV chains and forty-seven newspapers. Those who know their classics will not be surprised to learn that Charles Wallerstein has entered a second childhood.

Judge for yourselves. On 17 May last, Wallerstein was elected president of the American Puzzle Federation. On 21 July he laid the first stone of a Puzzle Museum, financed entirely out of his own pocket. Finally, on 8 September, he launched the Federation Tournament, the opening event of the JP Tour, the aim of which is to "bring together on a single circuit the fastest puzzlists on the planet" (*sic*).

Already I can hear the cohorts of *Life* readers, in their thirst for justice and objectivity, protest: where's the harm in promoting puzzling, that most inoffensive of pastimes, once so beloved of our grandmothers? And to be fair, setting aside the blatant ineptitude of the JP Tour, one might indeed find this sudden conversion, late in life, quite touching, and make a show of swallowing our man's explanations when he claims to want to "rediscover the thrill of his childhood pursuits." The sums in question may seem a little disproportionate with childish whim, but what the devil, if Charles Foster Kane had been alive today he would no doubt have had a sled made of solid gold and the blades of his skates studded with diamonds. The voice of reason would tell us to let Charles Wallerstein rip, if he wants; it's his own money he's throwing away.

But it would be an insult to the intelligence of the readers of *The Impertinent* to stop at that. Wallerstein is about as credible in the role of guardian of traditional arts and crafts as Ronald Reagan was when he tried to talk about the economy. Which raises one obvious question: what is it about the spectacle of a few epileptics assembling such gripping images as Davy Crockett killing his first bear that puts such a huge smile on the face of our man Wallerstein? And one very obvious answer: money.

A trusted technique: buy low, sell high

In 1988, according to reliable sources, Wallerstein bought, either directly or through front men acting on his behalf, more than four hundred collector's puzzles. In so doing, he created an artificial shortage, which pushed up the value of the puzzles he had acquired. Penny Kennan, a close associate of Wallerstein, made a profit of $2,400 by selling a copy of "Ablutions of Buffalo Bill" to a Chicago museum. By our estimate[13] the total profit for Wallerstein must be in the region of around $80,000 dollars, that is to say, peanuts: not enough to make a story.

In the same vein, but juicier by far, are Wallerstein's efforts to manipulate market values before he buys puzzle manufacturers. It is not widely known, in fact, that the president of Ubiquis personally controls four small producers and owns more than forty percent of Wicker Bros, the wholesaler with the biggest turnover in America.

---

13. Based on listings in the annual Anne Williams catalog, edited by Wallace-Homestead.

Each time, the method is the same. Through the various newspapers in his group, Wallerstein spreads rumors concerning the insolvency of those businesses that interest him. Once the price has dropped by about fifteen or twenty percent, Wallerstein "picks up" any share parcels lying around, until he controls a "blocking" minority of shares. It is then a fairly simple matter to persuade the other share-holders to sell. Generally they take such fright at the sinister name of the Wallerstein[14] family that they hand over their stocks, usually at a discount of around two-thirds of their real value. Net profit from these dealings to date: almost thirty-five million dollars. This is no doubt what our man is referring to in interviews when he talks of "rediscovering the feverish joys of childhood games...."

Wallerstein controls our investments, now he wants to control our leisure time. Brave New World!

Make no mistake, however: Wallerstein hopes to get a lot more out of his little adventure in the puzzle world than a few wretched mil-lions. His avowed objective is to transform the puzzle into one of the principal pastimes of the American people, on a par with base-ball or bowling. The day that happens, the jackpot will be in the order of hundreds of millions of dollars. As controller of every stage, from production through to broadcasting rights, Citizen Wallerstein will be in a position to dictate terms to us poor sheep. Wallerstein, and not Ubiquis, since the wily fox has been clever enough to invest as an individual. It's a well-known fact: the bigger the cake, the less inclined one is to share it!

---

14. To avoid landing ourselves in a libel case, we will refrain from mentioning the intimidation techniques employed by Wayne Wallerstein, father of Charles, to "persuade" reluctant shareholders. However, it is a well-known fact that one of them (John L. Willis, not to name names), who dared to pursue Wayne Senior through the courts, unfortunately smashed his jaw against a metal bar the night before the trial and was obliged to decline to give his testimony.

It's the hunting season, anything goes. Let us take, for example, the election of the aforesaid Wallerstein as head of the Federation. A ballot that passed off without a hitch, apparently, with every sign of being perfectly democratic. Result: almost too good to be true, unanimity minus one. Four months later, the pair of elderly spinsters who run the Federation receive a visit from the celebrated magnate Charles Wallerstein. He spouts his pretty speech about the feverish joys of childhood games, expresses bitter regret at the neglect of this wonderful pursuit in the world today, and reels off, with an air at once humble and sincere, various other hypocritical phrases which he has long used to touch the hearts of ladies. He then proposes, as an act of pure generosity, to make "some small payments to the Federation, by way of a contribution, commensurate with his means, to the development of the puzzle in the United States." No sooner said than done. Wallerstein makes out an initial check for $500,000 to Miss Milly Inglethorpe, president of the association, who almost has a heart attack to mark the occasion. "This is only the beginning," the good and munificent multimillionaire tells her, "you will be receiving the same sum every term—since this is the price of eternal youth."

Dear old Milly, infinitely trusting, consults the opinion of Carolyn, her sister, and also treasurer of the association, who is able to confirm that, yes, $500,000 is a large sum, almost thirty-five times the budget of the association, and with this money they will be able to rent bigger officers and hire a secretary, maybe two, a press officer, and organize an exhibition to which they can invite all the top drawer of Providence society, and bring out a new brochure on glossy paper, cardboard thick, et cetera, et cetera.

Four months later, the Federation is on the verge of bankruptcy. Their expenditures certainly rose, as anticipated, but were not met by the promised income. Milly tried to prompt Mr. Wallerstein but, one must accept, it's tricky, he's such a busy man. Finally, she is only too happy to give up her position in favor of the generous multimillionaire who agrees to pay all the creditors in exchange for her presidential chair at the Federation. As for Carolyn, she never really fully grasped what was happening.

Four months after that, Wallerstein launches the JP Tour. In the meantime, he elbowed out the two ladies and transferred the headquarters of the Federation from Providence to Las Vegas. The twelve thousand cameramen at his heels fall all over themselves to film the Federation tournament. It's the first time the American viewing public can see a puzzle competition on its screens, and they mustn't be disappointed.

Game fixing for viewing figures

To say that the rules of the JP Tour are absolute child's play is to understate the matter. Still, the disconcertingly low level of intelligence of some of the members of the circuit made it desirable, not to say necessary, for the general idea to be kept as simple as possible. The two players are each given the same puzzle (there are three categories: 500, 1,000 and 5,000 pieces): the winner is the one who finishes it first. A game in the 1,000-piece category lasts on average twenty-five minutes. The tournament operates on the principle of direct elimination; the justification given in the Wallerstein camp for this decision is that the Puerto Rican, Guerrero, would never have been able to get his head around the idea of a second chance.

To ensure the success of the first Federation tournament, the organizers pulled out all the stops. Every journalist is given a brochure containing a detailed biography of the thirty-two participants, an analysis of each player's style, and the projected performance of each competitor. For example, we are told that "the veneration received by the Argentinian Cortes, in his home country, is equal to that of a Fangio," or that "having won every amateur title going, Niels is now looking for his first professional title." The brochure even separates nice from nasty. Thus, on the subject of the German, Tackl: "His cold, calculating gaze, the way he storms through the monochrome sections, have earned him the name of Ice Cube among his colleagues." In short, the competition hasn't even started, and already we know that the Frenchman, who has recovered from his injury, won't get through the first round, that the Argentinian will crumble in the quarterfinals, and that the final will be between Niels and the rising star of the American puzzle scene, Texan Brad Callaway. This is what is meant by controlling the suspense factor.

It is obvious from the way this first tournament has been run that Wallerstein will stop at nothing to create a big splash. Every evening our puppet master flies to Los Angeles to join thousands of paid extras, leaping up and down before the skills of thirty-two mental retards. Installed in comfort in his private box, he nonchalantly puts his hands together to applaud.

The first rounds run according to plan. The Krijek–Cornillet match gets an audience of 4.2 percent, a very respectable rating considering it was up against Murphy Brown and the NBA play-offs. But everything stops dead in the quarterfinals, when Callaway finds himself in trouble against Casparelli. Halfway through the game, he is thirty-eight pieces behind the Italian. Watch out, danger: Callaway is the last American left in the competition. If he disappears from the scene before time, the level of interest in the tournament will drop dramatically.

Fortunately, Charles, our debonair multimillionaire, has his eye on things. While Callaway's scratching away at his head, we see Wallerstein lean over to his assistant, who immediately springs up and goes to have a word with Casparelli's trainer. The trainer then gets up too, goes and stands in front of the stage, and throws a wink at his protégé. Like a good little boy, Casparelli slows down. He goes through the motions of puzzler's block, allowing the hard-working Callaway to plod his way back into the lead to win by a nose.

Poor Charles Foster Kane...

It won't be the only fixed game of the tournament. *The Impertinent* is able to reveal that both the Dutchman Krijek, and the Dane Eriksen "lay down quietly" to allow Callaway to win. In recognition of their services, they were each paid $50,000 in cash and found themselves three weeks later in the final of the Buffalo tournament. As for this thickhead, Callaway, once Wallerstein realized he was no good after all, he put him back out to graze with a hefty check.

If I remember correctly, Citizen Kane put on an opera to allow his mistress, who prided herself on a pretty voice, to take the leading role. Despite all his contacts in the press, Kane got a roasting at the premiere, when his young lady took her bow to a chorus of boos and catcalls, and never appeared on stage again.

Poor old Kane, if only he'd known our friend Wallerstein...

In Praise of
The Missing Piece

Puzzology Review, April 1976

We have already mentioned in these pages[15] how highly we rate *Sky Blue,* Neville Batterson's debut monograph, published in 1968 and reissued in time for Christmas. "At the age of only twenty-four," we said in conclusion, "Batterson already possesses an admirable turn of phrase. His work is characterized by an inimitable mixture of erudition and instinct."

It is now eight years since *Sky Blue,* and during that time Neville Batterson has set up the Chair of Puzzology at the University of Rochester and produced two theoretical works, *Borders*[16] and *Seduction by Monochrome.* His new book is *The Missing Piece,* a work that defies classification, a veritable firework of puzzle philosophy, which

---

15. *Puzzology Review,* December 1973.
16. *Borders* is Batterson's contribution to the debate on Fissler's Theorem (1931), which states: the infinity of pieces in the world's largest puzzle renders all attempts at the production of such a puzzle entirely obsolete. Although it has been around for forty years, Fissler's Theorem was the subject of violent debate throughout the year 1972, which was sparked off by Fiodor Sadarov, a father of the Soviet school. Sadarov drew attention to the results brought back by Gagarin from outer space to deny the existence of limitless space, and, in the same breath, to proclaim the superiority of historical materialism to all other models of development. The greatest names in American puzzology responded to a call from Isaac Gilmar by signing *The "40" Manifesto* for Fissler. In paragraph 7 of the *Manifesto* Batterson calls on puzzologists throughout the world to keep the subject of their study outside the world of politics.

will undoubtedly succeed in satisfying the experts and attracting the uninitiated; a book that needs to be read twice over, a second reading of all four hundred and fifty utterly joyful pages being indispensable in the light of the final brilliant *coup de théâtre*.

What is it all about? Batterson writes modestly in his introduction that he hoped to "rehabilitate the famous 'last piece,'" which so often comes between the patient artisan and the contemplation of the finished work." In fact, he goes much farther, with a masterly demonstration of the mechanics of puzzle composition, in a work that goes beyond the known world of abstract puzzology and blows apart traditional modes of writing on the subject.

The book is composed of forty-eight numbered pieces, each one quite independent, each dealing in its own way with the theme of the missing piece. Some of them are only two lines long. The longest takes more than thirty pages. Each of them contributes to the effectiveness of the overall text. All literary genres are represented: essays, short stories, letters, fragments from novels, a diary. Two pieces may complement each other, or anticipate a third, which the reader will come across later; characters disappear suddenly, then pop up again equally suddenly two hundred pages farther on.

One group of characters provides a running thread through the book. They are the Bantamolians, a primitive people from the Zambezi delta, whose strange customs Batterson has already discussed in *Seduction by Monochrome*, from which he regularly quotes in support of his argument. The following text (piece 21) describes the relationship of the Bantamolians to the missing piece.

"The Bantamolians discovered the principle of the puzzle five thousand moons (around four hundred years) ago, almost a century before John Spilsbury. Their puzzles represent naïve motifs (usually hunting scenes), which occasionally carry a certain symbolic weight.[17] To each event in the life of the tribe corresponds a very particular kind of puzzle. The Bantamolians only get out their very best

---

17. See, for example, the thirty-four-piece puzzle in ebony and ivory in the Folk Museum in Bengui, which shows a lion being chased by an antelope.

puzzles once a year, to coincide with the flood of the River Niokolo, the ritual end to the rainy season. On that day, the Bantamolians intercede with the gods on behalf of hunters killed during the past year. By recreating various episodes in the lives of the dead men, they hope to help them cross over the swirling river waters. Indeed, legend has it that the dead live on the opposite bank of the Niokolo, where no Bantamolian ever sets foot in his lifetime.

"The widow of the deceased makes the puzzle that is intended to save her spouse's soul. The object usually takes the form of an ebony board with marquetry inlays in ivory and rhinoceros horn. The number of pieces reflects the number of catches achieved by the man in the year preceding his death; in no case may it exceed fifty-one. The puzzles are assembled with the left hand[18] by the youngest mother in the tribe, during a ceremony described by Tate in his *On the Banks of the River Niokolo: The Second Life of the Bantamolian Hunters*.

"For the Bantamolians, meaning does not come from the missing piece per se, but from its position within the puzzle. Tate lists around thirty possible scenarios, to each of which corresponds a prediction concerning the fate of the decreased. Thus, if the missing piece showed a four-legged animal, the prediction is highly favorable and the soul of the hunter is considered saved. On the other hand, a missing piece showing a specific part of a person's body indicates that the hunter's salvation is dependent on the sacrifice by their spouse of that same part of the body. For example, if the missing piece showed an arm, the soul of the hunter will be saved on condition that his widow agrees to have her arm chopped off. The woman is allowed one hourglass of time for reflection before announcing her decision to the witch doctor.[19] If the missing piece showed the face of the

---

18. Tate talks about the distinction drawn by the Bantamolians between simple intuitive functions (hunting, eating), which are all performed with the right hand, and elaborate functions (counting, doing puzzles) which necessitate the use of the left hand. Tate notes that it is said of left-handed children. "He hunts with his head and counts with his belly."

19. Tate notes that the witch doctor puts such pressure on the woman that she has no choice but to accept. The amputation may well entail the spouse's death.

hunter, his soul is irretrievably lost, drowned in the heaving waters of the River Niokolo. The fate of the spouse is scarcely more to be envied. She is condemned, for the rest of her days, to wear a mask made of smooth wood, pierced with two holes. These women are known, within the tribe, as 'balakés'—literally, faceless ones, but no one will pronounce the actual word, since it brings bad luck: they are simply called the 'nis,' literally the 'nothings.'"

Batterson devotes seven further pieces to the Bantamolians: piece fourteen, for instance, which is a good example of the inner logic that dominates the work: "Curiously enough, should two pieces happen to be missing, the Bantamolians will continue watching the young mother do her puzzle, as if nothing was amiss." This anomaly supports the principle of oneness. An account of this appears on page 320 of the book (piece thirty-seven): "It becomes abundantly clear that the variable which gives a piece its value obeys a constant law. On this basis, one missing piece is good, two missing pieces is commonplace, and three missing pieces is vulgar."

Stated thus abruptly, the principle of oneness is disconcerting. But in the light of piece nineteen it takes on its full meaning: that the value of a 500-piece puzzle should drop by thirty percent merely because one piece is missing is clearly excessive. If the piece is an important one, it may even depreciate by as much as fifty percent. Curiously, if three to five pieces are missing, the depreciation will not exceed seventy-five percent, and if ten percent of the pieces are missing the puzzle will fall to ten percent of its initial value. It is clear from these figures that the first missing piece has a quite particular status, taking away between thirty and forty percent of the puzzle's value, as compared to five percent for each subsequent missing piece. Why should this be?

It is possible that the puzzle has never before been paid such subtle tribute. Batterson gives a most delicate eulogy to the string puzzle, in which each piece determines the others. On a single page he throws in an amusing anecdote alongside a dialectical demonstration. All this in the sober style of an ethnologist, which highlights the contrasts and can occasionally make the reader laugh out loud.

"Latin peoples—the Spanish, Italian and French living around the Mediterranean—demonstrate a lack of control with regard to the missing piece that can on occasion prove dangerous for their fellow men. In 1962, Rodrigo Calmocha stabbed his wife, Manolita, chopped her body up and threw it down a well. He then gave himself up meekly to the police. He had discovered, on completion of a puzzle of a scene on the Costa del Sol, a free gift from the travel company Arriba Sur, that a key piece was missing, showing a vital aspect of a woman sunbathing on a beach. Calmocha declared he had immediately detected the hand of his wife at work in this apparent coincidence. Without even giving her a chance to explain, he plunged the blade of his pocketknife (which he had carefully sharpened on the grinder) between her third and fourth vertebrae. After a trial, which gripped the entire Spanish nation, the court in Valencia condemned the accused to fifteen years' imprisonment. It did, however, admit attenuating circumstances, and the magistrate conceded that Calmocha had been the victim of 'a vicious maneuver, little short of mental cruelty.'"[20]

Far from being swamped by this accumulation of trivial anecdote and crazy observation, Batterson's argument emerges all the more clearly for it. His premise is made clear as early as piece four, when the author explains that his dialectical training has taught him to consider both sides of every situation. Thus he observes, in a tone of wonder at his own discovery, that the negative, destructive power of the missing piece is necessarily counterbalanced by a positive, constructive power, which remains to be explored. "It became clear to me that the missing piece was not this black hole, a catalyst for

---

20. Batterson also mentions the case of the manufacturer from Vermont who was ordered to pay damages of $2.3 million to a private individual for having left a piece out of the puzzle he sold him. Charles T. Nanty, who was recovering from a breakdown, was being treated at St. Mary's Hospital in Bennington. When he realized he would never complete the view of the Golden Gate he had been working on for a week, he lapsed into a nonresponsive state, from which only the announcement of the verdict roused him. His lawyer accused the manufacturer of "faulty production leading to severe psychological problems." He also claimed $1.7 million from St. Mary's Hospital, for having failed to check that the puzzle was complete. Had this second claim been accepted, Batterson noted, it would no doubt have created an unfortunate precedent and provoked reconsideration of the entire notion of hospital care.

human frustration, as it has so long been presented by its detractors. I realized that at any moment it might brutally expose the entire accumulated energy of the last one hundred years to radiation. My head spun at the thought of a source of energy that was at once so immediate and at the same time unsuspected. The purpose of this book is to expound the basic principles of a methodology of liberation."

Batterson develops his arguments with minute attention to detail, albeit somewhat haphazardly. He begins by explaining that the denigration of the missing piece has gone too far: this is found in the wonderful nineteenth composition on the value of the missing piece.

He then proceeds to question the essential notion of the interchangeability of the missing piece. In painting the missing piece so irredeemably black, we tend to forget that, in fact, pure chance has led to the selection of this piece rather than of any other. Had a slap-dash worker happened to knock off a few seconds earlier, or a mischievous child stuffed a different handful of pieces into his pocket, the much-loathed piece of wood would never have acquired its infamous label of "missing piece" and would have been just one more piece in the vague and anonymous category of pieces that are present.[21] In other words, the missing piece is interchangeable. What conclusion can we draw from this? "The biggest mistake of the detractors of the missing piece is their failure to perceive its double-sidedness, at once both unique and indifferent. Because it is missing, it becomes a focus for the puzzlist's disappointment, and clouds his attention. Since it is only a piece, it is interchangeable, and undeserving of the opprobrium heaped upon it. Not until we manage to come to terms with this fundamental contradiction will we be able to unleash the energy within the missing piece."

Now we come to the core of the argument, which Batterson deliberately gives in piece twenty-four of his puzzle. Having revealed

---

21. A further example of that implacable dialecticism which seems to have haunted Batterson ever since his—unsuccessful—attempt at a Hegelian reading of *Who Speaks When I Am Silent?* by Fagot.

the existence of a "positive and constructive power" in connection with the missing piece, he now addresses the practical subject of how to liberate this power. But before we do that, how shall we describe this power? "The experience of the missing piece generates, in the heart of every puzzlist who encounters it, an inexhaustible source of mental energy. I am not talking about the common kind of energy, used to heat houses or run cars, but about a spiritual power that is stronger than spring torrents, more powerful than the tidal pull of the moon. The missing piece is like a battery, which charges up, year after year, while its detractors persist in reversing its poles."

There follows an astonishingly lyrical enumeration (piece twenty-eight), in which the author gives free rein to his enthusiasm. "Pure potentiality, the implosion of desire (...), paradigm of the core, the site of the possible, contingent on reality (...) caprice of the Creator, promise of the superman (...) plutonium of the spirit, hyper-plan of the imagination, the base, the seed..." Batterson playfully interweaves his ideas, evoking singly, then in concert, philosophy, geometry, material physics, trigonometry, cooking, fluid mechanics, psychoanalysis, theoretical astronomy, anthropology. So intent is he on finding the correct comparison, he has recourse to such varied tools as the periodic table, Latin versification, constant cosmology and differential calculus.

The next few sections (pieces thirty-three, thirty-six and forty-five) are deliberately designed to leave the reader unsatisfied. The author announces that he has discovered the necessary liberating gestures, a combination of ritual movements which, when executed to the rhythm of incantatory tropes, exorcize the curse on the missing piece and unleash the spiritual energy in the puzzle. But Batterson defers the revelation to the very last minute, for, as he writes on page 402, the truth is to be found in the forty-eighth piece, as the Bantamolians have long been aware.

Piece forty-seven, in fact, introduces us to a new aspect of Bantamolian custom. Some of their people believe that if a piece is missing, this is because in itself it represents the puzzle in its entirety. In other words, of the thirty pieces in a puzzle, twenty-nine make up an image that is to be found on the thirtieth piece, reduced to scale.

According to Batterson, the origin of this strange belief dates back more than two thousand moons. In order to save her husband's soul, a woman decided to draw the entire Bantamolian tribe. When she had finished fitting the pieces of the puzzle together, it was noticed that one piece was missing—the piece showing the head of the village chief. Preparations were underway for the beheading of the unthinking woman when the witch doctor—somewhat exceptionally—came to her defense. In the Bantamolian language, the word for village chief is "takonala," which means literally "the entire village."[22] So the final piece would have been a resumé of the motif of the rest of the puzzle: it was therefore redundant, and the spouse was reprieved.[23] To this very day, the Bantamolians are convinced that the last piece is a mere recapitulation of the statement made by the previous pieces. When they are told that a white man can actually lose sleep over a missing piece, they tap their temples lightly with the index finger, which, in the gestural language of the Bantamolians means that such men are soft in the head.[24]

At last we come to the forty-eighth piece.

Which is missing.

Under the heading forty-eight we find an insolent white page. The reader curses, rages against this unforgivable printing error, turns the page in search of a paragraph, a single line, which might tell him how to liberate the inexhaustible energy that resides in the missing piece.

And then he realizes.

---

22. The suffix "nala" expresses the idea of integrality. It is found, for example, in the term "Niokolonala," which means "the whole Niokolo, from shore to shore and from Matulu to Kyiki."

23. A few weeks later, torrential rain fell on the region. The Niokolo rose from its bed and swamped the entire harvest. A handful of Bantamolians saw in this catastrophe the proof of the sorcerer's error. They pointed to a flaw in his reasoning: "takonala" means "the whole village," that is, all those who live there, *plus* their chief. The widow's puzzle, from which the chief's head was missing, was therefore incomplete and the last piece therefore redundant. Firm in their conviction, the judges beheaded the widow while she slept and threw her head into the Niokolo.

24. The "Niokolotatéwaka," literally, "those through whom the Niokolo has flowed in one ear and out the other."

He realizes that in a book entitled *The Missing Piece,* the final piece must inevitably be missing.

That had it existed, it would have been a mere recapitulation of the preceding forty-seven pieces, and that its meaning arises from the fact that it is missing.

That if there do exist certain acts that will unleash its power, each of us must discover them for himself, in the solitude of his personal engagement with the puzzle.

That the Bantamolians are wrong, but also right, when they say that the truth is to be found in the final piece, for the piece is not missing after all. The final piece is, by definition, the one that precedes the missing piece.

On the Puzzology Society in General and the Gleaners Project in Particular

Puzzology Review, April 1991

The open letter you are about to read may well create a few shock waves. The seven signatories, all full members of the Society, hope to draw lessons from what is already being called the Gleaners disaster. Setting aside the financial damage caused by the Gleaners Project, they call into question the direction the Society has been taking over the last fifteen years, and demand that early elections be held. When contacted a few days before this issue went to press, President Sutter declined to exercise his right of reply.

Gleaners: postmortem on a fiasco

Over the last few years our association has had its fair share of setbacks, but a recent episode must surely rank as one of the most tragicomic in its entire history.

First, the basic facts.

On 4 December last, Melinda Plunket submitted a workshop project to the committee. She suggested we engage two workmen, set them in front of a wall, and instruct one of them to construct and the other to deconstruct it. There was more than a betting chance, our colleague advanced, that the two men's efforts would end up establishing an equilibrium configuration, which Plunket described somewhat pompously as "the truth of the wall." And should the results prove conclusive, the experiment might then be applied to the puzzle. The Committee was won over, and voted to allocate $6,000 to the project, which was put in the hands of Melinda Plunket and Doyle Evart, on condition they presented a report at each weekly meeting. Needless to say, no such reports were ever made.

Almost four months later—the experiment was meant to last only two—Plunket and Evart submitted their report, which made edifying reading. In the very first section (Experimental Protocol), the authors draw our attention to the fact that the significance of the results of the experiment should not be given too much credence. The protocol of our experiment, they explain with disarming candor, is linked directly to the two protagonists. In other words, the experiment cannot be repeated using two different workmen: this reservation alone is sufficient to render the experiment completely void in scientific terms.

Plunket and Evart go on to describe, in a style reminiscent of Suetonius's accounts of Hadrian's military campaigns, the different stages by which they arrive at "the truth of the wall." And what a truth that turns out to be! We are treated to such profound formulations as: "What strikes us about the equilibrium configuration is its air of provisionality; no single column or horizontal line is thoroughly complete; nor is any single one totally empty." The interpretation appears to rely on the authors' construction of a series of specious steps, punctuated with two gaping holes, whereby they admit in all honesty that "the equilibrium configuration remains entirely mysterious" and "is being subjected to more in-depth analysis, the conclusions of which will be given at a future meeting." Without wishing to cast aspersions in advance on our colleagues' abilities, we would be ill advised to hold our breath...

But the worst is yet to come.

Let us draw a veil over the rather alarming sixth section, in which Plunket and Evart finally work out that the two workmen may have relied on their own recollections in reconstructing the equilibrium configuration. A solution is at hand: the two men must be made to drink an amnesiac!

Nor will we insist unduly on their seventh paragraph, in which they attempt to amplify their research with a barrage of statistics, the manipulation of which is visible beyond their grasp.

Let us turn rather to the two final paragraphs, sufficient reward in themselves for wading through this indigestible nonsense.

The gist of Section Eight is that it would be pointless to transpose the Gleaners experiment to the case of the puzzle. The reasons given for this are precisely what one might have anticipated: the impossibility of establishing a protocol for the experiment, and the irreconcilable disparity between the two models. Was it really necessary to demolish and reconstruct the same wall eighty-seven times in twelve weeks in order to get our head around something quite so obvious? As for the final phrase: "There is doubtless still a great deal more to be learned from the study of the wall," the question surely arises: have we become a think tank for bricklayers? In which case, could it be that the Fraternity of Bricklayers is at this very moment giving thought to the future of the three-dimensional puzzle in the western world?

The ninth, and final, section notes, almost in passing, that the budget of $6,000 allocated to the project has been considerably exceeded. Each reason given is crazier than the last: they got the minimum wage wrong; they forgot to cost in the fringe benefits; the price of materials was abnormally high; Plunket ends with a reference to various incidents she is "determined to sort out, in the best interests of the Society." We don't doubt it.

A blind alley for thirteen years

This entire episode would be almost grotesque were it not such a tragic illustration of how the Puzzology Society has completely lost its way. For almost thirteen years now, our association has been indulging itself in a debate which is both completely sterile and increasingly removed from the reality of the puzzle. The puzzle as it features in our discussions is in fact not the puzzle at all, but simply the idea of the puzzle, a utopia, a chimera, no less. A quick glance at the evolution of our workshop themes will confirm this: we have gone from "Treatment of the Second World War in American, German and Japanese puzzles" in 1975, to "A psychoanalytic reading of 'Scenes from Family Life'" by Condoni in 1980, and, "Materialization of unlimited space" in 1985, culminating in Plunket and her "truth of walls" today.

In our opinion, the way the Gleaners Project was run is an illustration in itself of everything that is wrong with our society:

• Absence of proper guidelines
The Puzzology Society no longer knows what it is for nor where it's going. The recent Committee elections, which ought to have been the occasion for a debate on the aims and objectives of the association, instead took place in an atmosphere of apathy that was skillfully maintained by the cronyism of the outgoing incumbents. This explains why, when a project like Gleaners comes up, no one knows whether or not it comes under the remit of the Society.

• Anti-democratic organization
The minutes of the Committee meeting of 4 December make for particularly instructive reading. It is quite clear that the Committee members did not vote to approve the budget for the Gleaners Project. The President bulldozed his way through, saying: "If no one has any objection, I propose we accept Melinda's project under Section B1, and give her a grant of $6,000, which will be taken out of the budget for research." The statutes of the Society, however, make it quite clear: the President is under an obligation to make sure of a two-thirds favorable majority on the part of those present before committing money for research.

• Financial sloppiness threatening the survival of the association
Melinda Plunket asked for $6,000 without presenting a single document to show how she arrived at this figure. As it turns out, the bill comes to almost $20,000 dollars, that is to say, 230 percent over the estimate. For the third consecutive year the association's budget will be in deficit, and the society members will yet again be asked to

make it up, without receiving anything in return. The drop in income continues to accelerate, but no steps have been taken to counter the decline. The number of members is at its lowest in twenty-five years, leveling out at just thirty-four at the end of 1990. Weary of constant criticism, the puzzle manufacturers have withdrawn their funding. And, finally, the label "Puzzology Society" brings in not one single penny.

• Absence of controls or sanctions
This obviously goes hand in hand with undemocratic organization and financial sloppiness. If Plunket and Evart had stood by their commitment to supply intermediary reports, the committee members would have realized the Gleaners Project was going off the rails and could have demanded the workshop be suspended. Instead of which, they are presented with a fait accompli and asked to ratify this heap of total garbage. To our knowledge, Plunket and Evart have not been sanctioned in any way.

The world is changing

The way the Society is run is largely a hangover from the sixties, a golden age for the puzzle in this country. At that time, the popular craze for puzzling justified all sorts of extravagance and indulgence, even if some of the burning issues of the day now seem rather dated to us.

The situation has changed radically. In the mid-1970s our discipline entered one of its intermittent phases of eclipse, which usually last around twenty years. Common sense indicated that we should draw in our horns and consolidate forces in anticipation of a run of several years in the doldrums. The new president, elected in 1977, and reelected in 1981, 1985 and 1989, chose the completely opposite course. He played up to the intellectual inclinations of the Committee, depleted our meager resources, and made no effort to retain the services of our most able hands. We are now paying the price for that policy: a stuffy Committee that is disenchanted, demotivated, which unthinkingly approves pipe dreams with no feasible application; a dictatorial president, who's perpetually on the warpath; assets swilling away down the drain.

The puzzle has never been in such dire straits as it is today. According to the most recent *New York Times* survey, fewer than nine percent of children and two percent of adults regularly do puzzles. Sales of new puzzles are in decline. The secondhand and collectors' markets are collapsing. Several manufacturers, including some of the oldest and most prestigious, have shut down. In short, to misquote the words of Pete Carroll, the ideals of puzzology, in all their various forms, are fast being eroded.

Starting the Society afresh

The decline of the puzzle is not necessarily terminal. A few simple recipes, a few sensible commonsense principles would be enough to reverse the process and prepare for the next favorable tide. That, at least, is our belief. But we need to act quickly. That is why we demand that extraordinary elections be held. If the members of the Committee agree to seek renewal of their mandates—they can, of course, refuse, but we prefer to think they will avoid making that classic mistake, we too will put forward a list and unveil our program.

This is our last chance. Don't let's ruin it.

Beatrix Dale, Diana Dobbs, Cheradenine Eysenk,
Katherine Houtkooper, Lynn Moss, Hooper Targ, Wim Rhine

Extracts from the Minutes
of the Puzzology Society

Committee meeting, 8 April 1991

President Sutter opened the meeting at 1800 hours precisely.

1. President Sutter's response to the open letter published in the *Puzzology Review,* April issue

PRESIDENT SUTTER: Before we start on the agenda for the meeting, I should like to come back for a moment to the open letter published in the April issue of the *Review* in which, although I am not actually named, I am the target of a number of direct attacks.

What are we talking about here? An article signed by seven members of the Society (none of whom are on the Committee, which may well account for a certain bitterness of tone) that claims to draw lessons from the Gleaners Project. Their exposition of the facts is essentially accurate, and their analysis is not completely without foundation. I shall return to it in detail, if you wish. In the second part of the letter, Dale, Dobbs, Eysenk, Houtkooper, Moss, Targ and Rhine—let's name names, shall we?—attack my management of the association, which they describe as blind, antidemocratic, lax and complacent. They conclude their accusation with a demand for extraordinary elections.

Above all else, I would like to point out to the seven Society members that the fact that the *Review,* an organ of which I, as president of the Society, am also the director, agreed to publish such a violently critical letter, would seem to me to constitute excellent proof that our Society is run along democratic lines. Let me be quite clear about this: it was I who insisted to Bram Thouless, the editor of the review, that the article be published as quickly as possible, even if that meant having to reschedule the contents of the April issue. An instance of exemplary transparency, I might say.

That notwithstanding, I find it highly regrettable that members of our Society should have used the *Review* as a showcase for their squabbles. They could not have inflicted greater harm on our Society if they had tried. What have they gained by exposing our internal disagreements to full public view, when a lively discussion at an extraordinary committee meeting would most certainly have ironed out all our problems? No, I must say, an irregularity of this kind seems to me profoundly unhelpful, especially at a time when we have greatest need of unity.

And now I come to the core of the dispute. Yes, it is true, Gleaners has turned out to be a failure—a failure for which I, as a member of the Committee, must bear some responsibility. However, Melinda Plunket's idea seemed to me—and still does—to be an interesting one. In any case, hadn't the Committee already unanimously approved the allocation of $6,000 to the project? In fact, the authors of the article did, on the whole, put their finger on the principal shortcomings of the workshop: a weak experimental protocol, an overall conception that was scarcely, if at all, relevant to the puzzle, and considerable overspending on the budget. But allow me to draw your attention to the fact that the responsibility for all these elements lies directly, and quite clearly, with the leaders of the project. How can the members of the Committee be blamed for a protocol over which they had no control? How can they be reproached for failing to assure its relevance to the puzzle when the object of the workshop was precisely to establish how the two procedures could be linked? And, finally, how can they be accused of financial sloppiness when Plunket waited till the very last day of the workshop before handing over all the Bireley construction company's invoices at once?

If Gleaners brought to light certain weaknesses, they are weaknesses in two members of our Society who, by exceeding their powers, have shown themselves unworthy of the confidence we placed in them. I discussed the matter with the two people concerned only this morning, and, you will be pleased to hear, both have asked me to accept their resignation from the Committee of the Society.

TOM DE LAZIO: Really? I spoke to Melinda Plunket on the phone last Thursday. She was very upset by the letter in the *Review*. She was happy to admit she'd made some mistakes, but she found some of the accusations directed at herself and Doyle completely unjust. I got the impression she intended to fight to defend her point of view.

PRESIDENT SUTTER: She was obviously of a different mind this morning. In the meantime, Sol had shown her the accounts for the first quarter, which made it quite evident how much damage had been caused by her financial recklessness.

Accordingly, as of this morning, Melinda Plunket and Doyle Evart no longer officially belong to the Puzzology Society. That should silence those people who complain about the lack of control and of sanctions within our association.

TINA MANNING: There was more to the article in the *Review* than that. It talks about the decline in popularity of the puzzle in the United States. Do you concur with our colleagues' analysis?

PRESIDENT SUTTER: I was coming to that. I expect a number of you will be surprised to hear me express my gratitude to the authors of this article. Effectively, they draw our attention to a serious level of disaffection with the puzzle at the present time. How else are we to interpret the rejection of our colleague Ursula Carver, by the *Medway Independent*? And what other explanation could there be for the consistent depletion of the membership of the Society? You see, it's not the decline in the numbers of young kids doing their Mickey Mouses that bothers me, so much as the worrying fall in the average mark achieved in the selection test for entry into the Society! Young people today are quite extraordinary: they think they are fit to enter our lists the minute they can tell the difference between a Milton

Bradley and a Parker Brothers. Big deal! It reminds me of that performing seal Pasquale brought along—forgive me, Nicholas—last year. The man had the effrontery to spend a quarter of an hour—and I know he may have turned the heads of some of our ladies, including you, Ursula—reciting the entire list of one hundred and forty-one models of which there is no longer a complete set in circulation. And yet he was a great deal less sure of himself when it came to answering my question on the chromatic distribution of pieces in the work of Mrizek. "My dear boy," I said to him, "we have no need for heads crammed with facts in this assembly; come back and see us when you have learned to think for yourself!" I think we've probably seen the last of him for a while!

The reason I mention all this is because the ideals of puzzology are under threat. Yes, puzzling is in decline in this country, and yes, it is a setback that could have serious repercussions for the state of democracy. It starts with the refusal to publish an article of such key importance as Ursula's; the day may well come when books get burned, and their authors along with them. Consider the paucity of creative design at the present moment. The small independent manufacturers have folded, one after the other; only the bigger puzzle manufacturers remain, for the most part weak and lacking in imagination, guided purely and simply by profit margins. Our opposition to the industrial producers can never be too fierce. Their objectives are in complete opposition to our own. Their dream is to flood the country with twenty-four-piece cardboard puzzles of Dumbo the Elephant taking a bath. The very idea that my children might learn geography from a Spears puzzle makes my blood run cold.

I agree with the authors of this article—even if they appear to have dipped their pens in the gutter—when they say that the decline of the puzzle is not necessarily fatal. But, please, may they spare us their famous miracle remedies. I can imagine what they will come up with all too well. Nothing revolutionary—much the same as those proposed by Rudhyar when he was defeated by Betts in 1967: open the Society up to young people, organize puzzle scholarships, draw up a register of classic puzzles, join forces with a manufacturer to create a joint collection, and so on and so forth ad infinitum. No, believe me, that is not the way for us to go. You don't save a sinking ship by opening wide the bilges. The future of the Society will be guaranteed by ever-increasing vigilance and discipline. Otherwise, we're lost.

With the consent of the members of the Committee, I will accept the principle of extraordinary elections. As my detractors have observed, we are under no obligation to renew our mandates. We were reelected at the appropriate term in 1989 for a period of four years. We are only halfway through our mandate and, as yet, we have not had time to implement most of the measures on our program. But I think it would be petty of me to hide behind my legitimacy in order to avoid a fight. So be it. Let's have a vote. Our friends will put forward a list. That is their inalienable right. I will present a different list, and I have no intention of making a secret of my program. If you elect me, I shall devote my term in office to setting the Society on course again, placing an emphasis on the lively debate and the grass-roots research that have always been the touchstone of our reputation and a source of pride.

Extracts from the Minutes of the Board Meeting of the American Puzzle Federation

Committee meeting held 11 February 1995

1. Disappearance of Nicholas Spillsbury

WALLERSTEIN: Jimmy, go over the facts again to begin with.

BLYTHE: Spillsbury disappeared the day before yesterday on his way to the Hotel Excalibur to give an interview to Jessica Woodruff, a *New York Times* journalist. She spoke to him on the telephone at 1345 hours. Apparently, he said to her: "I'll call a taxi and come right over." He hasn't been seen since.

DOBBS: Has the taxi driver been traced?

BLYTHE: We checked, and not one of the taxi companies in town got a call of any kind at that time.

DOBBS: What about the journalist?

BLYTHE: She suspects nothing. We told her Spillsbury had been taken ill and that the doctors had told him to take a few days of complete rest. She took comfort in my promise to let her have an exclusive on the story of his convalescence.

WALLERSTEIN: Well, none of that gets us anywhere. Jimmy and Diana, if we haven't had any news from Spillsbury by 1800 hours, put out a release to the television channels. They can put out a missing-persons appeal in the evening bulletins. Oh, and remind them the season starts next week in Miami.

EARP: Aren't you going to tell the police first?

WALLERSTEIN: The chief of the LVPD was here in my office last night. I asked him to collaborate with Mischo's men. Just this once.

DOBBS: There's been no ransom demand so far?

WALLERSTEIN: No. But no one knows about it yet. As soon as TV breaks the story, all sorts of loonies will jump on it with glee. Cecil, you know him well, do you have any idea where he could be, assuming he's skipped camp of his own accord?

EARP: I thought of Pinewood, but Amy Forrester, whom I spoke to this morning, hasn't seen Spillsbury for two months. She was very worried. According to her, Nicholas took his first defeat very badly. He hadn't said anything, but he was dreading the start of the new season. "I hope he hasn't done anything stupid," she said.

WALLERSTEIN: The woman speaks precious words. And I mean that quite literally.

How I Discovered Spillsbury

Life, 28 June 1993

Since the start of the season, a nineteen-year-old boy has ruled the roost on the professional speed-puzzle circuit, the JP Tour. Up until eighteen months ago, he had hardly laid hands on a puzzle in his life. Cecil Earp, head of recruitment for the American Federation, tells *Life* the exclusive story of what he himself describes as a "miraculous discovery."

Billings, Montana. 1330 hours, 12 January 1992. The temperature outside is down to minus 22°C. There's a gusting blizzard outside, which means my plane probably won't be taking off. I'd be better off taking a room in a local Holiday Inn. The prospect of having to spend the night sitting in the freezing airport lounge at Billings doesn't exactly appeal.

"Do you know a decent hotel around here?" I ask the man who runs the café and has come to give me the check for my lunch. "With the weather like this, I'm afraid my flight to Chicago will be canceled."

"The 1950? No, I guess you're right. If I was you, I'd hire a car and drive to Helena. It's a three-hour drive, but you should be able to take off."

"Thanks. I'll bear it in mind. Unfortunately, I can't get away from Billings till six o'clock tonight. I'm with the trials for the JP Tour."

At these words, the café owner, already pleasant to us, turns distinctly jovial.

"Ah, it's you! You're going to be busy, let me tell you! With all that coverage in the papers, you've brought out the hidden puzzlist in more than a few of our citizens. Just wait here a second."

He returns with that day's copy of the *Montana Inquirer*, and waves it under my nose. Our ad appears on the last page: "Could you be the star America is looking for...?" It goes on to explain that a member of the Federation will be holding trials that very afternoon at four o'clock in Congress Hall in Billings and anyone interested should turn up "with their loved ones and an open mind."

"I'd like to come along myself, but I've got no one to mind the place. You may see my son; he's a big guy with ginger hair. It'd be great if you could take him on, he's a total waste of space around here."

"I'll see what I can do," I say politely. "And apart from him, do you know anyone who's into puzzling? Someone in your family? A friend, maybe?"

The man scratched his head.

"Not really, no. Football's more the thing around here. Wait a sec, why don't you pop down to Pinewood? It's a psychiatric hospital, a sort of rest home, as they call them. Dr. Forrester, she's the person in charge. Only yesterday she was sitting where you are now. We were talking about the trials and she said she was going to organize a little competition for her residents this afternoon. It might be worth going along for a quick look."

"Certainly," I said. "In any case, I've got two hours to kill. Have you got the address?"

Since that day I have often had cause to reflect on the coincidence that made me stop off at the very café where the director of the Pinewood happened to eat. When Charles Wallerstein put me in charge of recruitment, he insisted I shouldn't stop at local selection trials. "Keep your eyes and ears open. Get out there to campuses, into puzzle libraries, ask people if they've got a brother who's got a friend who knows someone who can do 'An Anxious Moment' by E. T. Price in under seven minutes. Don't stint your time or my money, and remember, all's fair in love and war!"

In fact, the results of the local trials had been rather disappointing. Not that the public weren't interested—quite the opposite. Four thousand five hundred people at Mobile, 2,800 at Bridgeport, Connecticut, nearly 8,000 in the gaming hot spot of Reno, all way above what we could possibly have hoped for, and, whatever happened, it had to bode well for the attendance at the Tour. When it came to the standard of performance, though, the results were less satisfactory. I sat the volunteers down in front of a dozen or so puzzles, five hundred pieces each, all of about the same level of difficulty. I knew that even the weakest Colombian, after training, could complete one of these in twenty minutes. I imposed a time limit of twenty-five minutes—equivalent to an absolute speed of twenty pieces a minute and a noticeably lower relative speed, around fourteen or fifteen.

So far I had found only three possible candidates: two men and one girl. All three were already aware of their talent and had been developing it for years. The margin for possible improvement therefore seemed likely to be fairly limited, the more so since their initial scores (an RS of nineteen for Libby Avalon, the best of the three) would not have earned them a place among the top ten on the circuit. However, I referred them to Diana Dobbs, the director of the Tour, who submitted them to more serious tests. I was pleased to see that Libby reached the quarterfinals in Pittsburgh last month.

My investigations around the fringes of the local trials paid off rather better. Wallerstein had been right to advise me to talk to people who ran puzzle libraries. It was a librarian in Des Moines who drew my attention to one of his most frequent clients, Clare Volney, aged fourteen. On average, Clare would take out a dozen puzzles a week. Unless she's keeping all her buddies from school supplied with Milton Bradleys, she must be pretty good, the librarian sensibly concluded. He wasn't wrong. I visited Clare that very same day, and was treated to a brilliant demonstration of her skills. I timed her to twenty minutes exactly on one of the test puzzles. The teenager told me she never missed a single round of the Tour and that she had a soft spot for Olof Niels. *Already,* I thought to myself, somewhat alarmed. It was agreed with her parents that Clare would spend the next summer at the Las Vegas Academy and that after that we would talk again about where to take her career from there.

The man who ran the café had told Amy Forrester I would be coming. She greeted me, a tall, very slim woman, bundled up in a sheepskin jacket. "You'll be disappointed," she warned. "You won't discover any future stars of the circuit here. We don't take our residents on for their dexterity." Her voice had a trace of irony unusual in psychiatric circles. Moreover, when I asked her why she had decided to organize this mini-tournament, she replied with a smile, "Usually on Tuesday afternoons we play bingo. I hope you will agree that the puzzle requires no less intelligence than bingo." There wasn't much I could say to that. So I said nothing.

Despite her apparently relaxed manner, Amy Forrester had organized things very well. She had bought fifteen sets of the same puzzle, which I recognized as Whitman Publishing's "Hopalong Cassidy and Topper," a rather rudimentary ninety-eight-piece puzzle, a fairly straightforward affair. Amy explained that out of the eighty-something residents in the institution, fifty-nine had volunteered to take part. As I later learned, Pinewood takes young men and women suffering from mental disabilities considered mild by the medical profession, but sufficiently serious to make it difficult for them to lead normal lives within the community.

For now, they all seemed fairly excited. The first fifteen to sit down at the tables were busy fending off the attempts of their comrades to unseat them. However, they all fell silent when Amy spoke:

"As you all know, this afternoon we won't be playing bingo. We're going to do a puzzle. I'll just recap what a puzzle is, for those of you who've never done one. John, leave Veronica alone and listen to me. Here's the picture: it's Hopalong, the cowboy from television, on his horse. Can anyone tell me the name of Hopalong's horse? Sandy? Yes, that's right, well done: Topper. Now, take a look in the box in front of you. We're going to use all those bits of wood to fit back together the picture of Hopalong and Topper. This piece, for example, shows Hopalong's head. What does a cowboy wear on his head? A hat, of course. And where is his hat? Ah, here it is. So I put that one next to the one I had already. Now I'm going to look for Hopalong's bandanna. And so on, till I get to the end. Everyone got it? Okay, now, settle yourselves down and we'll begin. And make sure you do your best—the gentleman over there has come a long way to see how well you can do. Ready. Off you go!"

It was apparent after only a few seconds that there was no one in the first round with a hidden talent. I used the time to make a quick calculation. The Whitman puzzle had ninety-eight pieces. To reach a relative speed of fifteen, you would have to do it in under two minutes, that is, at an absolute speed of about fifty.

I worked out the concepts of absolute speed (AS) and relative speed (RS) when I first started out on my talent search, to allow me to compare the different performances reported to me by talent scouts from all over the country. Is it better to be able to do a hundred pieces in four minutes than a thousand in fifty minutes? If one judges merely on the basis of the absolute speed, obtained by dividing the number of pieces by the time taken to fit them, then yes, it certainly is. In the first case the AS is twenty-five pieces a minute, as opposed to twenty in the second case. And yet everyone knows instinctively that it is proportionally more difficult to find a piece among a thousand others than among a hundred others. Hence it becomes necessary to modify the AS by the introduction of a second indicator, which takes account of the number of pieces in the puzzle. Other factors need to be taken into account as well, the shape of the pieces (interlocking or separate), the subject of the puzzle (figurative or abstract), the degree of difficulty (large areas of monochrome color), etc. After many painstaking sessions with the circuit players, I managed to come up with a mathematical formula with various different parameters that made it possible to determine the relative speed of a player, true for any and every puzzle.

As I say, I had set the upper limit for qualification at the trials at around fifteen pieces a minute, relative speed. Most people have a relative speed of between three and five. With a bit of training that quickly increases to seven or eight, rarely more than that. But work alone is not what makes for performances like those of Niels, Krijek and types like Mombala, who regularly score thirty-five and on rare occasions forty-five or even fifty. At that level, one has to speak in terms of talent—talent that is, of course, then carefully developed.

The girl who won the first round put down her last piece after seven minutes and forty-five seconds, which placed her well below average. Her RS was slightly under two. If my calculations were correct, she would have taken almost eight hours to complete one of the 500-piece puzzles I usually set in trials.

The next two rounds were not much quicker. Amy watched me write down the winning times in my black notebook, and was clearly a little disappointed by the mediocre performance of her residents. I suspected that, though she hadn't said so, she'd been hoping for a miracle.

Then she started off the fourth round, and right away I knew. At the back of the room, an adolescent boy was picking up pieces, one after the other, and putting them down in front of him without a moment's reflection. From where I was standing, I couldn't quite see the puzzle. For just a second, I thought I might be witnessing some kind of mirage. It wasn't possible to go that fast. The boy couldn't have understood the game: he must just be putting the pieces together without respecting the model. I went over to him quickly, to be rewarded—oh blessèd surprise—with the sight of the proud outline of Topper and the tough but slender form of Hopalong. I glanced at my chronometer. Less than a minute had passed since Amy's signal, and already the boy was up to the last part of the puzzle, a huge patch of blue sky. A few seconds later he put in the final piece, and looked up. Our eyes met; he must have realized, from my flustered air, that something had happened. "I've finished," he stated simply, before losing himself in contemplation of Topper's dappled mane.

My stopwatch said one minute and nine seconds. That gave an AS of eighty-five pieces a minute and a RS of twenty-five to thirty pieces. It was a performance that ranked him immediately among the top five players on the circuit. Amy Forrester brightened considerably. She came up to us at the back of the room and congratulated her protégé.

"Well, Spillsbury, I didn't realize you were so clever. Who taught you to do puzzles?"

"What did you call him?" I exclaimed.

"Spillsbury. Why?" asked Amy, taken aback by the abruptness of my question.

"That's my name," added the boy. "My name's Spillsbury."

"The man who invented the puzzle was John Spilsbury. He was a mapmaker who lived in London in the eighteenth century," I explained.

"He's called Nicholas," Amy added. "And his surname has two "l's."

"What's a mapmaker?" asked the boy.

Amy waited until all the residents had finished with Hopalong and Topper. Then she took them back to their rooms. Meanwhile I watched Spillsbury, who was wriggling in his seat, visibly ill at ease. He couldn't have been more than seventeen. He had that delicate constitution and very pale complexion you find in mentally retarded adolescents. I couldn't wait for Amy to get back. I got out "Keeper of the Flame" from my briefcase, a puzzle by the New York maker Squarecut Puzzle Company, which I often used in trials. Libby, my best recruit so far, had finished all 520 pieces in 21 minutes and 50 seconds. Could Spillsbury beat that?

As I watched him throw himself gamely into "Keeper of the Flame," I concentrated on identifying the main characteristics of his style, a most unusual style, which would before long be known as the "abstract" method. Spillsbury started by studying the image for about thirty seconds, as though committing every minute detail of it to memory, before he pushed it to the edge of the table. Then he grabbed a piece in his left hand, considered it for a tenth of a second, and placed it on the table in front of him, in exactly the place it would later occupy in the completed puzzle. When he had repeated this operation 519 times, Amy, whom I hadn't heard come back in, asked over my shoulder:

"How long?"

"18 minutes and 34 seconds. The same time, to the second, as Krijek in the semifinal last month at Pittsburgh."

"I sure like puzzles," Spillsbury said.

Later on that evening, Amy told me the story of Nicholas Spillsbury. He had grown up in Kalispell, a small town in the northwestern part of the state. His father was a truck driver. Until he went to secondary school, Nicholas was, to all appearances, a normal little boy, lively and, according to his teachers, even talented. But things began to decline after he reached the age of ten, when the neighbors began to draw the Sheriff's attention to the brutal behavior of Derek Spillsbury, Nicholas's father. Shortly afterward, Derek lost his job. Already a heavy drinker, he had started drinking more. He regularly beat his wife, until the day when, having thumped her rather harder than usual, she ended up in the hospital. Madeleine was in a coma for six days. The repeated blows had provoked a hemorrhage; a clot had formed on her brain. They tried to operate, but it was no good. She died on the operating table on 21 September 1985. Three days later was Nicholas's eleventh birthday.

The doctors didn't catch on right away to what was happening. The State of Montana sentenced Derek to five years in prison, and put Nicholas in a special home for orphans and abandoned children. He had to repeat his sixth year of school. The social worker in charge of his case attributed his failure to the effects of his mother's death. And yet the psychologists were agreed that the child had overcome— insofar as the word can have any meaning—the trauma: he rarely mentioned his mother, his father almost never; he spent his holidays with his aunt, Madeleine's sister; he had made lots of friends in class. But as far as his schoolwork was concerned, the following year was even more catastrophic. Although undeniably willing, Nicholas was hopeless at everything. The teachers who knew his background, did not stint their efforts; several of them made a point of giving him individual tuition to help him catch up; none of them managed to get his work back above average.

Eventually, they had to accept the obvious: Nicholas had stopped learning. His intellectual development had come to a halt eighteen months earlier. Perhaps one day it would start up again, but for the time being it would be better to take the child out of school. In 1987, Nicholas was admitted to Pinewood. Along with other young people with similar problems, he received appropriate teaching, based on acquiring basic, practical life skills.

During the first few months, Amy told me, she had given a great deal of thought to Spillsbury's case, and watched him carefully for the slightest sign of an intellectual reawakening. But in vain. Year after year, Nicholas remained exactly the same, charming, for the most part, given, if crossed, to sudden but harmless outbursts of anger. His mental age—that of an eleven-year-old—did not alter one jot.

In one respect, however, Spillsbury was different from his fellow pupils at Pinewood. He was blessed with an extraordinary photographic memory. After looking at a page of text for only a few seconds, he would recite it word for word, beginning anywhere on the page. He knew whole books by heart, often books of no particular interest. His computational skills were similarly impressive. He had, literally, at his fingertips, multiplication tables up to a hundred, he could give you the answer to any simple operation even before you'd finished asking it. Curiously, Nicholas's special skills had gone unnoticed until his fifteenth year. There were two possible explanations for this: he had always had them, but only the barrage of tests to which he was subjected on his arrival at Pinewood had brought them to the fore; or—and this was the explanation favored by Dr. Forrester—Spillsbury had actually acquired his extraordinary skills during adolescence, in the months following his mother's death. If this was the case, a remarkable skill had appeared at the same time as an intellectual retardation, which seriously impeded his very ability to use that skill.

Fortunately, both Amy and I immediately recognized the benefits that might accrue to Nicholas from his gift. He needed only a few seconds to memorize every single detail of even the most complex puzzle. He could then pick up any piece at random and work out, from its color or its subject, its exact position on the board. Unlike the other members of the JP Tour, or any amateur anywhere in the world, the composition of the puzzle presented no problem whatsoever for Nicholas Spillsbury; the speed of his hands was the only limiting factor in his game.

The trials that day at Congress Hall drew a blank. I couldn't have cared less. That evening, from my hotel room in Billings, I called Charles Wallerstein and informed him of my miraculous discovery.

Thunderbolt in Orlando

JP Magazine, no. 18, 1993

A thunderbolt has hit Orlando! Nicholas Spillsbury, a young nineteen-year-old American, completely unknown to the public, has blown away his fellow competitors and won the first tournament of the 1993 season hands down. Jean-Claude Cornillet, Spillsbury's unlucky opponent in the quarterfinals, summed up the general feeling: "The guy's from a totally different planet."

And to think some people were worried that they might get bored during this third JP Tour season. "Olof Niels is too good," you heard people saying, "he'll wipe out the competition yet again." In fact, the woodcutter from Jutland was as taken aback as anyone after the Orlando tournament, the first of the season. And no wonder. He had just been beaten in the final by seventy-seven pieces, the biggest gap to date in a Tour final. And who had dared humiliate King Olof in this way? Krijek, his runner-up in 1992? His fellow countryman, the promising Eriksen? One of those loose cannons from the African delegation? Oh no! Nicholas Spillsbury was the victor's name. He comes from Kalispell in Montana. He is just nineteen years old and until eleven months ago was a complete puzzle virgin.

   It was Cecil Earp, the director of recruitment for the Tour, who discovered Spillsbury in the darkest depths of Montana last February. The young lad was taking part in one of the selection trials organized by the Federation throughout the country, to discover new talent. The boy, who had never laid hands on a puzzle in his life, completed the 500-piece "Keeper of the Flame" in less than eighteen and a half minutes.

Spillsbury owes his superiority to a very simple technique, which will undoubtedly revolutionize the world of puzzling. Blessed with an incredible eye, he is able to memorize in a flash the most complex image, pick up any piece at random and instantly determine its position on the board. No doubt about the effectiveness of the method: it enabled its inventor to notch top scores of 56 RS![25]

You had only to watch his massacre of the Frenchman Jean-Claude Cornillet in the quarterfinal (a final lead of 138—unprecedented at this level of the competition) to realize that the future of speed puzzling lies with the technique perfected by Spillsbury. It is difficult to see how his opponents can hope to catch up with the young American by relying only on their existing skills. And, we should note, Spillsbury has not yet reached the top of his game. According to sources close to him, Nicholas still has considerable potential for further progress. His memory faculty already borders on perfect; but his dexterity may still be improved by training and competition. When asked why it was that fans of the tour had been deprived of Spillsbury's presence last season, his Pygmalion, Cecil Earp, explained that he had decided to wait until Nicholas's superiority was unassailable before dropping him in at the deep end of circuit competition. "Judging by his performances last February, Spillsbury could no doubt have won three or four tournaments and maybe, who knows, the overall title. However, on my advice, he decided that it would be better to work on his left-arm movement for a few months before making a really blazing entry onto the circuit.

---

25. And even as high as sixty-one on the "Townhall of Lijerbee," but the Italian judge, Oscar Finelli, expressed reservations regarding the allowances which had been made for the difficulty of the puzzle. The central committee will decide on 12 February whether or not to ratify this performance, which would constitute a new record in an official tournament. The existing record is held by Georges Montola (fifty-nine pieces in the semifinal of the World Championships held in Rome in 1988).

His avowed aim is to carry off the grand slam this season, and, to be quite honest, I think he has it in him."

The explosion at the highest level of a young American with a name written in the stars[26] has, in any case, perked up public interest in the Tour. Eight million of you tuned in on 24 January to watch Spillsbury receive his crown. That's three and a half million more viewers than last year. In 1992, the public became acquainted with the speed puzzle. In 1993 they'll be crowning it with ovations. Cheers to that—we'll see you on 8 February at Phoenix for the second round of the season!

---

26. His name differs from that of John Spilsbury, the inventor of the puzzle in the eighteenth century, by only one letter.

Newspaper Extract

New York Times, 25 April 1991

Upton Sutter, 52, was reelected head of the Puzzology Society on Monday evening last. This association, established in 1935, has around thirty-five members, whose aim is to promote the puzzle, both as an entertainment and as an intellectual discipline. The list headed by Sutter won the day after the third round with a vote of seventeen as opposed to the fifteen won by the opposition list, headed by Diana Dobbs. Dobbs had called for extraordinary elections to be held, provoking a lively debate on the role of the Puzzology Society. Sutter said he wished his fourth term of office to be characterized as a period of grass-roots research.

Extracts from the Minutes
of the Puzzology Society

Committee Meeting, 20 December 1994

6. Miscellaneous

TOM DE LAZIO: I'd like to ask the Committee's opinion of the interview given by our President to the *New York Times,* on the day following the defeat of Nicholas Spillsbury in the final of the Las Vegas Tournament.

PRESIDENT: And why would that be, Tom? Do you have something to say on the matter?

TOM DE LAZIO: I found the wording rather excessive. We all know your position with regard to the Federation and the JP Tour, and most of us are of the same view, more or less. But in the present case, I feel it was inappropriate to attack Spillsbury as you did. Surely it would be better to confine your criticism to Wallerstein? Spillsbury is just some poor kid with an IQ of eighty; his mother's dead, his father's rotting in jail, and he's got no other family. Do you really believe it's going to endear us to the public to call him a "vegetable," a "baboon"?

PRESIDENT: I'm not happy with your tone, Tom. Don't forget, as president of this Society, I and I alone am responsible for the way we, and our views, are put across to the public. I stand by everything I've said. This Spillsbury boy is a cretin and a walking insult to the puzzle. His mother's dead—so what? So's mine, come to that—the difference being that before she departed this life—with dignity, not punched out by some vile bruiser of a husband—she managed to pass on to me a few basic values. Never in a million years would the blessed woman have allowed me to make a mockery of her name by frantically pushing bits of wood around in front of the television cameras. As for my father, I don't even like to think about the thrashing I'd have got for such cheek. But that's the trouble nowadays: you can do what you like, say what you like, throw dollars at any old chimpanzee simply because he boosts the viewing figures! A pox on Wallerstein and his performing seal: believe me, these people are noxious, and should be wiped out, right away!

TOM DE LAZIO: I'm afraid I can't go along with you there. It's all very well to have a go at institutions, but I think we should draw the line at individuals....

PRESIDENT: And why, may I ask? Did that gilt-edged idiot Wallerstein reach for his kid gloves before he started criticizing my running of this society? Remember how his assistant summoned the TV cameras and declared that puzzling needed some fresh blood? We're dealing with vermin here, and I make no secret of my opinion: no pity for vermin. Honestly, just take a look at them, they're a bunch of degenerates: this Spillsbury boy, advertising some drink that's supposed to stimulate the neurones—I ask you! And that Viking, with his dysfunctional libido, and the tabloid press filling us in on the details of his boudoir skills! And Russkov, Davidoff, Iliakov, whatever his name is, who muddled up a Delalande and a Selchow & Righter last week! And worse besides! And Krijek, oh, let's not forget Krijek! Why, just the other evening I heard Krijek giving a subtle account of the method of assembling a puzzle by following the colors of the pieces...yes, young man, but I think if you go back to your books, you'll find that George Copeland wrote the definitive text on the matter as early as 1933!

TOM DE LAZIO: But you can't really blame them, can you? They're just sad cases, making the most of the talents Nature gave them. The one to blame is Wallerstein....

PRESIDENT: Oh, yes, Nature always carries the can! And do stop calling it a talent! Last Sunday I watched one of those Danes doing a demonstration on "Portrait of a Lady" by Harriet Bates. In God's name, if ever a young woman had grace... And this Baltic herring goes and polishes the whole thing off in three minutes and twenty-six seconds flat—three minutes and twenty-six seconds, Tom, can you credit it? Now you can call that a vice, call it a scourge, an idiosyncrasy, whatever you will, but please, do not call it a talent!

E-mail from Harry Dunlap to Cecil Earp

Date: 13/1/95–17.35
To: earp@jp-tour.com
From: hdunlap@compuserve.com
cc:-

Hello there, high priest of the wooden piece.

What are you up to? I wrote to you in Chicago but didn't hear back. I called Lynn yesterday; she said you were dividing your time between Chicago, Las Vegas and the various towns on the Tour. She sounded pretty fed up, if you ask me. "Tell Cecil, if you see him, that his daughter turned fourteen last week and that she hopes to see her father at least once, maybe twice, before she comes of age." That's the message she asked me to pass on, old chap. Maybe you'd better get your revered boss to let you in on the secret of ubiquity, and pop back home this weekend. But it's not my place to tell you what to do.

I'm writing from Boston, where I'm attending the Hourra hip convention. You didn't miss anything. The level of the papers is quite alarming. The way Dynamic Research is pushing its Hiptone; it's quite out of order—bordering on the indecent. The English put up with it more or less, but the Italians and Spanish were outraged. García, who was involved in Phase III, said he simply didn't recognize the figures they were putting out—ninety-eight percent success rate, according to them. As if. In his department alone, in Salamanca, he had seven rejections out of thirty-one operations! Well, anyway, you'll read all about it in February's *Lancet*.

Guess what, I ran into Thomas Carroll yesterday afternoon. Not at the Society—I had no reason to go by there—but at Moe's. I'd gone to try to find an interior-decorating book for Kate. He was buried in a history of Springfield County, written by some retired colonel. Proud as Punch, you can imagine, he showed me the passage on the Society of the Friends of the Puzzle. The author pays tribute to Pete Carroll's creation, calls it "one of the finest neighborhood initiatives of the Depression." Carroll was tickled pink. I bet he learns the whole page by heart.

On the same subject, he invited me over to his place this evening. Today's the thirtieth anniversary of old Pete's death (what are you meant to offer on these occasions: condolences? congratulations?). Every year, Carroll invites a few people to his house for what he pompously calls a "press conference." I do wonder what sort of scoops the journalists who turn up are hoping to get. By way of a revelation, he gets out his collection. He does have a few really wonderful things, and he always manages to get a couple of the really specialized papers. I asked him if Jessica Woodruff was invited. After all, she's the high priestess. But she's not coming. Carroll says she's sending someone along in her place. In other words, some trainee. To be fair, after all these years, she must know every last inch of Carroll's rarities. Besides, apparently it's the same every year; he always gets out his "Tulip Field," you know, the one he got runner-up prize for in 1969. It's sad to say it, but he's never actually got over being beaten by Rousselet. Mind you, I can understand it, the guy's an ass. Even so, to go to the lengths of getting ten journalists together every 13 January to rewrite history...

Weird guy, this Carroll...The Society's his whole life, but he never misses a chance—at least in private—to complain about the way it's changed course. We talked for about five minutes. He's really bitter. He's convinced Sutter despises him because he didn't go to college (knowing Sutter, he may well be right). He feels he's been treated like a second-class citizen, only good enough for scribbling down the minutes these last twenty years. I think he almost regrets turning down your offer three years back. He doesn't like the Tour, you can tell, but he's pleased about the new surge of interest in the puzzle. In my opinion, if you really want him to come over this is the time to make him another offer.

Anyway, that's all for now. It's 5:30 and I still haven't decided if I'll go to Carroll's or not. He said he was going to make an important announcement "and revive the fortunes of a sadly forgotten genre." He wouldn't say anything more. Oh, if I can't be bothered to go, I can always read the mention in the *New York Times*.

Hope to see you soon (where? when? who knows?) and don't forget to call Lynn if you can't make it home this weekend.

Harry

Newspaper Extract

New York Times, 2 August 1994

The American Nicholas Spillsbury, world champion, and the Dane Olof Niels advanced yesterday to the final of the Speed Puzzle Tournament in Providence.

Niels had an easy win (fifty-five pieces) over the Colombian Neto in the semifinal. This is the sixth time he's got through to the final this season and this time he'll be trying to break Spillsbury's incredible run (twenty-four tournaments and one hundred and twenty-four consecutive games without defeat). Spillsbury looked a bit shaky against the young Russian, Evgueni Kallisov, the rising star of the Tour. Although he trailed for the greater part of the match, Spillsbury finally got the better of his opponent, winning with a narrow margin of three pieces. It's the narrowest victory the American prodigy has had on the professional circuit.

The final will be broadcast this afternoon from 1600 hours or thereabouts on the various channels of the Ubiquis group.

Vitamix. Think Harder, for Longer

Spot TV, shown 145 times between 7 September
and 3 October 1993

Timing	Images/Text
1–5 secs	Image of Spillsbury, seated. He is doing a puzzle— the top section of the Eiffel Tower (puzzle: "Universal Exhibition" by Paul Rousselet). His hands seem to fly to the pieces, take them, fit them, without hesitation. Subtitle: Final of the Augusta Tournament, Maine, 25 July 1993).
6–20 secs	Setting: locker rooms, JP Tour. Close up of Spillsbury, holding a can of Vitamix in his left hand. Text, Spillsbury: "My job takes a lot of concentration. In a game, things go very fast; I can't afford to make mistakes. Vitamix is a delicious cocktail of fruits and vitamins. It's the perfect drink before a match or an exam. With Vitamix, my mind works better than my opponents', for longer."
21–24 secs	A Tournament official enters the frame and taps Spillsbury on the shoulder. Text, Official: "You're on in one minute." Spillsbury nods and takes a long drink of Vitamix.

25–27 secs   Camera tracks Spillsbury from behind, as he enters the arena and waves to the crowd. General ovation.

28–30 secs   Back to Vitamix, shown in cans, tablets and bottles. Voice-over, Spillsbury: "Vitamix. Think harder, for longer."

Newspaper Extract

New York Times, 15 January 1995

Is the mystery puzzle coming back into vogue? According to Thomas Carroll, it is. Yesterday he got together with some journalists to commemorate the thirtieth anniversary of the death of his father, the founder of the Puzzology Society. Having shown the journalists the jewels in his collection (in particular a Delalande, the only one left in the U.S.), Carroll went on to say that he hoped to take advantage of the current popularity of the JP Tour to bring the mystery puzzle back into vogue. He described it as a "fascinating, but now largely forgotten genre."

Indeed, the mystery puzzle was very popular during the Depression; more than twenty-five millions sets were sold during 1933 alone. The mystery puzzle consisted of a booklet giving the background to a detective story, and a puzzle that the puzzlist/reader has to do in order to discover the culprit's name. In Carroll's words, "All the pieces are in place to allow the mystery puzzle to resume its place center stage." We will have to wait and see if he is right.

The Detective Novel during the Depression

From the doctoral thesis of Mills Kelleher,
"History of the American Detective Novel," 1971

The mystery puzzle first appeared during the Depression. Although certain manufacturers have carried on the tradition to this day, it is still largely associated with the extraordinary popularity of the puzzle in American households during the thirties.

	1932	1933	1934	1935	1936
Number of models	124	187	93	26	11
Sales (in millions)	19,700	25,400	9,200	1,300	<500

Fig. 1   Sales history of the mystery puzzle during the Depression

1. The Idea

A mystery puzzle consists of a booklet and a traditional puzzle. To begin with, the puzzlist/reader studies the book, which sets out the situation and describes the first stages of the investigation. He then does the puzzle, which gives him the solution to the mystery, and usually depicts the scene of the murder. This very simple idea has a number of variants. The puzzles included in the *Jig Mysteries* series, by Einson-Freeman, did not immediately reveal the name of the murderer. They simply revealed details, hitherto unremarked, that would allow the puzzlist to work out the identity of the killer by deduction.[27] The solution was given at the back of the book, but was always hidden in such a way as to discourage the impatient reader. It was printed in tiny letters, which could only be deciphered with the aid of a magnifying glass; or else written in invisible ink, yielding its secret only when exposed to the heat of a flame.

Booklets	Puzzles	Manufacturers	Authors	Most famous titles
8–10 pages	200–500 pieces	Einson-Freeman	R. Wallace	"The Mystery of Walnut Creek"
			N. Thurow	"Three Men At Sea"
			A. Houston	"The Milkman Comes at Seven o'Clock"
		Wilshire Bros	R. McRae	"Murder in the South Seas"
50–100 pages	150–200 pieces	World Syndicate	D. Valentine	"The Jade Miniature"
		Pratt & Amro	A. Nough	"Traveler Without Luggage"
		Monclair Publishers	A. Nister	*No title*
150–300 pages	300–1,000 pieces	Samuel Leiser	S. Leiser	"The Paper Tiger"
				"The Grand Central Left-Luggage Mystery"
				"Francis or Duty"

Fig. 2 Typology of mystery puzzle manufacturers

---

27. Of course, the finished puzzle is not illustrated on the box lid.

2. Main subjects

Mystery puzzles are a good reflection of the contradictions of their time, torn between the thirst for lucre and a longing for purity. Most novels depict upper-class families afflicted by the economic crisis, whose inexhaustible optimism eventually wins over the reader's sympathy.

The most typical representatives of this pseudoaristocracy are perhaps the Willards, who feature in several adventures from the pen of Derek Valentine—for example, "The Bloodstained Curtain" and "The Jade Miniature." Tom Willard, 56, had lost his job as sales director at the textile firm Bernett & Finch after the main warehouse was destroyed in a fire. He is looking for a new job, but refuses to accept payment from the young unemployed people he helps with writing job applications. Mary, 47, works as a voluntary nurse in a hostel for the homeless. Paul, 18, dreams of becoming a pilot, and practices reconstructions of the aerobatics of the Bright Angels at the bottom of the garden. As for Lise-Ann, 15, a girl with a passion for animals, she seems destined for a career as a vet. It should be noted that the Willards are profoundly democratic. In the 1932 election, Tom and Mary voted for Roosevelt, disillusioned with Hoover's lethargy, and his announcement that economic recovery was just around the corner. Like the characters in Capra's later films, they have ultimate faith in the structure of the family, the only bulwark of the weak in the face of a society which, in all other respects, is tearing itself apart.

In "The Bloodstained Curtain," the Willards come up against the implacable financier George N. Harriman III, who made a fortune after the war by selling lightweight biplanes on credit. The author openly accuses Harriman of having taken advantage of his fellow citizens' credulity. He compares him to Bernett, Tom Willard's former boss, whom the police suspect of having deliberately set fire to his own warehouse for the insurance money. Valentine's message is clear: he doesn't question capitalism itself, but he blows the whistle on those profiteers who give it a bad name.[28]

---

28. It is interesting to note the extent to which the concepts of family and of virtue are closely linked in the mystery puzzle. Bernett is divorced. As for Harriman, he has gambled away the money set aside by his wife for their son's education.

The crime element (a vulgar story of insurance fiddling and overvalued stocks) is itself quite trivial. Its main function is to bring about a confrontation between the two poles of American society, the Willards on the one hand, who have entrusted their life to the care of the god of capitalism, and types like Harriman on the other, who, by shaking off the moral principles that this god presupposes, almost destroy their country. From this point of view, the death of Bernett in "The Jade Miniature" clearly performs a cathartic function. Nor is it pure chance that it coincides with a fresh start for Tom Willard, who finds a new job in the manufacturer of manure.[29]

3. Literary merit of mystery puzzles

The different manufacturers of mystery puzzles gave varying degrees of weight to the puzzle and the booklet that came with it. It is therefore necessary to draw up a typology of manufacturers based on the ratio of story to puzzle in their products.

a. Manufacturers who emphasize the puzzle
This is the most important category in terms of numbers of puzzles sold and numbers of titles published. It tends to include producers who are well established in the games industry and who became involved in publishing mystery puzzles more out of a wish to diversify their output than out of real interest in crime fiction.

Einson-Freeman, who in 1933 produced, all told, almost three million boxes a week right across the United States, is an example of a business that always placed more importance on the puzzle, and less on the book—and, consequently, on the plot. The dimensions of the

---

29. Agriculture is conspicuous by its absence from the mystery puzzle. Whereas a Steinbeck and a Caldwell were happy dealing with the subject of the Depression from the angle of the agricultural laborer, the mystery puzzle authors confined themselves almost exclusively to a large metropolis. Tom Willard's new job, however, breaks with the commonly accepted idea that the economic recovery in 1933–4 was led by industry; in "The Jade Miniature" it is agriculture that creates jobs in industry, and not the other way around.

boxes themselves confirm this: the book contains a dozen or so pages, while the puzzle has between two hundred and five hundred pieces.

The crime stories created by Edgar Wallace and Arthur Houston for the weekly *Crime Club* series by Einson-Freeman consist of little more than a description of the murder and the first few stages of the investigation. The characters are described with three epithets. Accordingly, Meg Tilden, the heroine of "The Milkman Comes at Seven o'Clock"[30] is described as "a beautiful woman of about thirty, enthusiastic, generous and detached." Colonel Abbott is "a most upright man, at peace with himself after his thirty years in the Navy. His greying temples and gentlemanly manner were typically British, and women adored him." The author contents himself with caricature, and indeed, the short format of the booklet relieves him of the need to develop character. He is at the extreme opposite pole of literary creation, in that he *says* things, rather than *shows* them.

The police elements used by Wallace, Thurow, Houston and others are likewise extremely rudimentary, in terms of motive (usually love or the prospect of an inheritance), the weapon (invariably a revolver or poison), or the clues that will eventually lead to the murderer. None of the mystery puzzles in this category, even if radically reworked, would stand up if published alone.

If the books can be criticized for their lack of originality, the Einson-Freeman puzzles, on the other hand, are quite clearly some of the most sophisticated of their time: pieces shaped like animals or characters, subjects cut along the color lines, the use, alongside each other, of interlocking and noninterlocking pieces, etc. A puzzle of five hundred pieces would take at least ten hours to do.

b. Manufacturers who give equal weight to puzzle and novel
These companies usually have their roots in games, and are competent and experienced in puzzle production, but are usually short on

---

30. "The Milkman Comes at Seven o'Clock," Einson-Freeman Co., Inc., Long Island City, NY, 1933. 14″ × 20″, 340 pieces. Cardboard box, 9″ × 7″, containing an eleven-page booklet signed by Arthur Houston. The solution, written in invisible ink, is revealed by a flame.

experience in the field of detective fiction. Even so, unlike the manufacturers in the first group, they try to use the fictional aspect to
stimulate the public's interest. The crime story is no longer subordi-
nate to the puzzle, and the authors refuse to make the discovery of
the crime's solution depend entirely on the assembling of the puzzle.
These makers, the finest of which include World Syndicate Publishing and Pratt & Amro, try to establish a balance between the two
media, hoping thereby, no doubt, to seduce both puzzlists and lovers
of crime stories.

These laudable intentions were not invariably rewarded with
success. Although their booklets were considerably longer than those
of Einson-Freeman (between fifty and a hundred pages), the novels
are still too short to really capture the interest of the reader. They
have to do without the accumulation of details and digressions that
are the crime writer's best means of creating interest. Nothing is included without a reason, so that the slightest element not immediately needed for the action to progress attracts attention. One can be
sure that, thirty pages from now, it will provide a motive for the person everyone always thought was the culprit, or, conversely, will ir-
revocably incriminate the victim's closet friend.

Botched exposition, worn-out conventions, and incoherent
character psychology are some of the most obvious faults in these
less than subtle constructions. Here again, stereotypes abound. Although they never sink as low as a speculator like Harriman, the victims are company bosses who have failed to anticipate the crisis and
whose lack of foresight leads to massive redundancies. The investigation is usually conducted by some young, energetic and wealthy
man, who plays at being detective between two rounds of tennis.

These puzzles are less carefully made than Einson-Freeman's.
They often include large monochrome areas, which expose laziness
in the piece-cutting. There are no outline pieces in Pratt & Amro's
puzzles, and certainly not in those by Montclair Publishing, which
scarcely ever got beyond noninterlocking pieces. Only Allen Nister
puzzles are still known today: made in beautiful lavender blue, they
carry not a single indication (title, number of pieces, even the author's name) that might give the player a clue.

c. Samuel Leiser and Co.

The third category consists of only one company, Samuel Leiser. Its founder, directing editor and spare-time novelist was quick to grasp the unique opportunity offered by this marriage between the puzzle and the crime novel. Rather than join up with a manufacturer in Philadelphia, Leiser decided to buy a small workshop in which he cut his own puzzles, with the help of his brother, William, and a handful of employees. Despite high prices, their puzzles were constantly in demand. Leiser received around 1,500 orders a month, whereas their output never exceeded 600. In its catalog for 1967, the Puzzology Society records nine different models. William Leiser, who today lives in a suburb of New York, recalls eleven or twelve models. Samuel died in a plane crash in 1952.

Leiser and Co.'s mystery puzzles illustrate more facets of police procedure than the novel alone would be capable of showing, according to their creator. This account will focus on three of the best-known examples.

The box for "The Paper Tiger"[31] contains a 152-page booklet and 441 wooden cubes. According to which side of the cube he turns face up, the player will get six different solutions to the problem outlined in the booklet. In one case, the gardener killed his boss. In another, the death of Captain Neels is in fact an accident, made to look like a murder to incriminate his older brother. In a third version, Pastor Wagner kills Neels, with whom he had been in competition ten years earlier for the hand of the lovely Carla, etc. In each of the six cases, the police make a different arrest; in each of the six cases, the accused is found guilty.

The second example, "The Grand Central Left-Luggage Mystery," owes its central idea to a forgotten novel by Steve de la Pena, *Urban Sierra*.[32] The puzzle, which, to look at, seems completely devoid of interest, is an illustration of Chapter IV. The employees at

---

31. "The Paper Tiger," Samuel Leiser & Co., Philadelphia, 1931. 38" × 13", 326 wooden pieces. Box in lacquered wood, 39" × 38", containing a booklet of 152 pages by Samuel Leiser. Solutions not given in the booklet.
32. *Urban Sierra,* Steve de la Pena ed. Homestead, Charleston, 1931.

the morgue lay out Eddie Cohen's corpse in a numbered drawer, after having emptied out his pockets on the table; a few coins, a bunch of keys, a chequered handkerchief and...a missing piece. The player turns the box over, dives under the table, lifts up the carpet—and all in vain. If he's lucky he'll notice on the box that the puzzle has 326 pieces, which, after numerous recounts, he establishes to be the number of pieces on the table. Thus the loyal Leiser puzzlist penetrates the master plan. The missing piece eloquently suggests that the solution to the crime is to be found in the contents of Cohen's pockets. From that point on, everything fits together. The reader realizes, from the fact that Cohen had no money and no train ticket in his pocket, that he was not about to leave New York, as the investigation assumed. So what was he doing carrying a heavy suitcase at six o'clock in the evening in Grand Central Station? There again, the contents of Cohen's pockets give the answer. Three quarters and a dime make eighty-five cents, the cost for a week of an automatic left luggage locker in the west aisle. But someone was waiting for Cohen as he came out of the lockers. In the Friday evening crowd, his aggressor failed to grab hold of the suitcase, which turned out to have a false bottom stuffed full of microfilms.

The most famous of the Samuel Leiser puzzles is quite rightly "Francis or Duty."[33] By the end of the 260-page booklet, everything points to poor Francis Northomb. The police accuse him of having pretended to discover the body of his uncle, an extremely wealthy businessman, mysteriously hit over the head in his library. The investigators have plenty to go on. Francis had financial problems and knew he was to inherit from old Mortimer. Added to that, the maid says she saw him go into the library. He only reemerged five minutes later, which conflicts with the accused man's own version, in which he claims to have called for help as soon as he discovered the body. The reader feverishly assembles the 738 pieces of the puzzle and sees his theory apparently strengthen as the image gradually emerges.

---

33. "Francis or Duty," Leiser Brothers, Philadelphia, 1933. 38″ × 38″, 738 wooden pieces. Box in lacquered wood, 20″ × 17″, containing a booklet, 260 pp, by Samuel Leiser. The solution is not given in the booklet.

Crouched beside his uncle's body, Francis wipes the heavy copper candlestick on his shirttail. Certain players stop there, and remain convinced that Francis killed his uncle. But those who completed the puzzle noticed a tobacco pouch which had rolled under an armchair. Francis had immediately remembered that, out of the entire family, only his father smoked a pipe, and, ever the perfect son, had attempted to eradicate the signs of his father's presence before calling for help.

4. The puzzle as metaphor for police procedure

Samuel Leiser must be credited with demonstrating how closely puzzling mirrored police procedure. The player and the detective move forward methodically, gradually gathering together all the pieces in the picture, but unable, until the end, to establish an overall image. The conscientious detective only closes the case when he finally has all the pieces in front of him and has fitted them smoothly together. If he has failed to do so, on the other hand, he runs the risk of catching the wrong culprit, as the unscrupulous reader might have been tempted to do had he not, at the last moment, noticed Charles Northomb's tobacco pouch.

And the similarity doesn't stop there. In the same way as each investigator ends up developing his own technique, so puzzlists develop different assembly methods. The Dutch colorist technique, the sorting procedure of the Scandinavians, the work of someone like Van de Kerkhof on the morphology of pieces, all these mark a player out as surely as deduction is the exclusive domain of Sherlock Holmes and psychological investigation the prerogative of Simon Ranicci. Leiser was also quick to exploit the tendency of players always to rely on one method that has already proved successful. He designed a multi-colored puzzle which the adherents of the Dutch method had to solve as quickly as possible, using a few basic precepts: building up small blocks of color (four to six pieces), finding light lines that run through the puzzle, and fitting together the different blocks. By this method the player arrived at a finished picture that gave him one culprit.

However, assuming years of blindly practicing the color method hadn't already robbed him of all critical faculties, he was bound to admit that it had been difficult to get the last few pieces in place, as evidenced by the sawdust on the carpet. So he'd break up the pieces and start over again with the morphological method this time, according to which the player allows himself to be guided by the form of the pieces alone. Behold the miracle: the image revealed a different culprit. This project, which, unfortunately, was never realized,[34] gave a perfect example of the relativity of police methods. It predated by ten years the skepticism expressed by Commissioner Owen: "The number of guilty men I've allowed to walk away scarcely exceeds the number of innocents I've locked up by mistake. But who cares? The first category just wants to be forgotten. As for the second, their constant ranting and recusal of juries ends up making them even less popular than the assassins whose crimes they're accused of...."

---

34. According to his brother William, Samuel Leiser completed a model of the puzzle after weeks spent filing each individual piece. This is formally denied by the five of his collaborators who agreed to be interviewed. On the other hand, we do know for certain, from a letter addressed to Pete Carroll, President of the Puzzology Society at the time, that Leiser shrank from the technical problems that would have been posed by mass production.

The Polaroid Killer
Strikes Again?

New York Times, 21 September 1995

Yesterday we brought you news of the death of the famous puzzle designer Paul Rousselet, whose body was discovered on 19 September in his hotel bedroom in Saint-Regis. For the last two years, Rousselet, 59, had been designing most of the models used on the professional speed puzzle circuit (the JP Tour). In 1969 he won an international competition (coorganized by the *New York Times*) to find the most difficult puzzle in the world. "Pantone 138" continues to be one of the best-selling puzzles worldwide.

An autopsy, carried out yesterday afternoon, revealed that Rousselet had indeed been murdered, using a method reminiscent of that used by the serial killer known as the Polaroid Killer, who has already claimed five victims in the world of the puzzle. Rousselet appears to have been initially put to sleep using Pentothal, an extremely powerful sleeping drug, before being poisoned with a massive injection of strychnine. But, unlike the other victims, Rousselet was not subject to mutilation of any kind. Nor was the usual hallmark of this assassin's work, the traditional fragment of Polaroid, found on his body.

There was no shortage of comment at NYPD headquarters yesterday evening. One man familiar with the file suggested this latest murder might be the last in the series. "In his own mind, the assassin may have run through the register of amputations now. This was the full stop to the series." Other experts were unfortunately less optimistic. Wilbur Kosh of the FBI observed that "the murderer now believes he no longer needs to put a signature to his crimes. He knows we'll recognize his method, whatever happens. I don't think we're out of the woods yet." Let's hope the FBI is wrong....

Wallerstein Tries to Reassure His Troops

Jessica Woodruff, *New York Times*, 11 July 1995

Following the murder of Evgueni Kallisov (July 8) multimillionaire Charles Wallerstein decided to bring together the entire retinue of the JP Tour for a summit on the wave of murders that has shaken the world of puzzling for the last few months. Players, trainers, technicians, aides—all told, over two hundred people—packed the auditorium at the Federation headquarters yesterday evening to listen to Charles Wallerstein in a particularly combative mood.

The magnate, who took over the presidency in 1991, began with a résumé of the facts. In the space of four months, two champions (Rijk Krijek and Evgueni Kallisov) and two people closely connected to the circuit (architect Irwin Weissberg and Wallerstein's personal secretary, James Blythe) have been murdered by the man known in the press as the Polaroid Killer. In addition, the police are not ruling out the possibility that the sudden disappearance of Nicholas Spillsbury on 9 February might also be linked to this affair.

Wallerstein paid fulsome homage to the four victims and expressed his confidence that the FBI would catch the murderer. At the same time, he said he intended to engage the services of private investigators in order to speed matters up. He called upon the members of the Tour and their retinues not to give in to panic, and assured them there would be increased security on the forthcoming rounds of the Tour (there has been talk of doubling, even tripling the existing measures); in addition, the personal protection offered to all the players will be stepped up.

The multimillionaire then invited questions from the audience. When asked about the possible motive of the Polaroid Killer, Wallerstein had nothing new to add. "I cannot completely rule out the hypothesis of personal vengeance," he stated, "but it seems extremely unlikely." He embraced the theory of the FBI, which believes the Federation is dealing with a lunatic who hopes to destabilize the JP Tour. "If that is the case," Wallerstein remarked, "he's on the wrong tack. The Tour is getting ever more popular and it would take a lot more than this to bring it to its knees." An unfortunate response, which was taken up, inevitably, by Olof Niels. "If I've understood you correctly," he parried, "what you're most worried about is that the killer's going to get to the sponsors." The Jutland Lumberjack's remarks were greeted with some applause.

Neto, the Colombian, said he spoke for his colleagues in asking for a reevaluation of the competition prize money, until such time as the murderer is arrested: "We are taking a big risk in continuing to play; you've got to pay us for that." Wallerstein is likely to be sensitive to this argument; his entourage says he is in fact prepared to go a long way to avoid defection of any kind.

Finally, anticipating the inevitable question, Wallerstein firmly denied the report in *The Impertinent*, which alleged that he had taken out life-insurance policies for his top players: "It's outrageous, but they're not going to take it back. I am going to come down like a ton of bricks on Mr. Nuss and his bunch of yes-men." His outburst speaks volumes for the somewhat strained atmosphere currently prevailing in the world of puzzling.

Spillsbury's First Defeat

Radio report by Leonard da Fonseca on WNDZ
Federation Cup, 11 December 1994

Welcome, ladies and gentlemen, to the holy of holies, the famous
sports arena of the Mirage Hotel, Las Vegas, packed solid tonight for
what promises to be the game of the year. On my left, Nicholas
Spillsbury, the young American prodigy, twenty years of age, as yet
unbeaten, who, whatever happens here tonight, will be ordained
World Champion, 1994, for the second year running. On my right,
Olof Niels, also known as the Jutland Lumberjack, the Mountain,
Juggernaut, and more besides, World Champion in 1992, relieved of
his title by Spillsbury, but still in, with a chance of winning it back.

Before the two players take their seats, let me quickly give you
the result of the Junior Final, which took place earlier this evening.
The winner was the Nigerian, Abouniké, who thrashed Duchemin,
the great hope of the French team. And what a revelation this Abouniké is. I've a feeling we'll be hearing a lot more about him. African
spontaneity laced with true Scandinavian discipline, picked up during his time in training with Jonas Lundqvist's boys. What a figure
he cuts, a strapping black, surrounded by Vikings! A sight to behold!
A practical joker to boot! He enjoys a good laugh. I'm told that in
Malmö, where he lives six months of the year, the girls are jostling to
be photographed at his side as he emerges from the Blue Herring, its
most fashionable nightspot.

But to get back to the final...I get the feeling Spillsbury's worried. He fiddles constantly with the medal around his neck. And, yes, the stakes are very high tonight. He's only thirty minutes away from the grand slam, the second of his career. And Las Vegas is a fixture like no other. It's the last of the season, and potentially the most lucrative: more than $250,000 goes to the winner, and half as much to the unlucky loser. Last year, Spillsbury concluded a breathtaking season in magisterial style. Niels—same opponent—played an indifferent final. But this year, there's a whiff of grapeshot in the air for the young prodigy. Only eight pieces ahead of Krijek in the quarterfinals in Indianapolis; just three over Kallisov a month later in Providence. The idol's still up on his pedestal—but he has wobbled. The slightest thing could turn that wobble into a topple!

Right now, Niels looks distinctly more at ease. I don't imagine metaphysical doubts keep him awake at night. The boy exudes a sense of power that is literally extraordinary. And those who know him say that's no exaggeration: yesterday, here at the Mirage, he actually cut up two of the stage doors to make firewood, a habit from his childhood days in Jutland. Fresh air, physical exercise...Nature, you could say! But not just pure and simple! One of the chambermaids was telling me this morning it's her job to fill up the minibar after Niels has been at it. Drinks, peanuts, dried raisins: all gone! Even the bottle opener, she told me, had disappeared....

But enough of the small talk, the Peruvian referee, the sprightly Señor Ayacho, is about to blow the whistle for them to start. First, he reminds them of the rules of the game, while the two players take this last chance to focus their minds, Spillsbury with his head in his hands, Niels with his two giant thrashers spread out on the table before him.

Hold on, what's happening? A ripple's spreading through the crowd. Spillsbury suddenly lifts his head. Even Niels looks alarmed. What can Señor Ayacho have said to produce this state of general astonishment? Aha! My goodness, this *is* one for the books. I'm told he has just announced that the length of time for which the picture on the box will be shown to the players has been reduced from the usual thirty down to just fifteen seconds! Spillsbury's asking for confirmation. Ayacho gives it. He gives the signal. Good Lord, what can this mean? Surely he can't have decided something like this alone. Besides, the Tournament officials aren't batting an eyelid; they must have been in on the secret, too. Well, this is all really quite astonishing. I have to say, I don't understand what's going on here and, by the look of things, I'm not the only one. The crowd sits in stunned silence. As for poor old Spillsbury, he looks completely dumbstruck. Will he even be able to start? Ah! Up goes his head! He's looking around for his coach. What will they decide? They could always try to get the start postponed, although I must say Señor Ayacho doesn't look disposed to grant them that particular wish. No, no postponement! Earp's giving his protégé the nod to continue.

And here we have the design for tonight's final. An unpublished puzzle by the Frenchman Paul Rousselet: "Ascent of Mont Blanc by Dr. Pacard and His Guide." What can I tell you about it? Two men walk along a snowy ridge. One carries a pack on his back, he struggles to advance, the upper half of his body stooping slightly forward. The other man has stopped: he examines the horizon, holding his hand to his face like a visor, protecting it, I imagine, from the sun. What with that huge expanse of blue sky, and those unruffled slopes of snow, our friends have certainly got their work cut out. Hard to say, at this point, whether this picture places either Niels or Spillsbury at an advantage. With his background, Niels should be at home with large areas of snow. On the other hand, Spillsbury's photographic memory should serve him well with a subject like this: unless fifteen seconds proves insufficient for him to fix every detail in his mind. We'll soon see. Right now, the two players are deep in concentration on the design, trying to engrave every last detail on their memories. That's it! The picture's gone, and indeed my suspicion was correct. Spillsbury appears to have been completely thrown by the change to the rules: he may even be in such a state that he hasn't made good use of the fifteen seconds he has been allowed. Not that he doesn't know where his pieces need to go; but each time his hand hesitates for just a fraction of a second. To the uninitiated, it might even go unnoticed, but believe you me, I know what I'm saying here; very shortly we should be getting confirmation as we pass the 100-piece

mark. There it is, Niels has just passed it, how many pieces is Spillsbury behind? Four, five, six, Holy Smoke, that many! Eight! Nine!
Nine pieces behind! After 100 pieces, that is truly incredible.... And
what's more, Niels has begun by tackling one of the more difficult
parts of the picture. He's got part of the sky done, and is now starting on the first of the two figures. He's looking as if he's got it made
from here, though I must say, force of nature is more the phrase that
comes to mind. Whatever, he's a helluva guy!

Ah! Now Spillsbury seems to be getting the bit back between his
teeth! He's just performed a truly beautiful sky-sky-snow-sky-snow
sequence. It's in moments like this that his eye works miracles, dis-
tinguishing between minute variations of shade and color. From
here in the commentary box, it goes without saying, they all look the
same: blue sky, white snow, and that's all there is to it. He seems to
be making a comeback. Yes, there's the confirmation: only five pieces
behind after 200; he's made up half of Niels's lead. The crowd knows
it too, it's starting to make itself heard. And this can be a real problem: should the referee impose a silence, to allow the players to concentrate? The debate was thrown open again last Tuesday evening,
when Cornillet, the popular French player, said during the press conference after the match that he'd been put off by the shouting of the
Mombala fan club. It must be said that the Cameroonian does have
a devoted following, and if I'd been in Corny's shoes, the horn-
blowing, hooting and the rest of the racket would have got on my
nerves pretty quickly too. Still, the Frenchman does seem a little
oversensitive. I remember last year in Cincinnati, he called for a
break in play because Tackl had shot him a dirty look.

But back to the game, where the Jutland Lumberjack is still
holding off Spillsbury's challenge. A quick look at the Relative Speed?
Thirty-six. Pretty disappointing for a final. No doubt due to the
change in the rules; it's quite clear that neither player really quite
managed to fully absorb the design. Ayacho's decision really was the
stuff of high drama! Thirty seconds is already pretty short, when it
comes to memorizing the position of a thousand pieces. If you recall, during the first season, the players kept the design on the table
throughout the game. The decision to limit the time of exposure was

taken in '93, when Spillsbury began to sweep the board. Nothing was said at the time, obviously, but the idea was clearly to reduce the young prodigy's superiority over his competitors. And I'm afraid this evening's iron fist in the velvet glove might be the coup de grâce.

Niels still has a five-piece lead at the 400-piece mark. The Dane has finished his figures. Spillsbury, on the other hand, is doing what we know he does best. I can't actually make out any logic at all in his choice of pieces: a bit of rock here, a bit of sky there, each time with the left hand, without a second's thought.

Or is there? Spillsbury seems to be slowing down his rhythm; he's flailing, as the jargon would have it. He must have examined his last piece for a good two seconds before putting it in position. As though, all of a sudden, the smooth machine had seized up, and he just couldn't work out where it went. It could be an expensive error for him. Niels must have noticed, he's taking double helpings, stocking up pieces in his left hand: extremely rare, that; I've only seen it done once before, in the Pittsburgh Final, when he was within sight of Mombala's record. As he moved in for the kill on Krijek, he began sliding two or three pieces into his left hand, which gained him a couple of hundredths of a second and, more to the point, allowed him to make a real show of his superiority. Snow-ridge-sky, there it goes, he slips them in from left to right, and back to collect again. Result: an eleven-piece lead at the halfway point. Ladies and gentlemen, something extraordinary is happening here at the sports arena of the Mirage Hotel tonight: a myth is beginning to crumble. This is quite unheard of, Spillsbury's odds at the bookmakers have just fallen to less than fifty-fifty. As you know, bets can continue to be placed during games. Until now, and even in his most critical moments, Spillsbury has always retained the punters' confidence in his ability to turn a game around. This time they've abandoned the sinking ship: 1.2 to 1 ... 1.3 ... 1.4. Niels's odds keep on rising. Spillsbury looks in deeper and deeper trouble. For the last three seconds, he's had a piece in his hand, he stares at the half-finished puzzle before him, trying to see where it goes. Ah, at last, it was a bit of sky, he snaps it into place. My own feeling is that Spillsbury has lost his mental picture. All he has to go on now is a dim recollection.

Oh, my word! The figures at 600 pieces are staggering. You may even have heard the furor that broke out as the statistics went up. Niels is now twenty pieces in front. Spillsbury's Relative Speed over the last hundred-piece leg has plummeted to twenty-four pieces: ten below Abouniké's score in the junior final. Roughly the score of a good player in a club in the suburbs of Copenhagen! And Niels's figures aren't looking exactly brilliant either: an overall RS of thirty-four, nothing to get excited about there....What a spectacle, my friends! The rhythm's slumped yet again. Clearly, both players have no more memory of the picture left to draw on. Now both men are coming to grips with live material! And Niels is by far the stronger in that department. He can always fall back on color-coding, or even, if it comes to it, on the morphological method. And that's, in fact, precisely what he's doing. A series of five sky pieces of decreasing intensity of blue—classic colorist technique...while poor old Spillsbury, an abstractionist through and through, is now all over the place. I cannot believe it, his RS counter is plummeting by the minute: nineteen, eighteen, sixteen...This time there's no doubt about it...the die is cast! Niels has just passed the 800-piece mark, with a lead of forty-three pieces. He's got the message now, he starts to ease off. No point taking risks, he must be saying to himself, my opponent's going under, the last bit's fairly easy. You almost wish he'd hurry up and finish, just to put Spillsbury out of his misery. Poor man! He lifts his head, scans the crowd to find his coach, Cecil Earp. Such distress in his eyes! And such bitterness too, no doubt, as this unexpected change to the rules deprives him of his second Grand Slam. I think we can expect ructions in the locker room after the match; there are going to be some tough questions to answer for those responsible for this last-minute decision. Only three pieces left for Niels, two, one; it's finished! The Dane has beaten Nicholas Spillsbury, World Champion, by seventy-nine pieces. Wait a second, if I'm not very much mistaken, it is actually the biggest margin in the entire history of the finals of the World Tour. Yes, that's right. I'm being told that the previous record was January 1993, when Spillsbury put his mark on the Tour by subjecting Niels to ridicule in the final of the Orlando Cup. What an extraordinary reversal of fate...

ah, the Dane is certainly a happy man! He's hopping up and down on the platform, surrounded by the entire Scandinavian delegation. There go Sundström and Uppal, dancing a demonic conga. Jonas Lundqvist should be with his team any moment. Here he comes! He makes his way through the crowd; Eriksen reaches out his hand, pulls him up onto the platform. It really is a joy to behold their delight, in such stark contrast to the loser, who is completely alone at this time. What a paradox: Spillsbury is World Champion for the second time, he's won fourteen out of the fifteen tournaments this season, yet he is the one weeping tears tonight, alone, all alone in his chair. For weep he does! Huge tears roll down his cheeks. And what wouldn't I give to know what he is thinking at this moment. Not only has he just suffered the first ever defeat of his brief career: he has been humiliated, and, more to the point, betrayed by the rules themselves. But no doubt Nicholas will be able to tell us more about that at the press conference. For now, stay with us, we'll be right back after the break.

Free-for-All in Puzzleland

Val Nuss in *The Impertinent*, 18 December 1994

It wasn't safe to linger in the locker rooms of the sports arena at the Mirage last Sunday at six-thirty, three-quarters of an hour after the end of the match between the Jutland Woodchopper and Nicholas "Egghead" Spillsbury, when Spillsbury finally realized he had been betrayed by his own people. Diana Dobbs, director of the Tour, was greeted with the delicate words "Get lost, you old trout." The faithful doormat of Citizen Wallerstein, Jim Blythe, who came to test the temperature, was dealt a resounding smack in the face. As for the Ubiquis reporter, the doctors are fairly optimistic; the operation to sew back his left ear was successful and he should be able to leave the clinic in about a week's time.

Chin up, Nicholas! Revolt is the first sign of awareness! No one ever saw a chimpanzee rebel against his master because the rules were changed to deprive him of his banana! Smart guy, Wallerstein! We don't exactly expect subtlety from him, but to actually hoodwink his own little monkey in front of twenty-three million viewers, well, you have to take your hat off! He's not one for fine details, our Charlie. On 2 October, the management of the JP Tour sent him a memo concerning the recent stagnation of advertising revenue on the circuit. They pointed to the guilty party: Spillsbury and his tiresome habit of winning everything. The author of the report had his own solution: give the likable cretin a good licking and bring him back down to the level of those in happy possession of a brain. All right, Wallerstein says to himself, but let's wait till the final of the Las Vegas Tournament, with its thirteen percent of the audience and five thousand auditorium seats at $60 each. As for the vanquisher, look no farther: let it be Olof Niels, known as the Organ to those ladies who have had the frequent pleasure.

The rest is mere child's play, or, rather, pure massacre. By reducing the time for which the image is shown to the players before the match from thirty to fifteen seconds, the referee left our simple-minded one without a chance. Poor Spillsbury! A sight to behold, as he struggled to get his synapses together! Not that Niels fared much better. Let us simply say that the few extra IQ points nature supplied him saved him from drowning. And he picks up the cash—$250,000 for the winner!

At least, if winner's the right word. For we know what it means to be the winner: with a seventeen percent market share for the final quarter of an hour of the game, and a 1995 season "that looks wide open from here" (you bet it does, if all you need to do to shuffle the league table is to change the rules!). Generalissimo Wallerstein has swept the board. Nice work, maestro!

Extracts from the Minutes of the Board Meeting of the American Puzzle Federation

Committee meeting, 2 October 1994

2. Quarterly report by the promotion department, JP Tour

SYKE: Income from advertising on the JP Tour grew for the twelfth consecutive quarter. This third quarter it has reached $67.2 million, which represents an increase of 84 percent over last year. However, growth is slowing noticeably. The rate of growth from one quarter to the next, which had previously never slipped below 25 percent last year, fell to seven percent from the second to the third quarter.

WALLERSTEIN: How d'you account for that?

SYKE: I'm afraid it's fairly simple. The latest audience figures aren't good. The viewing share for the Tour's broadcasts is being eroded. The Baltimore final got only 11.3 percent of TV viewers watching at the time.

BLYTHE: If I recall correctly, we often used to get 13 percent at the start of the season....

SYKE: Your memory's excellent. If we look at the figures a little closer, we see that the audience began to decline in May, which is the time when Spillsbury practically sewed up the title for the second time running, by winning the Chicago tournament. They've picked up every time Spillsbury's been in trouble, as, for example, in the semifinal at Augusta, when he was eleven pieces behind Neto, the Colombian, at the halfway point.

DOBBS: If I've understood you correctly, what you're saying is that Spillsbury's reputation for being unbeatable is now starting to count against us...

EARP: When it was the very thing that gave the Tour liftoff in the first place...

SYKE: You have to accept the facts.

WALLERSTEIN: So, the Tour's going to be struggling as long as there's no proof Spillsbury can be beaten. Is that it?

SYKE: That's what I meant, yes.

WALLERSTEIN: Well, say it then, don't bother to beat about the bush. Next!

46

Extracts from the Minutes of the Puzzology Society

Committee meeting, 30 June, 1995

President Sutter opened the proceedings at 1800 hours precisely.

1. Committee elections

PRESIDENT: My dear friends, this meeting is a little unusual in that we must now proceed to a vote by the Committee that will govern the future of the association over the coming few years. Before I invite prospective candidates to put themselves forward, I should like to clear up any doubts regarding my own candidacy.

As you know, by the statutes of our association I am entitled to seek a fifth mandate. Over the last few months I have searched my innermost conscience as to the best interest of this Society. Several factors argue in favor of my candidacy: my numerous, solid contacts in the academic world; the opportunity to go on to consolidate our association, which might well suffer from constant changes in its leadership; and finally, and most important, my wish to see through the long-term projects I have been managing for several years. But let it not be thought that I was in any way clinging to my position. A little voice told me that the time had perhaps come to make way for a younger man.

An unexpected event put an end to my procrastination. Several daily papers and magazines, better known for their TV listings than for the seriousness of their journalism, began to circulate the rumor that I was seriously ill. Obviously, I have my own ideas about the source of these rumors, as well as the identity of those who spread them. They are clearly intended to weaken the Society for the benefit of other organizations, whose interests we threaten by our intransigence and our loyalty to the basic values of puzzling. Once I had understood that our adversaries hoped to see me abandon my duties, I decided to posit my candidacy for my own position!

I hope you will understand my reasons, and that you will share them. I now invite the other candidates for the post of president to make themselves known. I need not remind you that a unanimous election would only give strength to my legitimacy and, consequently, to our entire organization.

THOMAS CARROLL: I have the honor of offering my candidacy for the position of president of the Puzzology Society.

PRESIDENT: You, Thomas? But you're not allowed!

THOMAS CARROLL: Who's stopping me? I pay my subscriptions like the others and, if I'm not mistaken, it's thanks to my father that we're all here today....

PRESIDENT: Come now, Thomas, be reasonable...

THOMAS CARROLL: Let me speak, Upton. We spent twenty years listening to you in silence. Now it's my turn to say something.

I won't make a long speech. I don't like them, and I'm no good at them. I didn't go to college, as has often been remarked on here. My father didn't either, or hardly. That didn't stop his spreading happiness all around him, and creating something people will remember.

I'm putting myself forward today for Upton's position simply because I'm ashamed. Ashamed of what this Society has become, ashamed of the way we have squandered Pete's legacy to us.

PRESIDENT: Careful, Thomas. Watch what you're saying...

THOMAS CARROLL: Shut up, Upton. I spent some time this morning going through the figures for the membership of the Society since you were first elected. Here they are. Let me warn you, they are devastating. 1977: eighty-five members. 1982: sixty-eight. 1987: forty-four. 1991: thirty-two. 1995: nineteen. Let me ask you this, why have we gone along with this?

PRESIDENT: We've always prized quality over quantity. I would rather have nineteen motivated, competent members than hundreds of housewives doing "Pinocchios."

THOMAS CARROLL: That's where you're mistaken, Upton. What quality are we talking about here? What good does it do you to know the names of every single manufacturer in New England or the official supplier to the Court of Denmark? And what's the use of knowing how many pieces there are in a Samuel Leiser when there isn't a single copy of it left, anyway? Face up to it, you haven't done a puzzle yourself for ten years. Please don't try to tell me you actually like puzzles. You're a historian who's chosen the puzzle as the subject of his research; that's quite different. And the proof is, you despise today's manufacturers simply because they didn't disappear after the Depression. You'll praise a 1933 Einson-Freeman to the skies, even though it's inferior to half the things being made now by Mattel or Parker Brothers.

PRESIDENT: Don't talk to me about Parker Brothers. Their puzzles are appallingly vulgar. . . .

THOMAS CARROLL: There we go, the dirty word's out, Upton. You know, Pete was quite capable of calling a puzzle banal, ordinary, weak, ugly, or meretricious, but never vulgar. He had too much respect for the people. Never forget that the first three presidents of the Society were a surveyor, a butcher and a gas station attendant, in that order. Oh, I wonder what you'd have to say if the local gas station attendant took it into his head to come to our meetings! Or, rather, I know perfectly well. You would interrogate him subtly on his university career before humiliating him with two or three really tricky questions, like you did that young boy Pasquale brought a few years ago. I'm very sorry to undermine your certainties, Upton, but not all gas station attendants are cretins, and even if they were, if they love puzzling, they belong in this gathering.

PRESIDENT: That's going too far! I cannot allow you to accuse me of sectarianism. Look at Libby, she's a secretary, yet we allow her to attend our meetings....

LIBBY CULLINS: Too kind of you, Upton. It's always nice to learn you're considered the token idiot!

PRESIDENT: Oh, come on, Libby, that's not what I meant....

THOMAS CARROLL: But you said it, Upton, and you might at least have the courage to stand by what you say, though it doesn't really surprise me coming from you. You must let me tell you, ladies and gentlemen, how I first came to be recruited by Upton. It was in 1977; I'd been working at the Town Hall in Boston since I'd left school. For ten or so years I'd been doing the minutes for these committee meetings, which had earned me the unofficial title of secretary. Upton had just been elected. He considered, for some reason, that the Society needed a permanent employee. Out of respect for my father I felt obliged to accept. And, anyway, I was proud to be asked; I'll admit that now. However, I should have realized that something would go wrong. The day I came to sign my contract, Upton said to me, and I remember it perfectly: "Thomas, in the future you will record the minutes of our discussions. You will be this association's memory. But you know the finest quality in a scribe: discretion. I am counting on you, Thomas. Get it all down, but never open your mouth."

PRESIDENT: That's a lowdown jibe! How can you possibly maintain I said, or even thought, such a thing?

THOMAS CARROLL: Quite simply because it's the truth. Remember the day in 1985 when Jessica Woodruff called the Society. She was preparing an article on the fiftieth anniversary of the association, and in your absence I answered her questions. When you heard about it, I thought you were going mad. You had me call Jessica back, to demand that she send us her article in advance. You entirely rewrote my version of the prewar years, which is really a bit rich given that at the time the meetings were held at my parents' house and you weren't even born. And that's not all: not content with having introduced some total contradictions into my text, you sent it back to the *New York Times*, demanding that the remarks be credited to you.

TOM DE LAZIO: I remember now thinking it was a dreadful article...

THOMAS CARROLL: Thank you, Tom. But the real problem lies elsewhere. Why do we meet at all, that's the question. I must admit that over the last ten years I've asked myself that more and more frequently, which can't be a good sign. You know me, I'm not exactly what you'd call an intellectual. When you all started talking about the Fissler Theorem or configurations of equilibrium in the seventies, I asked myself where on earth that was going to get us. We spent whole evenings discussing trifles that Pete and his friends wouldn't have wasted a single second on. I remember the famous seminar on transversalism/idealism, which was only meant to last one Friday evening but ended at six o'clock on Monday morning. I didn't understand much of it, and yet I was happy. It reminded me a bit of the atmosphere of those evenings back in my childhood. Cold pizza had replaced my mother's brownies, but the fervor was the same. Everyone pitched in without reserve, without thinking; at that stage, we still weren't frightened of saying something stupid.

And then the enthusiasm plummeted. I'm sorry to have to say this, Upton, but it does seem as though that dates from the time of your election. Oh, of course, there'd been some warning signs already: the ridiculous awarding of that prize to Rousselet for his "Pantone 138," the departure of some of the Society's more brilliant members. Farewell Dunlap, Earp, Dwain... where once you'd been students, you became academics, not necessarily less brilliant, but certainly much more serious-minded. I suspect some of them were just embarrassed to be seen doing "Mickey Mouse" at their age. They must have felt it was far more respectable to talk about puzzles than to do them. And Upton wasn't going to contradict them. His first action, if I remember correctly, was to abolish the initial hour of the meeting, which had traditionally been devoted to doing a puzzle. Make way for interminable discussions! The agendas became incomprehensible to ordinary folk, whom I am not ashamed to represent, to the point where I began to make mistakes in the minutes, something that had never happened before.

And finally, we had Gleaners. I can't remember whose idea it was now, but I'm grateful to them for it. In three months, it achieved what Upton had been trying to do for thirteen years: to ruin the Society by exposing it to the ridicule of, I was going to say the whole world, but, thank God, it's a good while since even the *Medway Independent* has bothered writing so much as a line about us.

Is it worth my even mentioning here the fact that we spent precisely $18,765 on proving the existence of an EJ–1/5 staircase in a four hundred-block wall? When I think that out of the thirty-two members of the Society at that time, only seven asked the committee for an explanation! And since we did, after all, need to blame someone, we kicked Melinda and Doyle out without even allowing them to have their say. Upton was no doubt too frightened of what they might say in their defense. As for the idea of offering his own resignation, I doubt it even occurred to him for a moment. As a result, the budget has sunk farther into the red every year. The only thing that reduces the running costs is if the photocopier breaks down, and each of you has already made an "advance" to the Society of six or seven thousand dollars, for which I am very grateful. Each time we have a quarterly report, Upton goes into his little dream world, trying to calculate when Old Ma Creenshaw's going to snuff it and leave us her cash, and in the meantime all he can come up with is refusing some dear farmer's wife from Missouri the right to exhibit her Whitmans at the town's fair with the Society's label on them.

At least Gleaners had one positive outcome: it blew up the Society and released a dozen members who were genuine puzzle lovers. Do me a favor and ask yourselves just this once whether Diana, Beatrix, Cheradenine and the others aren't happier building up an outright-professional circuit than we are sitting here debating for the nth time what color the lifeboats were on the *Titanic* in a Krazy-saw puzzle that no longer exists.

Everyone's free to have an opinion on the JP Tour. Personally, I feel puzzling is somehow above competition, and I don't much like Wallerstein, ever since he made use of the Society to get his hands on Rousselet's "Pantone." But putting that aside, I have to admit that he is in the process of getting the puzzle out of the blind alley where it had ended up. I don't suppose many of you have read *JP Magazine*. It's a pity, because it is a remarkable publication. There isn't that much talk either of the secondhand and exchange market or of the regional forums organized by the Federation. I went to have a look at the one in Springfield, out of curiosity; it's pretty well done, a bit on the showy side, maybe, but pretty authentic on the whole. As for the prize they award annually to a small-scale manufacturer, well, that's easy, they've come in to fill the gap we've left empty for twenty years.

Anyway, however badly disposed you are toward him, it is impossible to reject the sum total of what Wallerstein's achieved. But here we are—it is impossible even to mention his name at this table without provoking the most vicious attacks on the man. All right, compare him to Al Capone if you will, but I was ashamed—and I don't think I was alone in this—to hear Spillsbury referred to as a baboon and Niels as a Baltic herring. That's pretty low you've sunk, Upton, that it should come to that....

TOM DE LAZIO: You're right, Thomas, we've kept silent for too long. What's your program?

THOMAS CARROLL: I'd better come clean. I haven't got one. All I can say is that if you elect me, I will try to bring honor to my family name. I'll begin by getting back our independence, by asking you to wave good-bye to the sums of money you have advanced. For my own part, I'm prepared to take a salary cut of thirty percent. Then I'll get busy on recruitment; we need some new blood, urgently. No more quizzes, no more victimization; I never saw my father refuse entry to anyone at one of his meetings. Following the same lines, I'm in favor of relaxing the rules for the use of the Puzzology Society label. This label is probably the one good idea Upton ever had. And we need to liven up the *Review,* the design hasn't been changed for fifteen years. And we need it to include a backlist of old puzzles. This is the area where we have the best chance of competing with the Federation; between the lot of us, we know virtually every collector in the country....

PAUL FAIRCHILD: This is beginning to sound like a real program....

THOMAS CARROLL: You think so? Maybe you're right. There's certainly no shortage of ideas. Upton, shall we take the vote now?

Thomas Carroll was elected by sixteen votes to two for Upton Sutter, with one abstention. The incoming President thanked the members of the Committee and said he hoped to show himself worthy of the confidence they had placed in him. Also elected were Tom De Lazio, Vice President, and Maria Andrees, Treasurer.

The outgoing President acknowledged his defeat and announced his intention to quit the Puzzology Society.

Extracts from the Minutes of the Board Meeting of the American Puzzle Federation

Committee meeting, 10 October 1995

2. Investigation report from Mischo Detective Agency

MISCHO: You'll find a résumé of the facts of the case in the first part of the report we've handed out.

WALLERSTEIN: We know the facts. What we're interested in are your deductions.

MISCHO: Quite so. Then let's start, if you will, with a quick summary of the autopsy report. From this we can build up a picture of the assassin's method. He anesthetizes his victims by putting a Pentothal mask over their faces, amputates one of their limbs and finally finishes them off with a massive injection of strychnine.

The murderer uses a surgical saw and cuts through the flesh right down to the bone in taking off the limb, be it an arm or a leg. In either case, we should really talk about dismemberment rather than amputation. Niels's right arm was taken clean off. Operations like this, according to the police doctors, require an average amount of strength, no more. A reasonably strong woman could do it.

WALLERSTEIN: Come on, Diana, own up, you did it. Okay, no more jokes, how's the official inquiry going?

MISCHO: In the absence of any physical clues, it's pretty much treading water. The FBI has drawn up a list of people who were in town each time a murder was committed. You'll find the list in the appendix, but it tells us nothing new: the four hundred people on it are all members of the JP Tour (players, trainers, aides, Federation staff, journalists, guests). The traditional procedures (comparison of hotel bookings, air, bus and train tickets, car hire, etc.) didn't turn up a single name that wasn't already on the list.

It's quite clear that the murderer knows his victims. Three of them opened their door to him (Blythe, Niels and Rousselet), two of them (Krijek and Kallisov) went to meet him. In my view, that confirms beyond doubt that the assassin belongs to the puzzling world.

Finally, I should add that the presence of the fragments of a single Polaroid photo on all the victims except the last (but I'll come back to that) seems to quash the theory that the crimes were committed by two different murderers; the "imitation" phenomenon, as it's called, is classic.

EARP: What do you know about the killer's psychological profile?

MISCHO: First, the killer is very sure of himself. With each murder, virtually, he has taken considerable risks. Krijek and Kallisov could easily have mentioned the name of the person they were meeting to someone in their circle; Blythe was killed at four o'clock in the afternoon. His hotel room overlooked an office block, but not one person working there could tell us anything. The hotel room Rousselet was killed in was at the far end of an eighty-foot corridor. What's more, the elevator was out of order. The assassin must have left by the staircase, where he could have run into anyone. The assassin is intelligent. The very fact that we haven't caught him yet proves that. He is playing with the police. Witness the arrangement of the "discovery" scenarios, or the whole business with the scrap of Polaroid, which is somehow intended to lead us back to him.

One thing we can be quite sure of, he is pursuing some sort of goal. He's never taken the same limb off twice, and he progresses systematically: he started off with legs, then moved on to hands, then arms, and so on. There must be some kind of plan behind all that.

WALLERSTEIN: And you're going to tell us what it is.

MISCHO: I'd love to, believe me. Having said that, I think I've uncovered some interesting things regarding the choice of victims.

Let's start with the fact that, apart from the fact that they are involved with the JP Tour, they have nothing in common. We've tested and rejected the following parameters: age, personal particulars, geographical origin, marital status, religion, sexual history, style of play, taste in puzzles, hobbies. And the research we did on common acquaintances was likewise pretty inconclusive. The only two people who definitely knew all four of the victims are Nicholas Spillsbury and yourself, Mr. Wallerstein, which is in itself a piece of non-information.

WALLERSTEIN: Too right it is. Go on.

MISCHO: A certain pattern does emerge, however, in the choice of amputations. The first five murders were all orchestrated in such a way as to emphasize the absence of the missing limb. With a little imagination, in four out of the five cases, one can guess why he chose to take off one limb rather than another.

Krijek was found at the wheel of a rented car with a stick shift. His right hand was placed on top of the shift, as though he was just about to change gear, but he couldn't because his left leg was missing. Now it was public knowledge that Krijek drove racing cars whenever he had a spare moment.

The assassin propped Irwin Weissberg up against a wall after removing his right leg. He placed a ball in front of him, reminding us that Weissberg had won the University Soccer Championship with the Georgia Tech team in 1969. He played center forward.

A violin was fixed under Kallisov's chin. The fingers of his left hand clutched weakly at the strings. His right arm, which should have held the bow, was gone. Let me remind you that Kallisov had been picking up prizes for his violin playing from a very early age.

Finally, Niels was killed while seated at a table finishing a practice puzzle. He was famous for the speed of his left arm.

EARP: "Slow Arm" was one of his nicknames.

MISCHO: Out of the first five victims, the only one for whom there is no obvious theme is Blythe. The assassin left his body in the position of a rock climber, cruelly underlining the absence of his right hand, but as far as anyone knew he wasn't interested in rock climbing.

WALLERSTEIN: I can confirm that.

MISCHO: I come back to the suspects, and the list of four hundred people who were, each time, in the town where the crimes were committed. After careful checking, it seems that twenty-one people have no alibi in all six cases (see the list in the Appendix). Niels's murder, for which we have a very precise timing (Niels's girlfriend discovered his body less than thirty minutes after his death) allowed us to eliminate a great number of suspects.

These twenty-one people divide into fifteen men and six women. Although we can't rule it out completely, I do think it's very unlikely the assassin is a woman.

WALLERSTEIN: That's good for you, Diana: you're off the hook.

MISCHO: Of the fifteen men, two have a criminal record: Raul Sánchez, 28, an American security officer on the tour, served six months in prison in 1990 for getting into a knife fight during a brawl; Fernando Neto, 23, Colombian, was given a three-month suspended sentence for possession of cocaine—we managed to hush up the affair at the time.

DOBBS: I remember Neto very well. A real little bastard!

MISCHO: There are three names I'd add to this list of suspects. The first is Upton Sutter, the president of the Puzzology Society. Sutter utterly loathes and despises the JP Tour and its founder. We've had access to the minutes of the weekly committee meetings for the Puzzology Society. I'll read you a few extracts:

—"Don't expect me to condemn this Polaroid Killer; personally, I think he's acting in the interests of public health and safety. Someone should give him a medal." (11 June)

—(on the death of Irwin Weissberg): "If he'd stuck to building schools instead of dancing attendance on some third-rate Citizen Kane, he wouldn't be where he is today!"

—(on the death of Evgueni Kallisov): "One less mollusc on the face of the earth!" (10 July)

—(on the death of Paul Rousselet): "He had his moments, but by the end of his career he'd completely lost his marbles." (20 September)

Sutter has no alibi. As for a motive, it's glaringly obvious: to put a stop to the JP Tour and restore his own supremacy in the puzzling world.

WALLERSTEIN: What do you think, Cecil, since you know the nature of the beast?

EARP: He's good with words, but I don't believe he could actually translate them into action.

MISCHO: The second suspect is Thomas Carroll, the son of Pete Carroll, the late founder of the Puzzology Society. For the last twenty years he's been the permanent secretary of the Society. He doesn't get on that well with Sutter. According to the members of the Society I questioned, Sutter thinks he's not worthy to participate in the committee's discussions, since he's not well educated.

Even though he hasn't said so officially, one can imagine that Carroll might take a dim view of the expansion of the JP Tour, which partially destroys the work of his father (all the witnesses emphasized Carroll's strong attachment to his father's memory).

Carroll also drew attention to himself by organizing a press conference on the theme of the mystery puzzle on 13 January 1995—three days before Spillsbury disappeared. At the conference he announced his intention to "offer a little glimpse of a magnificent work, a true masterpiece of the genre." And he has no alibis.

WALLERSTEIN: Cecil—same question again.

EARP: I'm inclined to give the same answer as before, but I must say I'm intrigued by this press conference.

MISCHO: Finally, even if it may seem a little tasteless, I must add the name of Nicholas Spillsbury to the list of suspects. Spillsbury disappeared on 16 January, seven weeks before the first murder. His intellectual weaknesses, when set against the profile of the killer, would seem to be sufficient to eliminate him from suspicion. However, there are a certain number of striking coincidences.

First, Niels was the only player to have beaten Spillsbury in an official match. After Niels, the two players who'd given him the most problems were Krijek and Kallisov.

Second, as everyone has remarked, Spillsbury reacted very badly to his first defeat. He was dreading the 1995 season and was afraid he would lose his title. Moreover, he knew Weissberg well, and had spent a week's holiday in his home in Hazlewood in May 1994.

And last, Mr. Wallerstein had detailed Blythe to take special care of Spillsbury's interests. Among other things, he had managed to land him several advertising contracts.

WALLERSTEIN: Is that it for the suspects?

MISCHO: More or less. I should just add that the idea of a professional killer in the pay of some organization out to damage you doesn't seem credible to us. The soaring viewing figures in the wake of every murder are far too beneficial to the interests of the Ubiquis group for them to be the work of one of its enemies.

WALLERSTEIN: It wouldn't be the first time my enemies did me a favor when trying to harm me....

MISCHO: We've also dismissed the theory of a human puzzle, put forward by the *New York Times*. Besides the fact that so far the amputations have been carried out only on limbs (no trunk, head or organ has been removed), such a hypothesis just seems like pure intellectual fantasy, and is not worth spending time over.

EARP: Do you think the assassin could strike again?

MISCHO: Yes, I do think so. I know the FBI investigators interpret the murder of Rousselet as a sign that the assassin has given up on the amputations and the scene-of-the-crime set pieces he's indulged in up till now. Personally, I'd be wary of drawing any conclusions. Except for a few most unusual cases, a serial killer never voluntarily stops killing. The lists of JP Tour members who are personally acquainted with Spillsbury or Mr. Wallerstein is still a long one. It is important that everyone continue to consider himself at risk and to exercise the utmost vigilance. And that warning goes especially for you, Mr. Wallerstein.

WALLERSTEIN: To sum up, you're advising me to reinforce my personal security.

MISCHO: I strongly recommend that.

WALLERSTEIN: If I remember correctly, your own organization is responsible for providing my bodyguards. I congratulate you, Mischo: your report's told us absolutely nothing, apart from the fact that your own turnover is going to go up in the next few weeks.

The Solution

And so, here we are on 17 June 1996 AD, and you come knocking at my door. Cecilia shows you in, and comes to find me in my study, where I'm marking papers. "A reader wants to see you," she announces. "I didn't know you'd written a book."

I take my time before I join you, gathering up the scattered papers into a little pile, pausing to straighten it against the table top, locking the drawers one by one before pushing the chair neatly under the desk. At last, I go down.

Your back is turned slightly toward the door. I see you jump when I arrive, and make as though to get up from the couch, where you've been sitting waiting for me.

Over a glass of whisky, we chat for around twenty minutes: about the time it takes to get here from the airport, the countless micro-climates of the Great Lakes region, the new Chicago Bulls team, of which you are a fervent supporter. No doubt you weren't expecting to talk about such neutral subjects. Judging by your feet, which constantly slide about on the carpet, I can see you are gradually getting more relaxed and that you are already in less of a hurry to come to the purpose of your visit. At this point, Cecilia appears in the doorway to announce that the meal is ready.

All this happened only a few hours ago, and yet, it seems to belong to another age, as though your ring at the doorbell (I remember it as long, determined, precise) had suddenly split my existence in two, as though twenty-five years of painstaking work had at last found their justification in this final denouement.

I let Cecilia carry the conversation. She who complains so often of our lack of social life, graciously answers your questions on my behalf. I hear her sorting out a few hazy passages in my biography, relating in detail the occasion of our first meeting at a ball in Boston, how I asked her father, Walter N. Coppelkan, one of the biggest manufacturers on the East Coast, for her hand, how we moved to Chicago in 1973, and my meteoric rise within the scientific community. I am amused by your attempts to focus the conversation on certain aspects of my personality, the nature of my relationship with Harry, my taste in puzzles (of which, I admit, I gave you precious little indication), the circumstances under which I met Charles Wallerstein. Poor Cecilia, in the belief she is simply fueling the conversation, in fact submits to what begins increasingly to resemble an interrogation, and acquits herself quite well. From time to time, naturally, I have to correct her, changing a date, modifying a judgment, making a connection between two events, where she had seen none. You pay close, one might even say excessive, attention to each of my interventions, excessive even if one considers that your presence at my table is quite sufficient proof that you have understood—if not the overall picture—then at least the general theme.

After dinner, Cecilia excuses herself, and goes upstairs to her room. It is just after ten o'clock. Back on the couch again, you indicate you'd be happy to take a liqueur. I am obliged to refuse you, for reasons which, I trust, will be clear to you later.

EARP: So, you've read the mystery, you've held the puzzle pieces in your hands; what solution do you suggest?

READER: You kidnapped Nicholas Spillsbury, murdered Rijk Krijek, Irwin Weissberg, James Blythe, Evgueni Kallisov, Olof Niels and Paul Rousselet, in order to create the first ever human puzzle.

EARP: I hear what you say.

READER: You grafted onto Spillsbury the limbs you had removed from your victims. God only knows what you did with the poor man's own arms and legs....

EARP: If that's the only question you've got, I actually threw them in the garbage. What was I going to do with extra pieces?

READER: The limbs shown in the photos that you left on the bodies of your victims were Spillsbury's and not your own, as the police believed.

EARP: I must say, I'm impressed. What else?

READER: The only piece of Spillsbury you used was his left hand.

EARP: His famous left hand, you mean? Is that all?

READER: What do you mean, is that all?

EARP: Is that all you know?

READER: Well, obviously, there are a few details I haven't worked out yet, but I've got the essential elements.

EARP: Oh, excellent! So, just because our learned friend has worked out that I carved up the corpses of half a dozen good folk, he thinks he's "got the essential elements." But what with the anesthetic and the surgical saw, everything pointed to a doctor! Don't go and tell me you suspected someone else . . . Sutter? I'll bet his wife doesn't even let him cut up the Christmas roast! Carroll? He faints at the sight of blood! The essential elements, don't make me laugh! Except for total cretins, maybe, the question of "who" was sewn up in the first eighty pages. Did you really think for one moment that I would be satisfied with the name of the guilty party, or have you also had some ideas on the "how" and the "why"? Why Spillsbury? Why Krijek's left leg and Blythe's right hand? Why Gleaners, why the JP Tour? Why all these bits of Polaroid on the victims, except for Rousselet? Why Val Nuss and his vitriolic articles? What about the Bantamolians? I do hope you've got an answer to all these questions, because otherwise it's looking like a long night. The essential elements . . . You remind me of those kids who lose interest in their puzzles the minute they've finished the border. . . . So, let's go back. What put you onto the scent of a human puzzle?

READER: Er, I don't know really. Gleaners, maybe.

EARP: Gleaners maybe! You're priceless. Very well, Gleaners then. Be more precise.

READER: The idea behind Gleaners is that there exists an equilibrium configuration, which will emerge out of the opposing efforts of the two workmen, one building, one dismantling.

EARP: That's correct.

READER: From the beginning of the experiment to the end, the number of cinder-blocks in the wall scarcely varies. On the other hand, the wall gradually moves toward a definitive state. One might almost speak of communicating vessels, between the wall and the pile of blocks the workmen are working on. The volume held in the two vessels remains constant, but the composition of the liquid gradually changes. . . .

EARP: Keep going. You're on the right track.

READER: I felt I was onto something important there, but I couldn't see how to fit the argument together. The similarity with the investigation was striking: on the one hand, limbs that kept disappearing, one at a time; on the other, this photo, which was being put together piece by piece with each murder.

EARP: Until the article by Louise Coldren. That showed you the way, I imagine?

READER: Yes, how did you know that? She speculates on why it is that most serial killers amputate, dismember or remove the bones of their victims. She writes: "In our opinion, dismemberment constitutes a reversal of the natural process. The serial killer is measuring up against the great architect who made man, and whose work he is in some sense undoing. He creates by destroying, or, to be exact, by deconstructing."

EARP: And later she adds: "It seems more appropriate to talk of a *deconstructive* rather than of a *destructive* impulse."

READER: That's right. I was back to the same dialectic, construction/deconstruction, but this time formulated much more clearly. The Polaroid Killer deconstructed his victims, in other words, he removed parts of them—let's call them building blocks—which he intended to use to different ends.

EARP: Good, very good. You have already got through more work in a few hours than the FBI has in a year. Notice, in passing, that Irwin Weissberg was an architect, but I won't insist on it. It's simply a coincidence. What was the next step?

READER: The next step was to ask what the assassin was going to do with all these limbs. Once I asked the question in these terms, the answer was obvious: a human puzzle, each victim providing a building block, his block, in the construction.

EARP: On that point, Louise Coldren got it wrong, in fact. In the same article, she wrote: "The fact that he [the assassin] takes a different limb from each of his victims should be interpreted as an affirmation of his power: the Polaroid killer is showing his contempt for the systematic assassin, by showing that he can remove *any limb he chooses*. He is not the victim, but, rather, the master of his impulses."

READER: At this point, I found myself up something of a blind alley. I'd unraveled part of the mystery, but there were still some knots there, quite a few.

EARP: I suppose the next one you tackled was the missing piece.

READER: Obviously, that was one of the motifs that featured in more puzzles than any other.

EARP: The Bantamolians, the mystery puzzle, and even the fragment of photo the FBI couldn't find on Rousselet's body.

READER: Not to mention Carroll's mother, doing all the puzzles in Gladys Fretts's library to check that none of the pieces were missing.

EARP: Which of these references really set you off? The Bantamolians, I suppose.

READER: Actually, no, not exactly. Of course, the book's title— *The Missing Piece*—caught my attention. But I found the Samuel Leiser puzzle "The Grand Central Station Left-Luggage Mystery" much more explicit. Kelleher writes: "The missing piece eloquently suggests that the solution to the crime lies in the contents of Cohen's pockets. From that point on, everything falls into place. The reader realizes Cohen has no money, and no train ticket in his pocket, from the fact that he wasn't about to leave New York, as the investigators supposed. So what was he doing carrying a large suitcase at six in the evening in Grand Central Station?" When applied to our investigation, that amounts roughly to this: why did the assassin go out and get a right leg, a left one, a right arm and a left one, but only a right hand? What about the left hand?

EARP: Anyone who hears the words "left hand" thinks immediately "Nicholas Spillsbury." Agreed?

READER: More or less. I drew the conclusion that the murderer had kidnapped Spillsbury and that, if his body was never discovered, it was undoubtedly because it didn't exist. In other words, Spillsbury was the matrix onto which the Polaroid killer grafted each new limb.

EARP: And, just as the Gleaners wall received one new block for every one it lost, so Spillsbury had each of his limbs replaced, except for his left hand, the one fixed point in the whole construction.

READER: So I got it right. That's really how it happened?

EARP: Absolutely. Your clever move wasn't in realizing it was a puzzle: the police and the public guessed that right from the start.

But they mistook the model; all they could think of was the puzzle that the pieces of Polaroid built up as time went on; now, what would it have given them? A full-length photo of Spillsbury, just like any you could have found in a newspaper a few years ago. Paradoxically, the real puzzle was building up *beyond* the looking glass. But that still doesn't tell me how you got on to me. Don't tell me you went and played the same bluff on all the other suspects as you did with me?

READER: No, of course not. But I admit I haven't got anything really big on you, just an accumulation of things that seem to point in your direction, nothing truly decisive.

EARP: Let's hear what you've got. I'll fill in if necessary....

READER: First, as you pointed out yourself, certain practical details show that the murderer had a sound medical background: the Pentothal anesthetic, the injection of strychnine, the amputation by surgical saw (as quoted in the Mischo Agency report), everything carried out under exemplary conditions of sterility. Now, along with Dunlap, you are the only protagonist who went through medical school.

EARP: Poor Harry, if he knew you'd suspected him of murder...

READER: Not for long. It was clear he'd broken off virtually all his links with the puzzling world, while you, on the other hand, seemed never to have been so involved as you were from the start of the JP Tour. Not to mention that you were also Spillsbury's inventor, his trainer and probably his confidant as well.

EARP: Anyone who's ever spent two minutes talking to Spillsbury could tell you that the term "confidant" is somewhat inappropriate given the scope of his conversation. Whatever else, Spillsbury was even dumber than the average idiot. You didn't need to be his trainer to slip a sleeping drug into his milkshake.

READER: I still believe you didn't choose him simply at random.

EARP: And indeed you're right. We'll come back to that later. Do you have anything else on me?

READER: I suspect you of being Melinda Plunket's mysterious friend, the one who was with her on the way to the university the day she saw the building site that gave her the idea for the Gleaners Project.

EARP: You astonish me. And what do you base this on?

READER: Not much, really. Intuition. And the fact that, in 1969, in a letter he sent you from Indiana, Dunlap mentions a mutual friend, a certain Melinda.

EARP: Well spotted. Anything else?

READER: No, except for one thing, which has been bugging me ever since the beginning, and which I still haven't found the answer to: Why didn't you take part in the competition for the most difficult puzzle in the world?

EARP: But I did!

READER: Oh, come on! That's not mentioned. Even Dunlap doesn't know about it.

EARP: Of course not. I haven't sent in my entry yet.

READER: For your information, the closing date for entries was 31 October 1969.

EARP: And for your information, let me tell you I am not going to participate in the same contest as people like Paul Rousselet or Thomas Carroll. My puzzle will be completed tomorrow morning. The fact that it took me twenty-five years to make it does not, I believe, detract from its worth.

READER: You mean all this butchery is your answer to a competition launched by the Puzzology Society in 1969?

EARP: My word, you're quicker than I would have dared hope! Perhaps the time has now come for me to tell you the whole story.

READER: Please do.

EARP: I first became involved with the Puzzology Society in 1967, through Harry Dunlap, a friend in medical school. Nothing you've read on the subject—I'm thinking, for instance, of the interview with Walter Nukestead—will give you any idea of the sheer scale of the puzzle craze on campuses at that time. Its Monday evening meetings attracted a crowd almost as big as the protest meetings against American engagement in Vietnam. Puzzology was a brand-new discipline, the field was wide open. I think I can say without false modesty that I possessed all the necessary qualities to carve out whatever position I wanted for myself within it. Better still, for the first time I had the feeling I could make full use of my extraordinary abilities.

READER: That alone...

EARP: Do you want to hear the rest, or would you rather go straight to bed?

READER: Please go on.

EARP: I was an only child and, to put it mildly, my parents never overburdened me with their presence. I was free to give a great deal of thought to the subject of myself. You see, my kind of intelligence is not of the normal kind....

READER: I had noticed that.

EARP: Silence! One more word and I'll send you back to your books! So, my intelligence is out of the ordinary. I'll spare you the scientific jargon; suffice it to say that the reason I chose medicine was in order to be able to study my own case. You should bear in mind that Nature blessed me with an extraordinary capacity for synthesis....

READER: Dunlap says something about your memory....

EARP: Like most people, you confuse the notions of memory and synthesis. A foolish error: a "clever" monkey is incapable of making connections. Inversely, certain scientists claim that the memory is actually the enemy of synthesis, that an excess of information somehow weighs down the brain. This, again, is a foolish error: you can't reason on thin air.

I certainly don't have the visual, purely photographic memory of a Spillsbury, say. On the contrary, the ease with which I retain things comes entirely from my ability to assimilate them, qualify them, classify them. I read five daily newspapers and, on a fairly regular basis, two dozen magazines. I have no area of special interest: I'm as interested in medicine as I am in puzzling, economics, literature, heraldic theory or entomology. I make highly improbable connections between all these different disciplines, opening breaches into intuitive method, which one day will swallow up whole hordes of scholars. On the other hand, I'm not some old scribbler. I don't answer the mail, I never take notes, and in thirty years I have produced only those articles that were strictly required for the furthering of my career, and even then with some distaste, given the impossibility of ever reproducing the complexity and breadth of thought in a piece of writing.

READER: With the exception, perhaps, of puzzle theory...

EARP: The puzzle elevates dispersion to the level of a fundamental value. It celebrates the fecundity of the idea of dispersal, whereas all other disciplines fight shy of its potential risks. Puzzology is the science that gives us the greatest insight into the way the human spirit works, every single recent discovery in the areas of neurology or cognition appeared in concept form in the minutes of our meetings at the end of the sixties.

READER: Why does the Society have only a handful of members now?

EARP: Because no one, not even Sutter, has grasped that puzzological research goes a great deal farther than the study of the catalogs of out-of-print puzzles from Delalande. Kelleher is perhaps the only one who did touch on its possibilities, in his thesis on the detective novel...

READER: When he points out that the puzzle is a metaphor for police procedure?

EARP: Of course. Unfortunately, he comes to it via the detective novel. If he had approached it from the point of view of the puzzle, he would have noticed that the puzzle is also a metaphor for the brain, or for life itself. I myself realized the use I could make of the puzzle as early as 1967. I threw myself headlong into my research, going through and making notes on the few European studies I could get hold of (I learned Italian to be able to read one of them), classifying the American manufacturers' catalogs according to criteria I devised for myself, devouring endless essays, articles and other pieces of writing by my fellow Society members late into the night. I was also careful never to actually join the Society myself. I attended the meetings as an independent, undoubtedly of the most assiduous kind, but free of the obligation ever to take up a position in the wretched power struggles that were at that time already tearing the association apart. On the other hand, I was one of the first people to take out a subscription to *Puzzology Review*, the editorial quality of which has declined for twenty years now, but which I nevertheless continue to read.

READER: Let's get back to 1969. How did you get to hear about the competition?

EARP: From Dunlap's letter, with which he enclosed the clipping from the *Review*. For three years I'd been looking for a vehicle to express a synthesis of my reading and reflections. Reading through Harry's brief sketch of various people's projects, I began to see the amazing possibilities this competition opened up. The debate about the biggest puzzle in the world had long since been resolved, but as far as I knew, no one had ever written anything on the most difficult puzzle.

READER: Why didn't you enter along with the others?

EARP: Because I already knew what the other participants' puzzles would be like, and I had no desire whatsoever to compete with a "Tulip Field," or "Monochrome." Rousselet is an imposter; in 1993, Wallerstein told me he voted for "Pantone 138," after the Frenchman had promised to give him the rights to it for $100,000. The only interesting entry was the one by the Japanese Hakematsu, "In the Footsteps of Buddha," even if the links between his pieces lack boldness. As for my own project, I knew it would take a lot longer than the three months allowed in the competition rules.

READER: When did you get the idea for a human puzzle?

EARP: After the awards. All the prizewinning puzzles seemed to me to have two main defects. They had too many pieces, as though all you had to do to make a puzzle difficult was cut it into smaller and smaller pieces. And also, none of the five puzzles, except maybe Hakematsu's, really had anything profound to say about "the puzzle." That was particularly true of "Pantone 138," in which Rousselet clearly assumed that his fancy gimmick exempted him from any need to put the puzzle in its proper perspective. From then on, I knew that my puzzle would contain only a very small number of pieces—no more than a dozen—and would in some sense be the puzzle to end all puzzles.

READER: What do you mean?

EARP: At the end of the sixties, our discussions always came back to the idea of transversality. Inspired orators were constantly flirting with the idea of a new genre of puzzles, in which the ideas would be borrowed from the arts or from quite unrelated disciplines. They examined the concept from every conceivable angle in their debates, burying it under layers of references, before digging it up again, to construct fanciful prototypes, drawing from music, silent cinema, or history. They were playing with an idea. I chose to grapple with something real.

READER: And how does that fit in with putting the puzzle into perspective?

EARP: I'm coming to that. Right from the start I was conscious of wanting to construct my work on two levels. On one level, the matrix body, fitting together the Polaroids as the deconstruction of that body progressed; and on the other level, our meeting tonight, which has been made possible by my careful planting of clues over the last twenty-five years. Although all the subjects are different, the puzzles are all one in the end, and the one cannot exist without the other, as you will shortly understand.

READER: Why did you make Spillsbury the central piece of your puzzle?

EARP: It was the least I could do, to take the best puzzlist in the world as the basis of my project. I'd been looking for this rare bird for years, without much idea of what he would be like. Each month I hoped to read a name in the *Review*. I dismissed Hakematsu—his later work, now on display in Hiroshima, quite sickened me. I had some hopes for a young law student at Yale, who wrote three important articles between April 1976 and March 1977. Unfortunately, he died in a car accident in the summer of 1977. Two other young men, almost as promising as him, emigrated to Brazil and Europe. The years went by and still I didn't have my central concept. More seriously the Puzzology Society was going through difficult times, and even the survival of the *Review* looked doubtful. So I invented the character of Mrs. Creenshaw, a kindly widow from Pittsburgh, whose generous donation arrived annually at a given time, to keep the association afloat....

READER: You mean it was thanks to you that the Society managed to balance its books all those years?

EARP: If we'd had to rely on that incompetent, Sol Draving, the *Review* would have folded long ago. Nonetheless, when I realized in 1989 that the level of debate within the society was rapidly declining, I decided to concentrate on a new criterion altogether, and one that was much easier to assess: speed.

READER: I thought the idea for speed competitions came from Wallerstein himself.

EARP: That's not correct. In fact, he talks about having witnessed a demonstration by one Jack Marietta in 1969. At that time, speed competitions were often held on the Harvard campus. I tried to rediscover the champions from that time, in the hope that one of them might have kept up his skill, or carried it to inconceivable heights. But they had all left the world of puzzling. Marietta had a brilliant career as a barrister in Philadelphia. When I was passing through Philadelphia, under the pretext of some common relatives, I managed to persuade him to meet me one evening in a jazz club. I brought the conversation around to his youthful exploits, asking if he kept up with it today, and if he had exercised his talent. He told me he had stopped training in 1974, the day he realized that his talent had no effect on the opposite sex any more. He agreed to turn his hand to it once more for me, and showed no surprise that I happened to have in my briefcase a copy of "Pennsylvania Road" by Grif Teller. In less than a minute it was obvious that he had lost all his skill. I packed away my puzzle, and abandoned him then and there.

READER: Then what did you do?

EARP: I thought for a while, and realized that the best way to test the virtuosos of the puzzle world was to get them to compete with one another, within an organized circuit that was attractive enough to get them all to take part.

READER: The JP Tour...

EARP: Exactly. The JP Tour. But since I couldn't implement the idea without immediately drawing attention to myself, I had to inspire other people, while letting them think it was their idea. Besides,

I knew the Society's aversion to any kind of nonintellectual activity. From there I came up with the idea of getting the Society to implode and rebuild the JP Tour from its ashes.

READER: With Melinda Plunket's cooperation...

EARP: With Melinda's entirely involuntary cooperation. It was at my suggestion that we walked part of the way together that Monday morning, 4 December 1990. I knew she was on her way to the Society, so I chose for us to meet in such a way that we would have to turn off at the corner of Hancock and Derney. I was the one who drew her attention to the two workmen, whose services I had engaged that very morning for $100. I was the one who drew her attention to the absurdity of their task and the similarity with the puzzle, before encouraging her to bring the subject up with the Committee.

READER: How did you know that Sutter would react so favorably?

EARP: If you had read, as I have, the minutes of all the Committee meetings for the last twenty-five years, you wouldn't have had a moment's doubt about it. The Gleaners Project was foolish, theoretical and woolly—in short, it had all the ingredients of a project that would appeal to Sutter.

READER: How did you choose the subject?

EARP: It had to be one that would lead you, or one of your fellow readers, back to myself. Construction and deconstruction, the same as ever.

READER: I can hardly believe that you limited your role in the breakup of the Society to a simple visit to a building site.

EARP: You're right. But even so, I was very careful not to intervene in the running of the workshop itself. Given Melinda's lack of both common sense and responsibility, there was no need to. I discovered, as did everyone else on reading their report, the extent of their incompetence. On some trumped-up pretext, I called Diana Dobbs, whom I knew had a grudge against Sutter. Let's say I didn't do anything to calm her anger. Then I asked her, incidentally, what action she planned to take in the wake of this affair, and I whispered in her ear the names of a few fellow members who would doubtless be prepared to sign an open letter to the *Review* along with her. The rest you know....

READER: Well, yes, the revival of the Federation by Wallerstein coincided exactly with the split in the Society. Could it be that...

EARP: That I had a hand in it? Indeed, yes! A few months before launching Gleaners, I got in touch with Blythe, Wallerstein's closest confidant. An old Harvard man, the network, you know...

READER: That didn't stop you from cutting his right hand off! His right hand! My God!

EARP: At last, you've got it! Spillsbury gave me the idea: he was always referring to Jeffrey as Wallerstein's right-hand man. I wonder where he got this expression from. At any rate, in autumn 1990, I sold him the idea of the JP Tour by showing him how, with very little investment, his boss could build up a very profitable circuit. Blythe gave exactly the answer I'd expected: it's an interesting project but we don't have the skills or the legitimacy to carry it through. I responded by talking to him about the Puzzology Society, suggesting he might entice away a few of its members. It was Wallerstein's idea to get his hands on the Federation by ousting the two old dears who'd been running it for the last thirty years.

READER: So it was on your recommendation that Blythe went and sweet-talked each of the members of the Society in turn?

EARP: It's more complicated than that. In fact, we shared it between us. I persuaded Diana and the others on her list to come over to the other side after their electoral defeat by Sutter. Jeffrey didn't get involved until later, once Wallerstein had taken over the Federation. We didn't want anyone to think Wallerstein had played any kind of role in Gleaners.

READER: And Carroll?

EARP: He's the only one I approached individually. I knew he'd refuse but I wanted to be sure of leaving written evidence of my action. Without my letter, you might not have been here this evening.

READER: What about you? Why did you accept a place in the Federation management when you never actually signed up for the Society?

EARP: I'm disappointed by your question. It's obvious. What position did I choose?

READER: Head of recruitment and talent spotting.

EARP: Precisely. And who was my greatest discovery?

READER: Spillsbury, without a doubt.

EARP: Obviously, Spillsbury. Having gone to all this trouble to bring about the creation of the JP Tour, I wasn't going to leave someone else the job of recruiting the champions. When I say I chose the fastest puzzlist in the world for my project, I know what I'm talking about: I personally auditioned thousands of them. Would you like some fruit juice?

3

I hope you didn't think I was concerned for your comfort. To tell you the truth, I could care less what you choose for your final drink. You were meant to see my suggestion as an offer of a truce, a short interlude during which I would leave you time to reflect on what you had just learned. And you have clearly accepted it as such. While I was out in the kitchen getting you your drink, you stood up and walked three, maybe four times around the couch with your eyes lowered, your hands in your pockets. To be honest, it's rather a pity that after these few minutes' reflection you were able to come up with nothing more inspired than "Why Spillsbury?"

4

EARP: Is that your question?

READER: That's my question.

EARP: Didn't you read my article in *Life*? Not only was Spillsbury miles ahead of the competition right from the start, but he also had the same name as the inventor of the puzzle. I was particularly interested in the fact that, since the day he lost both his mother and his father, his entire development seemed to have centered on the puzzle. Whole regions of his brain seemed to have remained undeveloped; the only thing he was good for was doing puzzles. You could almost have said that he existed only in terms of his left hand. I didn't hesitate for a second before deciding to make him my lynchpin.

READER: So why did you wait so long before killing him?

EARP: First of all, I didn't kill him, I kidnapped him. I had decided at the outset that the project would begin with his first defeat.

READER: Ah. Let's talk a little about that defeat.

EARP: There's not much to say. You've read the report by the publicity team for the JP Tour. Where once he'd been their main weapon, Spillsbury began to do damage to the circuit. If he'd won a second grand slam, it would have seriously eroded the public's interest. Wallerstein did what might have been expected of him, changing the rules of the game without warning.

READER: You hadn't been warned?

EARP: No, believe me; otherwise I would have prepared Spillsbury for his defeat. When I saw his reaction in the locker room after the match, I knew the moment had come. The public adored Spillsbury when he was winning; they would have hated him as a loser.

READER: Poor Spillsbury...

EARP: He could not have dreamed of a greater destiny.

READER: Not everyone dreams of destiny, and certainly not of that particular one.

EARP: Spillsbury is happy.

READER: Happy but dead.

EARP: Would you like to meet him?

READER: Is he here? In this house?

EARP: Right under your feet. If you'd like to follow me...

5

You rise, haggard, slightly dizzy for a second, which I imagine comes from the long period of inactivity. It's still too soon for the sleeping draft I slipped into your drink to take effect.

When I converted the basement into an operating suite several years ago, I was careful to forbid Cecilia access. "My word," she exclaimed, "you'd think it was Bluebeard's castle!" Little did she realize the truth of her words.

Spillsbury's stretched out, inert, on the operating table. I glance at the control screens, while observing your reaction. You've suddenly turned as white as a sheet.

READER: Is he alive?

EARP: Of course.

READER: But he's not moving.

EARP: Most of the day he's unconscious. I feed him through a tube at regular intervals.

READER: How long have you been holding him here?

EARP: Since the day he disappeared, 9 February 1995.

READER: And he's never left this room?

EARP: More than that—I strapped him to this bed to take the Polaroid, and he's never left it since.

READER: You're a monster!

EARP: That's a very relative concept....

READER: He'll die.

EARP: Yes; in fact, he'll die this evening. These last few months he's given me some cause for concern. I had to assist his breathing for a couple of days, but he got over that. He's a soundly built young man.

READER: Those marks on his shoulders...

EARP: Yes, that's where I sewed on the arms. The marks on the wrists are more discreet. And the ones on the legs have had time to heal now. You really have to look closely to see them.

READER: His eyelids are moving. He looks like he's going to wake up.

EARP: He is. I gave him an injection a little while back. Don't expect any great speeches, though. That's never been his strong point.

The human puzzle opens its eyes, turns its head slightly to one side, as though to test the leather collar around his neck. His eyes meet mine, then yours. "Maestro," he says, speaking clearly, before slipping back into unconsciousness.

READER: He calls you Maestro, after what you've done to him?

EARP: He is quite devoted to me.

READER: Body and soul!

EARP: If you like. He has placed his life in my hands.

READER: While you have chopped his hands off . . .

EARP: Keep your childish remarks to yourself. Do you want to see the Polaroid?

READER: I'm dying to.

It's hidden away in a drawer. You hold the remaining two pieces; the head and the trunk, and the left hand, turning them slowly. You look up at Spillsbury, as though to check off the different stages of his long metamorphosis.

READER: Why Rousselet?

EARP: To close the circle. To show the world I didn't need the left hand. To finally beat that cretin who, right up to the day he died, believed he'd given the world the most difficult puzzle ever.

READER: Are you sure it was nothing to do with jealousy?

EARP: For me, Rousselet's just another piece in the puzzle.

READER: Who chose the pieces? You said earlier that the right arm thing was Spillsbury's idea.

EARP: One evening, at the Memphis tournament, I asked him what pieces he'd choose to make a human puzzle.

READER: Weird question!

EARP: Which, however, he took very seriously. "Forget the left hand for a moment," I said to him. "Obviously we'd have to use yours. Who do you suggest for the rest?"

READER: What did he say?

EARP: Olof Niels for the left arm. Spillsbury admired Olof a lot. You know his nickname for him was "Slow Arm."

READER: I didn't know that.

EARP: Well, it's written in the report from the Mischo Agency.

READER: Possibly.

EARP: Certainly! And the right arm was an obvious choice as well: Kallisov gave a violin recital at the Federation gala in September 1994. Spillsbury found the legs a bit harder. He came up with Weissberg for himself—Blythe had told him stories about Weissberg's days on the Georgia Tech soccer team. I had to help him for Rijk Krijek: left to his own devices, I don't think he'd have seen the connection between the left leg and motor racing.

READER: And that's how you created your masterpiece! By heeding the ravings of a mental retard.

EARP: On the contrary. In my opinion, Spillsbury showed great discernment in his choices. I'm sure you couldn't have done any better. Tell me, who would you have chosen for the head?

READER: For the head?

EARP: A body isn't made up of just arms and legs; you need a head as well. Spillsbury certainly thought so, anyway. Who do you suppose he thought of?

READER: You, obviously.

EARP: Exactly. He even added that, in my area, I was a champion of sorts.

READER: You didn't deny it?

EARP: Should I have?

READER: At least we know you'll never finish your project. I can't really see you cutting your own head off to provide the missing piece so dear to the Bantamolians.

EARP: Indeed, I'd say it's extremely unlikely. Just as it's extremely unlikely that I'll leave my puzzle unfinished.

READER: You'll just have to come to terms with that.

EARP: I've tried, but I can't. You see, a head like mine may be extremely rare, but it's not entirely unique. If you consider there are half a dozen or so in each age group, that still makes three hundred in the United States alone.

READER: You underestimate yourself!

EARP: If you knew me better, you would know that wasn't something I'm accustomed to do. But let me put the problem to you in exactly the same way as it occurred to me, and I'm sure you'll arrive at the same answer as I did.

READER: I doubt it, but try it anyway.

EARP: In order to complete my puzzle, I needed a head that was perfect, a mind capable, as mine is, of making rigorous deductions and imaginative connections...

READER: Go on.

EARP: Capable of demonstrating these qualities in the very area for which he himself was the metaphor...

READER: The puzzle.

EARP: Capable of picking up, rearranging and interpreting the forty-eight clues I'd left behind....

READER: In short, the only reader capable of working it out was you.

EARP: You.

READER: Me.

EARP: I knew you'd understand.

I can tell from your silence, broken only by Spillsbury's pained, laborious breathing, that you find my conclusion irrefutable. It may help alleviate the pain of your position if I say a little to put it in context.

EARP: At the start of our conversation, I spoke to you about my desire to construct a puzzle on two levels. The first level is here, stretched out before you. It consists of seven pieces, it breathes noisily, and I doubt whether it will survive the final graft, which I intend to make shortly, for longer than a few seconds. The second level reaches completion this evening, with your visit. It contains forty-eight pieces, which I have carefully fitted into place over the years, in anticipation of the person who'd come ringing at my door announcing he had the solution, without realizing that he himself *was* the solution. And since you have successfully, in part at least, put together the second picture, you have earned yourself the right to feature in the first. Your place in history is assured.

My words do not get the reception they deserve. You cannot suppress a yawn, which I attribute to the effects of the Pentothal. No doubt you now realize that it's pointless to fight; that substances are already at work in your body to bring you to your knees. So you throw all your energy into a final declamation, which, I must admit, has a certain grandeur.

READER: How dare you call this ragbag of seams and stitches, this puppet who cannot even move his fingers, a human puzzle? Can you not see that you have dedicated your life to the production of a monster, a circus beast, with one leg shorter than the other? That with your series of grafts you have made, out of a boy who was perhaps stupid but certainly uniquely gifted, an invalid who can just about mumble your name? You rant on about Sutter, Plunket and types like Draving, or whoever, but you're no better than they are. Worse than that, you're just like them: all you care about is putting your own indelible mark on the history of the puzzle. Admittedly, their efforts were clumsy and at times downright ridiculous, but they never hurt anyone. Being in love with the sound of your own voice isn't a criminal offense, and no one ever got thrown in jail for having made random piles of cinder-blocks. Does it really seem that much more subtle, to you, to play at Meccano with people's arms and legs? You're so proud of being the first person ever to make a human puzzle, but did you ever seriously think you were the first to come up with the idea? Gepetto and Doctor Frankenstein got there rather a long time before you, my friend. As for a passion for slotting together bits and pieces, it's one of those fads that normal people simply brush quickly aside.... I really think that taking six good men apart, without counting Spillsbury and yours truly, just to make a puzzle is, well, a little beyond the pale. But Sir obviously has expensive tastes, Sir no doubt beheads little boys when he feels in the mood for a game of croquet.... The worst thing about it, you see, is that your puzzle isn't even a puzzle. What is a puzzle? Let me just ask you that. Surely you must have some idea, what with your thirty years' research and your father-in-law being in the business.

EARP: The dictionary defines it as a game of patience made of separate fragments, which must be assembled to reconstruct the original image.

READER: All praise to the lexicographer, who sheds light on even the most difficult concepts! The definition pleases me, but at the same time I am surprised that, since you are acquainted with it, you feel able to give the name of puzzle to something that quite clearly isn't one. What's the image you are trying to reconstruct? Where were the scattered pieces, and what gave you the idea they belonged together? The truth lies in quite the opposite direction, with those perfect bodies you mutilated in order to construct something that only ever existed in your own imagination. Assembling a puzzle follows an inner necessity: each piece slots in with its neighbor, because it cannot be otherwise, because there is no choice about it. Your model has no real *raison d'être.* Just because some dimwitted young man sat about in a hotel room one night and remembered that Evgueni Kallisov played the violin, his right arm turns up six months later, in your garbage can. But perhaps Kallisov also played tennis. Maybe Olof Niels had other talents that had nothing to do with his left arm. Did it not occur to you to cut off another part of his anatomy, which, according to the press, he made prodigious use of as well? The moment it becomes clear that I, or you, could have made a choice that was not the choice that Spillsbury made, your puzzle ceases to be a puzzle, and becomes at worst a patchwork, and at best a piece of artful butchery.

The more you talk, the more confident you become. I have to listen to you ranting on until the Pentothal finally gets the better of you. You flop to the floor like a limp rag. I check your pulse, establish it's regular, and then lay you out on the second operating table, not far from Spillsbury (should he still be called Spillsbury, when half his body is no longer his?), so you could touch him by stretching out your arm.

It takes me almost an hour to prepare the operation. By the time I put on my smock, gloves, and adjust my mask over my face, the sound of your snoring is in time with that of Spillsbury. My instruments have long been sharpened and ready. The blade of the saw sinks effortlessly into your throat, and blood spurts out onto my gown. Your left leg jerks, your eyes open, but the life has already gone from them: they stare stupidly at me, as I cut your head off. It is 1325 hours, and it occurs to me that, for some inexplicable reason, the temperature in the room is well over the usual thirty degrees.

Then I leave your head in a basin and turn to Spillsbury. He murmurs inconsequentially in his sleep; he is dreaming. I can't take my eyes off his lips, and their beatific smile. I think I can safely say that this boy has me to thank for the few hours of happiness he's ever known. He is still smiling when, standing behind him, I gently lift his head and cut his throat.

9

It takes me over two hours to sew your head onto Spillsbury's trunk. Your neck is rather bull-like, while Spillsbury's is fine, almost slender. The difference in color is rather disturbing too. Never mind, there's not much I can do about it.

It's getting hotter all the time. For the first time in many years, I'm unsettled by the smell of blood. I step back carefully to admire my puzzle, now at last complete, and snatching my Polaroid camera from where it sits surrounded by compresses, I immortalize the picture on film.

It's five thirty. I'm nearly at the end of my tale. I decided to write down the last installment in my day book. Whoever finds it should tear out these few pages and add them to the forty-eight pieces in the drawer of my writing desk. And should he feel so inclined, he may add the Polaroid photo, which I'm watching, as the contours emerge on the shiny paper, appearing limb by limb, in the order of construction, left leg first, then right leg, the arms, left and right, the right hand, then the left hand, then the head, your head, with your huge eyes staring out at me.

It will soon be dawn. I must hurry now, roll Spillsbury up in a blanket, and load him onto the back seat of my car. I've already worked out my route. I'll plant the left arm at the foot of a pier of the Thomas Banks Bridge. I'll leave the right arm on the steps of the

Town Hall. I'll stuff the left leg into a locker at the left luggage in the main station and the right leg in a garbage can in Frank Lloyd Square. As for your head and Spillsbury's body, the Chief of Police of Chicago will find them on his lawn. Maybe he'll even manage to work out the whole story.

If all goes well, it will be six fifteen. Michigan Avenue will be virtually empty. No one will take any notice when I get out of my car, open the trunk, and wrap a coil of dynamite around my neck.

If what the salesman said was right, pieces of me will be blown to all four corners of the city.